Also by Jonathan Kellerman
Available from Random House Large Print

City of the Dead
The Burning (with Jesse Kellerman)
Serpentine

UNNATURAL HISTORY

JONATHAN KELLERMAN

UNNATURAL HISTORY

AN ALEX DELAWARE NOVEL

RANDOM HOUSE
LARGE PRINT

All rights reserved. Published in the United States of America by Random House Large Print in association with Ballantine Books, an imprint of Random House, a division of Penguin Random House LLC, New York.

Cover design: Scott Biel
Cover image: Carl Larson Photography/Getty Images

The Library of Congress has established a Cataloging-in-Publication record for this title.

ISBN: 978-0-593-67838-1

www.penguinrandomhouse.com/large-print-format-books

FIRST LARGE PRINT EDITION

Printed in the United States of America

1st Printing

To Henry and Abram

UNNATURAL HISTORY

1

When I go to crime scenes, I'm ready to focus on terrible things.

I end up at crime scenes because my best friend, a homicide lieutenant, thinks I have something to offer on the cases he calls "different."

He rarely gives me details, wanting me to form my own impressions. As I pulled up to the yellow tape on a Monday morning just after ten, I knew nothing.

No evidence markers outside. Whatever had happened was limited to the interior of a navy-blue, two-story stucco building.

I gave my name to a uniform guarding the tape and was allowed to park in a red zone.

The blue building sat on the north side of Venice Boulevard, perched on a grubby corner, the entrance on a side street. At the back was a parking area, also taped, with the rear end of a black Prius just visible. Beyond the alley was a residential block; seventy-year-old apartments and a few straggling bungalows.

A little pocket of L.A. that had managed to elude Culver City when borders were drawn.

The automotive mix out front was the usual. Black-and-whites plus vehicles dispatched from the crypt on North Mission Road. Two vans for transporting techs and their gear, meaning lots of scraping and sampling; one for transporting bodies; a Chevy Volt sedan used by coroners' assistants as they traveled around the county ministering to dead people.

No signage on the blue building. Rust-crusted security bars grilled two narrow windows on each floor. So narrow they evoked castle bow-slits.

I slipped under the tape and headed for the front door, a gray metal slab left slightly ajar. No one had told me to glove up but I covered my hand with a corner of my blazer and prepared to nudge. Before I made contact, the door swung open and Milo Sturgis came out.

He wore a pessimistic black suit, a beige shirt stretched tight over his gut, and a skinny brown tie whose origins could be traced to a chemistry lab. Paper booties covered his desert boots. He had gloved up and latex glistened as it strained over hands the size of strip steaks. His black hair alternated between gelled obedience and random flight. His face was chalky in the sunlight, UV rays advertising pits and lumps that harked back to teenage acne.

Nothing to interpret; his default pallor. Startling green eyes remained calm but his mouth was set in a sour frown.

Annoyed.

"Thanks for coming," he said. "Ready to put on your therapist hat?"

"For who?

"C'mon, I'll show you."

The door opened to a blank white wall. To the right was an alarm keypad. Less wall than knock-up partition; pebbled, whitewashed fiberboard, no ability to mute sound.

Lots of sound from behind the wall. Moans and gasps and sobs then a moment of breath-catching quiet during which a woman said, "Try to relax," with no great sincerity.

More sobbing.

I said, "Someone's having a bad day."

Milo said, "Not compared with the decedent. Hopefully you can calm things down so I can **concentrate** on the decedent."

CHAPTER

2

By the time I reached the crying woman, I knew the decedent's name and hers after Milo showed me her California driver's license.

Melissa Lee-Ann Gornick.

"But," said Milo, "she goes by Melissande."

The license pegged her as twenty years old, five-four, ninety-eight pounds, BRN eyes and hair. Why DMV bothers to record hair color has always mystified me and Melissande Gornick proved my point with a hot-pink, teased-up do. Since being photographed three years ago, she'd also added steel piercings to her left eyebrow, her left cheek, her right nostril, and the soft spot between lower lip and chin.

For all that, both ears remained untouched by metal. Maybe that was now a **thing.** My patients are generally well below the piercing age so I sometimes miss out on current events.

Melissande Gornick rocked back and forth in a chair and gripped the sides of her face with black-nailed hands. Her spare frame barely impacted the seating, an oversized love seat of brick-colored tweed. One of half a dozen pieces of furniture strewn randomly in cold, white space. Two techs worked in corners, scraping, bottling, bagging, labeling.

As we approached, she let out three gulping sobs then switched to high-pitched keening whistles. Then back to crying.

Like a teapot undecided if brewing was complete.

Milo's look said, **See what I mean.**

The female officer stationed behind Gornick said, "Try to relax," with even less enthusiasm than a moment ago.

When you're all strung up, there's nothing less helpful than being told to calm down. But cops aren't therapists and confronting anxiety kicks in their own fears of madness and impulse. So they keep saying it and getting nowhere and the beat goes on.

Melissande Gornick wailed louder. The uniform rolled her eyes.

Milo said, "We're okay, Officer Bourget."

Bourget's look said he was Santa and she'd been a good girl.

"Yessir." She trotted away.

Melissande Gornick seemed unaware of her surroundings. Rosy, welt-like marks striped her cheeks where her nails had taken hold. I wondered if she was prone to self-injury. A long-sleeved black jersey and gray skinny jeans blocked diagnosis.

Milo bent close to her. "So sorry you had to go through this."

Using the ideal tone, soft and nonthreatening, but nothing indicated she'd heard. He shook his head, stepped away, and waved me forward.

I'd been checking out the white space. The entire ground floor of the building was a single open area with an iron spiral staircase tucked in the rear right corner. Walls were blank, cement floors painted glossy black. The mismatched furniture—chairs, table, an old desk—ranged from gently used to stuff that looked as if it had been rescued from the curb.

The only clue to the building's function was a section, rear and central, lit by overhead tracks and containing a single, straight-backed chair, three high wooden Victorian armoires, a trio of silver light baffles, and two cameras on tripods, one of which looked antique.

Robin has a camera like that, a Hasselblad she inherited from her father and has never used. Neither of us photographs much. Robin because she prefers to draw and paint, I because there are enough images in my head.

Black drapes hung from a ring of metal pipe running high near the ceiling of the posing area. A curtain capable of blocking the front was furled, leaving the space open to view.

I approached Melissande Gornick. Her soundtrack changed and she began hyperventilating.

In movies, heroes use paper bags to treat hyperventilation, but it's an iffy technique at best and can sometimes be dangerous.

Gearing up my hypnosis voice—soft, rhythmic, and, most important, monotonous—I said, "You're doing fine . . . if you feel like it, slow your breathing . . . not a lot, just a bit."

She continued to gulp. Caught her breath. Arched her back.

Trying.

No success but I said, "Excellent . . . keep doing that . . . just breathe . . . you're in charge . . . that's it . . . great . . . perfect . . . breathe nice and easy . . . great . . . think you can slow down a tiny bit more?"

She tensed.

I said, "Or not. Up to you."

She loosened.

"Excellent. Now see if you can breathe in through your nose and out through your mouth."

I timed her respiration with my watch. Good old analog Omega with a second hand.

Another couple dozen respirations before her rate had slowed to just above normal.

I said, "Fantastic, so whatever you need to do."

She exhaled. Sat still. Stared straight ahead.

"Good job, Melissande."

"I felt like I was . . . gonna . . ." Her chest rose and fell.

"Sure," I said. "You've been through something tough."

BRN eyes widened. "What . . . now?"

Someone else might've said, **Try to stay relaxed.**

I said, "Do whatever you need to."

That confused her, which was the point. The power of constructive distraction.

She stared at me. Her hands dropped from her face, wrists and forearms vibrating. If she'd had a fleshier face, it would've jiggled. This face was narrow, delicately boned, the sweaty skin stretched drum-tight, and it remained still.

Milo fidgeted.

Melissande Gornick said, "I don't . . . fuck, I don't . . . know."

I said, "Know . . . ?"

"What to do."

"You don't have to do anything, Melissande."

Unsatisfactory answer. She grimaced and tightened up.

I said, "Do whatever it takes."

"I'll **never** get through this!"

"It's a terrible thing."

"It's—fucked **up.**"

"Totally."

"I got here and it . . . he . . ." Her eyes clenched shut. More rocking. More whistling.

Milo's bushy black brows tented. **So much for that.**

I held up a wait-a-sec finger. The science of

therapy is knowing what to do. The art is knowing what not to do.

Melissande Gornick, eyes closed, said, "I feel . . . I don't know what I feel."

"You don't need to know."

She opened her eyes.

I said, "Is there someone we can call for you?"

"Just my mom . . . no, no, no, not **her** . . . she'll try to talk me out of . . ."

I waited.

She said, "She doesn't want me working for Donny." Her eyes sparked in terror. "Now I **can't** work for Donny! But don't call her! Please! Don't!"

I said, "Of course not. You're an adult."

Her mouth dropped open. "Really?"

"Really."

More silence. Milo's eyes were jumpy. I ignored him. Even good friends need to wait.

Melissande Gornick slumped. Nice, slow breathing. "What do you want?"

"When you're ready, we'd appreciate hearing about what happened. So we can find out who did this to Donny."

"Ready? That'll be never."

Then she sat up straight and said, "**Fuck.** Let's do it **now.**"

We guided her outside the building toward Milo's latest unmarked, an Impala the color of oxidized avocado, the interior redolent of taco sauce and pine deodorizer. I kept my eye on my impromptu patient. Her breathing was regular but her gait was unsteady and I was ready to brace her.

But she made it to the car and allowed Milo to settle her in the front passenger seat, protecting her head with his hand. Once in place, she stared through the windshield blankly. Then she suddenly touched her throat and looked alarmed.

Milo said, "You okay?"

Breathy whisper, inaudible.

He leaned in closer. She croaked again.

He said, "Thirsty? Get you something right now."

I stood outside the car keeping watch as he circled to the rear, popped the trunk, and returned with a plastic bottle of no-brand springwater from the case he keeps there. Ready lubrication for his own thirst during long surveillances and for situations like this. The rest of his supply stash includes a few empties that can double as urinals, several twelve-packs of tissues, and a knapsack stuffed with beef jerky, pork rind, trail mix, cookies, pretzels, and roasted nuts. Plus police gear, including his shotgun.

Former Boy Scout, like me. The gospel of preparedness.

He uncapped the water, handed it to Melissande Gornick, and drew me aside. "What was that, reverse psychology?"

"Maybe good luck."

"Meaning?"

"She was ready to wind down."

"Seriously, Alex."

"What feels bad about anxiety is loss of control. Anything that restores control can help."

"You gave her permission to freak out?"

"I didn't fight it or order her to relax."

"Huh. Sounds like reverse psych to me . . . if I'da tried it, whole damn thing probably woulda gone south."

He returned to Melissande Gornick. She looked weary and drained. The bottle wasn't. She hadn't touched a drop.

Aftermath of an adrenaline O.D. She'd hit the fatigue wall soon, so best to question her now.

He said, "Not thirsty anymore, Melissande?"

"Mel's okay." She looked at the bottle. "Could you . . . like help me. I'm feeling like . . . my arms . . . like . . . they can't."

"No prob." He held the water to her lips. She latched on and began sucking greedily.

Like a baby bottle-feeding. What the Freudians called regression in service of the ego.

I call it understandable. At murder scenes, anything is.

Melissande Gornick finished the water and asked for more. When she'd emptied the second bottle, she burped without apology and said, "What now?" Better color, normal breathing.

Milo sat down next to her, behind the wheel. Looked past her to where I remained, outside, wanting to read her expressions. And his.

His said, **What next?**

I said, "If you can, Mel, go through what happened from the time you got here."

"It started before," she said.

"Then start from before."

Long silence.

I said, "What happened before, Mel?"

"I brought the bread. From the SproutBake outlet. He likes the multigrain with flaxseeds and craisins. He **doesn't** like raisins."

"You brought him breakfast."

Several emphatic nods. "I always bring it to him, the bread and Danish butter that I get from Whole Foods."

I said, "You bring Donny breakfast every morning."

"Not every morning. When I work."

"Which is . . ."

That took a while to process. "Four days a week? Or if he needs me for something I also come in."

"You're his assistant."

"Personal **and** technical."

"You help with the photography?"

"I help with whatever he needs."

"Got it. So you arrived with the bread and the butter at . . ."

"Eight thirty. That's when he wants me."

I said, "Sounds like he depends on you." Going with her present-tense fantasy.

"He **does.**" She turned her head to the side. Her hands began to shake.

"So you showed up at eight thirty and . . ."

"He's always upstairs. I said, 'Hey.' He says **Hey** back. It's like . . . what we do. He didn't say **Hey** so I'm like I said it too soft so I said, 'Hey,' a little louder but he still **didn't** say it back. So I'm like, maybe he's got someone up there. So I went over to the sitting room and sat. Then I opened the chests like he likes and fluffed the clothes."

"We're talking those three wooden chests in the posing area."

"The **studio.** They're antiques, he likes them 'cause they're tall so he can put long stuff in there."

"Got it."

Milo exhaled. **Get her to the point.**

I said, "So you fluffed."

Mel Gornick nodded. "Then I listened some more. But there was nothing so I waited some more. Then I thought maybe he overslept and I should check. He likes me to do that when he oversleeps. So I did."

Black nails flew back to her cheeks, a burst of tiny ravens clawing. The welts had faded to pale-pink diagonals as new markings cropped up.

I said, "You went upstairs and saw him."

"I saw **it** first," she said.

"It . . ."

"The red! Part of it was dark. Part of it was . . . red. Like when you manipulate an image when it's wet, he showed me once . . . what am I **talking** about? It's his **blood** and he's . . . oh God!"

She hunched low, touched her knees with her brow.

I said, "Terrible thing to find, Mel. What did you do then?"

"I ran downstairs screaming."

Milo said, "Then you called 911."

She sat up and turned to him. "No. I fucked it

up, my fingers were all . . . I called 922, then 912. Then finally."

Her face creased with shame. "Can I go **home**? I don't want to **be** here!"

Milo said, "Real soon, Mel. We need to contact Donny's family. How can we do that?"

"It's huge."

"His family?"

"All sorts of brothers and sisters."

"How many?"

Shrug. "There's all kinds of mothers."

"His father's been married several times?"

She shot him a sharp look, as if he'd failed a history test. "His. Father. Is. Victor. Klement."

Milo glanced at me. I shook my head. He said, "Ah," and got busy with his phone.

"Wow," I said. "Victor Klement."

"Totally," said Mel Gornick.

"Does Victor live here in L.A.?"

Another pedantic frown. "He lives everywhere. That's what Donny said. Victor's of the world."

"You ever meet him?"

"Uh-uh."

I said, "Okay, here's a tough question, Mel, but it's important. Can you think of anyone who'd want to hurt Donny?"

"Everyone loves him!"

"No one's threatened him recently."

"Not anyone," she said.

"No one he worked with?"

"For sure not **them.** Even though you're gonna think it 'cause you're cops."

"Them, being . . ."

"The Wishers."

"The Wishers . . ."

Her hands left her face. She held them out toward me, palms up. **Idiot, don't you get it?**

I said, "Sorry, never heard about the Wishers."

"It's the most epic project he's ever done. It's human psychology. It's society and passion and privilege. It's going to win a **prize!**"

Something on Milo's phone widened his eyes.

I said, "The Wishers. We'll check it out."

"It's not them," she insisted. "It's not anyone. He's loved!"

Suddenly she sprang out of the car, stumbling and nearly falling, catching herself with a slap on the hood, just below the windshield. Hurrying past me, she stationed herself by the Impala's front bumper, arms clamped across her chest.

"I want to go **home!**"

Milo got out and joined her. I hung back.

"I want to—"

"Absolutely, Mel. Thanks for taking the time."

Frantic head shakes. "Let me **go.** I don't want to **be** here."

"Where's your car? We'll walk you."

Her look said he'd inquired if she boiled and ate babies for dinner.

He said, "You Ubered."

"**Lyft.** They do carbon offsets."

"No prob, I've got both."

As she tapped her foot, he worked his phone. Another personal outlay that would never see a reimbursement request. "Okay, four minutes, your driver is Andre. We'll wait with you."

The three of us stood on the sidewalk as Venice Boulevard traffic streamed by.

Lots of traffic. The new Culver City.

During Prohibition days the town had been a corrupt oasis for bootleggers, with local cops notifying the criminals in advance of raids. Four decades later, the town settled in as a sleepy adjunct to the southernmost tip of West L.A. Now it was Hipster Central, housing cruel-looking, knife-edged buildings that clogged the business district from Venice Boulevard to Jefferson. Home bases for streaming services, software giants, game developers, and the kinds of start-ups that hatch nineteen-year-old moguls.

All that also brought the enterprises that sprouted on islands of youthful affluence: gourmet food trucks, bars pretending to be dives, **the-latest-thing** cafés. Mandatory nods to organic, vegan, sustainable, and any other trendoid deemed virtuous.

A truck advertising Halal Gourmet Caribbean Jerk Chicken rumbled by. Nice aromas—lamb and allspice and cumin—distracted Mel Gornick for an instant until she recovered her grief. She sidled away from us.

Giving it one last push, Milo said, "All those sibs you mentioned, Mel. Do you recall any of their names?"

"No," she said. "Just the one I met."

"Who's that?"

"**Colin.**" As if pronouncing a diagnosis. "He's not like Donny."

"How so?"

"He's like a banker. Even though . . ."

"Even though what?"

She shook her head. "He's not like Donny but he's okay."

Milo said, "Colin's been by the studio."

"Uh-huh."

"Regularly?"

"Once."

"Once in how long?"

"I only worked here four months."

Shrug.

Milo said, "Colin and Donny get along?"

"They went out."

"For?"

"It was dinnertime so probably dinner." She pouted. Not invited.

Her eyes shifted to the curb where a white-and-green Smart car had pulled up. The driver, bald and bearded and hollow-cheeked, gave a world-weary

finger-wave. His eyes drifted to
began drumming the steering wheel.

Mel Gornick threw open the passe
and got in, her lack of size enabling an easy entry
making the tiny car appear a bit less toy-like.

Andre putt-putted away.

Milo said, "You'd need Crisco and a wedge to
get me inside that . . . okay, brother Colin, it's a
start . . . here we go . . . Colin M. Klement, CMK
Investments, Beverly Hills. If I can't reach Daddy
soon, which is likely, I'll go local."

I said, "Daddy's looking elusive?"

"If the Web's to be believed, Daddy's a multibil-
lionaire with either a dozen mega-homes all over
the globe or no permanent residence and a taste for
hotel rooms."

"Man of mystery."

"Just what I need, more question marks. At some
point, someone's gonna have to take possession of
the body."

I said, "Speaking of which."

4

Milo fetched two sets of booties and gloves from the car trunk and we returned to the blue building.

I pointed to the alarm pad.

He said, "Checked with the company. Not activated last night."

I said, "Underdeveloped sense of threat?"

"Maybe having a billionaire daddy does that. But it doesn't seem to be a robbery. His wallet was on his nightstand, had ten twenties in it and credit cards. Same for his phone and a pad, which was all music streaming. He liked neo-folk and Seattle stuff."

We walked around the partition. A third tech had joined the first two, taking samples from the chair in the posing area.

Milo went up to him. "Body fluids?"

"Not so far."

"Anything?"

"Not so far."

We climbed the spiral staircase. Iron steps were embossed with triangles designed to minimize slippage. Perfect surface for catching blood and other evidence. The absence of tape-off and Milo's bounding up said no such luck.

At the top of the stairs was a small stainless-steel kitchen, to the left of that, a black granite bathroom.

The rest of the second floor was a huge bedroom, at least fifteen hundred square feet of loft-like space. Twelve-foot white walls, flat white ceiling. No furniture except a king-sized bed set up with charcoal-gray linens and a black faux-fur throw and flanked on the right by a gunmetal nightstand. The entire wall to the left was taken up by a series of steel gym lockers.

Nothing decorative on the walls, not a trace of photographic bragging.

Donny Klement separating work from play? Or just a modest guy.

Whatever his priorities, privacy hadn't ranked high. Not a single door anywhere, even to the lav, which was visible through a wide open entry. Two of the slit-like windows I'd noticed on the street pierced the wall behind the bed. The scant light they'd have admitted was blocked by panes painted black, limiting illumination to the same kind of overhead tracks as in the posing room.

Unforgiving light, focused away from the bed and toward the nightstand and the black cement floor. On the stand were a white-noise machine, eyeshades, earplugs, and a bottle of Benadryl.

Sleep issues.

Two techs worked well away from the bed, where a brown splotch had violated the fur, stiffening it and setting off a gloss. Traces of moisture and tackiness; death hadn't arrived long ago.

Donny Klement half sat, half slumped in the center of the bed, atop the fur spread. A black silk robe hung open, revealing a naked, gray-green torso vertically striped with several streams of blood.

Three trails; one for each of the bullet holes peppering his chest in a rough triangle. His head drooped, face hidden by dense black hair dangling like the drapes in the studio.

Death changes the body steadily, but it takes a while to alter body mass patterns. This body was lean and hairless but for a black pubic thatch and a sparse sprinkle where the bullets had invaded. Not much visible body fat save for a rim of flab between navel and groin.

No apparent rigor mortis but the process can be subtle and it begins in the jaw, which was out of view. Still, the glowing blood suggested the stiffening of muscles hadn't come and gone.

If so, Mel Gornick hadn't arrived long after Donny Klement had died. I said so.

Milo said, "There's some in the face but C.I. best-guesses two to five a.m. when it was still dark."

I looked for closed-circuit cameras, found none. Consistent with someone who neglected to turn on his alarm.

"Am I missing any CC?"

"Unfortunately not."

"Exit wounds?"

"Nope, all three slugs are still in there."

He walked to the bed and lifted the head with his usual tenderness, revealing a face that had once been well beyond handsome. Aquiline, symmetrical, fashionably stubbled. One of those faces you see in would-be actors all over L.A. This face was marred by the jut of a jaw frozen forward and high-tension tendons in the neck.

I got closer to the chest wounds. "Don't see any powder."

"None to see. Same for forced entry or defense wounds."

I said, "Lying in bed, having a conversation with the shooter. Or he woke up to a nightmare."

"Or ready to do what people do in bed."

"Sexual encounter gone wrong?"

He shrugged. "We'll see what the pathologist says."

I looked at the floor beyond the bed. "Footprints?"

"If only. No, this was bang bang bang, then walk away without a trace. There could've been passion but I'm leaning toward cold and professional. And now that I know about Daddy, my mind's going all sorts of interesting places."

One of the techs said, "Who's Daddy?"

"A prosperous fellow." He motioned me away and into the kitchen. Windowless and not much more than an alcove but equipped with a massive hood and expensive appliances.

I pointed to the cabinets. "May I?"

"Nothing in there but a few boxes of brown rice and a couple of baggies of weed but suit yourself."

He opened the fridge. Ginger beer, vodka, white wine.

I said, "Anything in the bathroom?"

"Lunesta, Ambien, organic melatonin, more weed, vitamins, and boring stuff."

"Sleep was a challenge. Who prescribed the pharmaceuticals?"

"No one. What looks like samples in blister packs."

"Friends with a doctor?"

"Or he got it on the street."

I said, "Problems sleeping could explain his being up in the wee hours. Or just the opposite, so heavily medicated he couldn't defend himself."

"Or it was a booty-call gone wrong. I have no idea if he was into women, men, all of the above, none of the above. Little Mel did seem rather enamored of him, so maybe he was straight."

"Or she hoped he was."

"Yeah. That was a bit of emotion she just showed

us. Over the top, no? Think she coulda been involved?"

"If so, she's Oscar-caliber."

"This is the city for it, Alex. I'll give her time to calm down, see what she's like when she's not hyperventilating. In any event, it's a weird scene. Ergo I called you."

"Not to do therapy with Ms. Gornick?"

"That came up later." He grinned. "You're the gift that keeps giving."

"Find casings?"

"Two on the mattress, one on the floor, 9mm." He pointed to an evidence bag in the collection amassed by the tech closest to the bathroom.

She said, "Soon as we get back, Ballistics will have it."

"Thank you, Terri."

"Anything for you, Lieutenant."

"Bet you say that to all the detectives."

"I do and everyone appreciates it."

I spent more time absorbing the scene, took a closer look at the body. The triangular wound pattern was arranged two on top, one at the bottom. It felt calculated, almost code-like. Not the product of a semi-automatic tantrum.

I said, "I'd like to know more about that project Gornick talked about—the Wishers."

"Me, too. My first thought was some kinda cult but so far haven't found anything on the Web."

"Where did he keep his records?"

"Haven't found any, yet." He strode to the metal lockers and opened them. No sense of discovery said it was for my sake, he'd already looked.

Men's clothing, black, gray, and blue denim, took up the first three compartments. The rest were empty.

He eyed the tech who'd asked about the victim's father, turned to me, touched his lips, and motioned me back to the kitchen.

When we got there, I said, "Loose lips sink investigations. Pretty sparse setup."

"Empty lockers could mean evidence taken by the bad guy. Or he lived simply."

"I can see simple as rebellion against a parent with a dozen mansions. Same for joining a cult. Those groups always end up being about money and with a father like that, he'd have been a twenty-four-karat trophy."

He said, "Then maybe he got disillusioned and wanted to leave and they did a roach-motel on him."

"Go in but don't come out." I glanced back at the body. "Photographers hold on to prints, they have to be somewhere."

"With my luck, he rented a storage locker in Saugus under a false name."

"If you haven't checked the cases in the studio, I'm going to allow myself some optimism."

He headed for the stairs. "Haven't, yet. It was all

I could do to stop little Mel from melting down and creating an environmental hazard."

The armoires were a hundred or so years old, made of finely grained French walnut carved with vines and chrysanthemums. The first two contained what looked like a stash lifted from a studio costume lot. Clothing spanning decades, everything from men's suits to beaded flapper dresses and Victorian gowns, military uniforms complete with regalia, white lab coats, khaki trench coats, dark-blue police duds. At the bottom of each case were triple-level racks of shoes, everything from ballet slippers to combat boots.

Milo said, "Guy liked playing dress-up. Feels like one of those tourist places, more carny than arty."

He kneeled and slid open six drawers at the bottom of the first case. Hats; from pith helmets to feathery cloches. Same for the lowest compartments of the second and the third armoires.

Muttering "Saugus," he shifted to the next drawer. Inside was a stack of oversized black books. Hardback folios, held together by beefy chrome screws.

"Don't say it."

"Say what?"

"Optimists are the true realists."

I smiled and he lifted the top folio and flipped it open.

Inside were photographic prints protected by

clear plastic sleeves. The first image was an aspen grove. Next came Joshua trees in the desert. A hundred or so images, harmless as milk.

As Milo continued to examine, my eyes shifted to something to the right of the stack.

Eight-by-ten box, dark-green crocodile leather, likely synthetic like the bedspread.

I lifted it out. Heavy, the substructure a dense, hard wood. Covered in what turned out to be genuine reptile hide glossed by decades of handling. A rose-gold monogram was stamped above a keyhole and two clasps of the same finish.

V K.

A gift from Dad. Maybe Victor Klement admired his son's work. I wondered what the notification would be like once Milo found him.

I tried a clasp. Unlocked, as was its mate. Taped to the inside of the lid was a rose-gold key. All that luxe protected a thin collection of paper, maybe half a dozen sheets folded in half to accommodate the space.

A scatter of internet reviews, all dating ten years ago. A group show featuring several student artists at UC Santa Cruz. The exhibit had traveled among California colleges, garnering positive reviews for all concerned.

No specific mention of Donny other than as a name in a list. Yet he'd held on to the write-ups, suggesting that not much had occurred in his professional life over the past decade.

But the final sheet of paper, resting at the bottom, said that might be changing. Not a reprint, actual paper snipped from a magazine called **Angel City.** One of those ad-filled, glossy throwaways that get tossed onto high-income driveways.

The article was a "Preview" of a "planned" solo show by "new-line photographer Donny Klement." No scheduled opening or venue but the writer had seen Klement's photos and was certain the exhibit would be "as groundbreaking as the next seism sexing up the bump-meters at Caltech."

Title of the project: **Wishing Makes It So.**

The author was someone named Deandra Sparrow. I re-read the piece. Generous dollops of adolescent gushing brought to mind Mel Gornick's hero worship. Donny Klement, good looking even in death, appeared to be thirty or so. Maybe he'd had a talent for charming ingénues.

I was about to show Milo the review when he said, "Guy was actually pretty good. I was expecting edgy but it's mostly pretty stuff—flowers, trees, the ocean, sunsets in the desert."

I said, "All that plus homeless people decked out in costumes."

"What?"

I held up the **Angel City** piece. "His next show was going to feature street people that he dressed up in order to fulfill their dreams."

He took the review and scanned. " 'Virtuosity behind the lens uncompromised by virtue' . . . 'a neurology more yen than Zen . . .' " Jesus. **Wishing Makes It So.** Talk about the big lie. Doesn't say where or when it happened."

I said, "He saved reviews from a ten-year-old college show. If this one had already happened, he'd have documented it."

"He wished but didn't make it so . . . maybe he pissed one of his subjects off and learned about permanent cancel culture."

I pointed to the folios. "The prints aren't in there?"

"Haven't gone through all of it." He lifted a book, went through it, shut it, and put it aside. Same for the next one. And the one after that. Several hundred pretty images.

Nothing until the last folio, when he said, "My my my."

5

Eight pairs of color portraits displayed side by side.

The camera capturing faces and torsos down to the waist.

Crisp lightly colored images were heightened by a black background. A wooden slat ran just above each subject's shoulders. The top rail of the posing chair a few feet away.

In each set the left-hand photo featured faces eroded by life on the streets, eyes incandesced by psychosis, fear, intoxication, or some other affliction. The clothes that were visible were drab, torn, unraveling at the seams.

To the right, the same faces been scrubbed clean and veneered with makeup and, in the cases of the men, given a shave or a precise beard-trim. The women wore lipstick, mascara, and eye shadow. Everything well applied and tasteful, no obvious intention to caricature with clownish excess. Hats for everyone.

Aspirational headgear.

A name typed in capitals had been affixed to the top of each "before" shot. Each "after" was tagged with a single-sentence "wish summary."

"Stella," sun-scorched, bloated, and bleary-eyed, dreamed of being a society woman. Donny Klement had interpreted that as Gilded Age dowager and provided her with a ruby velvet lace-trimmed gown, cut-glass pendant earrings, a silver lorgnette on a chain, and an elaborate high-piled wig of sausage-like golden curls that propped a wide-brimmed red hat banded with white feathers.

Nose in the air, smug smile.

"Jack," gaunt, snaggle-toothed, most of his face concealed by a mass of gray beard, yearned to be a Top Gun, and had merited a shave that exposed a long, large-boned face that might've once been attractive. Removal of the hair mask knocked ten years from his appearance despite the network of deep wrinkles it revealed. Donny Klement had gone to the extent of providing temporary teeth. Cheap-looking, too-white, too-large bridgework that created the smarmy smile of a political candidate.

Borderline comical, but again, the effort seemed honestly cosmetic with no aim at ridicule.

Jack's new outfit was an olive-drab flight suit peppered with patches, and an aviator cap and goggles from decades previous. Chronological hash, but the subject didn't mind, displaying his slip-on incisors with satisfaction and flashing a V-sign.

Squinting as if peering at the great blue yonder. If you didn't look too closely, the clash of a glossy manicure and gnarled, scarred fingers didn't disturb the image.

Milo remained wide-eyed as we examined each pairing.

The fine-boned substructure of "Beverly's" emaciated face suggested she might once have been pretty. Her wish had been conventional, almost to the point of pathos: movie goddess, meaning tiara, platinum wig, white satin, off-the-shoulder dress, and false eyelashes. I'd once spotted Mae West during her final years, dining at Musso on Hollywood Boulevard with three young men.

"Solomon" became a surgeon. Scrubs, O.R. cap, oversized scholarly eyeglasses. Looking grave as he held up a stethoscope.

"Louis": world explorer. Monocle, handlebar mustache, khaki shirt with epaulets. The pith helmet I'd just seen.

"Maria": ballerina.

"Katie": another would-be physician, this time with a specialty in pediatrics. White coat over a pale-pink dress, another surgical cap, holding a thermometer in one hand and a copy of **What to Expect the First Year** in the other.

Last came "Eugene," an aspiring corporate CEO. Pin-striped suit, starched white shirt, repp-stripe tie, scant white hair slicked down but for a pencil mustache. A scowling expression behind rimless glasses fought with a smile budding the corners of thin lips. The pink pages of the **Financial Times** in his grasp. Rough hands fought the pampered-executive theme. He, too, brandished glossy nails.

I said, "Wonder where the props are."

That was answered by the final set of drawers. Three of them filled with what looked like a random toss of thrift-shop finds.

Returning to the Wishers folio, he paged through again.

"Amazingly, no one wanted to be a master sleuth."

I said, "Or a psychologist."

"Puts us in our places." He stood and stretched, holding the book in one hand. "Thoughts?"

"It could've been exploitive but to my eye it looks sincere."

"I guess. But there's something about it, Alex . . . one thing for sure, he paid them. Wonder how much and if it got complicated."

I said, "What I'm curious about is how they reacted after it was all over and they returned to their usual lives."

"Shifting gears too fast?"

"Not good for the psyche. When I worked at Western Peds, seriously ill kids would get visits from celebrities—actors, singers, athletes. A few seemed sincere but I also saw a lot of obvious P.R.

stunts. They'd blow in with an entourage, pose, get to read about it the next day in **Variety** or the sports pages. The kids enjoyed the attention but after the hoopla died down I noticed they often got depressed. These people were impaired to begin with. That could make confronting reality even tougher."

"Depression." He lofted the folio. "Or maybe anger."

I said, "Eight potential suspects."

"Occupational hazard," he said. "It's how I see the world."

We left the blue building. The morning had turned warm and dry and noisy. Milo fetched two bottles of water from the trunk and we both drank.

He said, "Now all I have to do is find eight homeless people—'scuse me, unhomed individuals. You're the social scientist. Tell me why people think renaming anything makes a difference."

"It's easier than finding a real solution."

"Wishing makes it so . . . guess Donny was a man of our times . . . finding them's not gonna be easy."

I said, "Mel Gornick assisted during the shoots so she might know something. Same for any makeup artists or other staff."

"I was gonna reinterview her after she had time to settle down. I'm not minimizing finding your boss dead but her reaction was intense, no? Maybe because she really did have a thing for the boss."

"Could be. You might check out the **Angel City** reviewer."

"Why her?"

"The gushing seemed over the top."

He took out his pad. "Remember her name?"

"Deandra Sparrow."

"Sounds like a toon."

He returned to his phone. Instagram pulled up the headshot of a pie-faced bespectacled woman around Mel Gornick's age who self-labeled as a "truth-teller / heretic / journalist / tide-watcher."

Deandra Sparrow wore a black pageboy with one-inch bangs. Her eyeglass frames were red plastic, the lenses oversized and owlish. Squinting eyes behind the glass plus a tiny mouth implied years of habitual disapproval.

Milo said, "That's the best she could do for a selfie? Okay, she's real, so she goes on the list. Think there were other young ones with crushes on him?"

I said, "What was he, thirty, thirty-five?"

"Twenty-nine."

"Sophisticated older guy, comes from money, good looking, glamorous profession? Is his phone crammed with contacts?"

"Big-time, take a while to go through it, I'll get Reed, maybe one of the others to help." He pocketed his own cell. "Good looking," he said. "His mother thought so, too."

"You've talked to her?"

"Nope, no idea who or where she is, yet. But she named him accordingly."

"Donny?"

"It's not short for Donald. Wanna guess?"

"Dante?"

"Adonis."

I said, "A mother's love."

"She loved him," he said. "Someone else didn't."

He walked me to the Seville.

I pointed to the Prius behind the building. "That his?"

"Yup, unlocked but miraculously untouched." He scowled. "Toss in the untriggered alarm and we've got a non-genius when it came to self-protection. Okay, next step: Get brother Colin to tell me more about him and direct me to at least one parent. What's your schedule like for the rest of the day?"

"Consults all afternoon, free by five. Tomorrow and Wednesday it reverses—busy in the morning."

"The custody waltz never ends."

"Some of those," I said. "But also injury cases."

He grimaced. "Kids getting hurt. The ones in the hospital, were you able to settle them down after the bullshit was over?"

"Usually. The problem was every time some flack contacted the hospital, there'd be another round of bullshit."

"You ever try to set the hospital straight?"

I laughed.

He said, "What?"

"The head of Oncology was sympathetic but didn't seem to really get it so I talked to the chief administrator. He told me my work was useful but not 'heroic.' Meaning it didn't make the papers and raise awareness in a way that brought in donations. As opposed to a kid helicoptered in for heart surgery."

"Sounds like my situation. If I may be so bold."

"Closing murders isn't heroic?"

"Think about it, Alex: I do all the spadework, then the lawyers take over. Does anyone remember a detective, unless he turns out to be corrupt or craps his pants on the stand? Which is just peachy with me. If I could work under a pseudonym, I would. And your office décor tells me you agree. Nothing personal in there."

"True." Professional distance but there was another reason: Other than Robin, I had no attachments to showcase.

He said, "Now that I think about it, Gorgeous also keeps it low-profile."

I said, "People know how to find her."

He laughed. "Obviously all three of us are all highly evolved. Anyway, if I can work it out time-wise, I'd appreciate you being there when I reinterview Little Ms. Emo, seeing as you cured her anxiety attack. Maybe also that reviewer—Sparrow. She looks like she could use some cheering up."

◆

I drove away, redirecting my focus to the two patients I'd be seeing soon. A five-year-old whose legs had been broken in a collision caused by a lane-cutting motorcyclist on the 405 freeway and a seven-year-old who'd fallen off a low ridge during a school outing in Thousand Oaks.

Healed up physically; now it was my turn.

When it comes to legal cases, the basics of injury evaluations are comparatively simple: Know your patient's history, get a handle on their specific reactions to trauma, and draw upon research to try to predict the future.

The first time I'd been contacted by an injury lawyer, I'd resisted, having no enthusiasm for the legal system. That attorney had worked on me by emphasizing the suffering of his four-year-old client. I'd told him I'd evaluate but not to expect anything dramatic in my findings.

"Meaning?"

"All I'll be able to say honestly is that children with facial scars are more likely to have problems than if they're not scarred."

"That's perfect, Doctor."

"Sounds like common sense to me."

"Sure is, Doctor. But I need **you** to say it."

I'd seen both of this afternoon's patients several times, had enough to write reports. But as I usually do, I sneak treatment into the evaluation and wanted to make sure they were doing as well as I thought.

None of that would find its way into the report. I'd tried it once, learned that plaintiffs' lawyers don't like pre-settlement good news.

At five p.m., if Robin or Blanche didn't need me, I'd try to learn more about Adonis Klement and the family that produced him.

The woman I live with was one of those kids with an inborn talent for drawing, painting, and design. She makes a good living building and repairing high-end stringed instruments. Had also used her talents to create the house we share.

Our half acre sits on a high, forested lot with distant ocean views on clear days. It's easy to miss, set well above a section of Beverly Glen filled with randomly styled structures on small parcels that tilt perilously close to the road.

To get there, you turn off an unmarked road that hooks above the Glen and connects to a former bridle path. Even when you locate the access, the property's hard to find, sitting on an unmarked lane. Sometimes patients' parents comment about that. I thank them for their effort and guide them to my office.

Years before meeting Robin, I'd bought the

place cheap because the lot was considered unfit for rehabilitation and lived in the structure that came with the land: a bare-bones wooden thing knocked up haphazardly by a bipolar artist. Not much more than a cabin. The first thing of substance I'd ever owned, and I was happy.

All that timber was kindling for a psychopath's arson and Robin replaced it with a series of white cubes that could've been cold if she weren't warm-hearted. High walls, pale-oak floors, thermal glass, everything in modest proportion. The foundation was a challenge and she ended up using deeply sunk pylons, creating a high entry and a wraparound terrace where we sometimes sit and drink and think. The garage is taken up by Robin's materials and extra tools, neatly stacked and labeled. She parks her truck out in front and the same goes for my old Seville. I'm the car wash guy.

When I got back from the Klement murder scene, the house was its usual cool, bright self and my footsteps echoed reassuringly. No greeting from Robin and no toddle-up by Blanche, our little French bulldog, meaning the two of them were back in the studio. My first patient was due in twenty minutes, just enough time for a day-old bagel washed down by the high-octane coffee that's my narcotic.

When the bell rang, I was still thinking about what I'd seen in the blue building. By the time I reached the door to smile at an eight-year-old bitten by two dogs, thoughts of Donny Klement had dissipated.

Ready to do the job for which I'd gone to school.

The afternoon went well; both children making progress, parents grateful, attorneys who, so far, weren't acting like scumbags.

Now I could get back to a young man shot in bed and left to bleed out. Starting with his father.

"Enigmatic billionaire."

"Shadowy mogul."

"Financial mastermind."

When it came to Victor Klement, the internet did what it always does when facts are lacking: substituted random guesswork, borderline libel, and paranoid nonsense.

Anti-Semites knew for a **fact** that Victor Klement was an "Ashkenazi Jew with Russian roots" and hence part of a creepy cabal in control of world finance and the mass media. Just in case that didn't inflame you, he was also the chief warlock of a satanic / anti-Christian / anti-Muslim / anti-freedom / anti-everything-that's-decent secret movement responsible for falling income in the Third World and rising tides in the Antarctic.

At the other end of the lunatic spectrum were rabid anarchists and self-described revolutionaries who **knew for a fact** that Victor Klement was a reactionary tool of the rapaciously capitalist, white male privileged banking elite, holed up in an impenetrable, tax-sheltered aerie atop a mountain of gold coins as he orchestrated the destruction of the working class.

One thing both camps had in common: lousy spelling.

Theorizing about Klement didn't end with the fringe. His name had come up years ago in side-bar articles published by supposedly mainstream newspapers. The dominant theme was a man too secretive to be virtuous. I supposed that assumption had a twisted logic in the age of look-at-me, but maybe the guy just liked his privacy. In any event, Klement's low profile had led to theories about his political leanings and wonderings if his contribu-tions of "dark money" were designed to pervert the electoral process.

I found no indication Klement had ever reacted to any of that.

If Milo had begun the same research process, I knew what he was thinking.

Guy's controversial, meaning a whole bunch of goddamn motives.

Wading through the dross finally brought me to what seemed to be dispassionate and factual: a brief piece in **Forbes** that focused on Klement's gift for currency trading, stock picking, and arbitrage.

No photos of the man or his residences were provided, but the magazine discounted the conspir-atorial hubbub and had taken the time to actually trace Klement's birth to sixty-three years ago in Ames, Iowa, where he'd grown up as the only child of a Lutheran minister and a teacher.

The rest of his bio was sketchy: psychology degree from the University of Iowa, rejection by the Wharton business school at Penn, a move to New York where he began as apprentice at a small brokerage and climbed the ranks at a larger trading firm before striking out on his own.

His pattern was to lay huge, risky bets, a policy that had led to several massive failures. But over four decades, Klement's wins had outnumbered his losses and the magazine estimated his net worth as $1.5 billion. A figure admittedly imprecise because Klement worked hard at avoiding publicity and operated through a labyrinth of trusts and shadow companies.

The part that stuck with me was "only child."

Sometimes people who grow up without siblings develop a lifelong craving for the company of others and opt for large families. Sometimes, just the opposite. Despite my degree, I'm not one to overly psychologize but it was hard to avoid wondering about the solitaire when another chunk of Klement's history surfaced in, of all places, a French tabloid, author unspecified.

Le famille de Victor Klement.

The piece had been published four months ago. I google-translated and lucked out with relative readability. Brief note of Klement's wealth but cheerful emphasis on his love life. That made sense when you considered that Paris hosts a Museum of Romance.

Lots of love life.

Klement had married his college sweetheart in Iowa, a woman named Mary with whom he had one son. Divorce followed two years later. No further mention of her, other than the name of the child she and Klement had produced.

Hugh Klement was described as "an American cowboy and entrepreneur."

Soon after that, Klement married Sharlene, a secretary at the New York firm where he traded options. Two years later, they split up and she was reported as deceased, cause not specified.

That brief union had produced Colin Klement, a "banker in California."

Wife Number Three was Moira who'd been Wife Number Two's personal trainer, and with whom Klement had "grown friendly."

No mention of acrimony in the Sharlene/Victor dissolution, and the same went for the Moira/Victor split following an eighteen-month union that produced a daughter.

Bianca Klement-Steen was identified as an interior designer living in New York. No status report on Moira.

Following Klement's third divorce, he was described as fabulously rich and receiving treatment for an unknown "condition" in Beverly Hills.

The treating physician, Dr. Leona Gustafson, was described as "glamorous and trained at the finest schools."

Elite training hadn't stopped her from blurring boundaries and marrying her patient.

Another year and a half passed before Klement's fourth marital dissolution. In the interim a daughter: Danielle. She, the paper reported, had perished, date and place unspecified, in an "accident."

Almost immediately after splitting with Leona, Victor Klement had hooked up with his fifth wife, an actress named Vanessa Charles whom he allegedly met at a "Hollywood movie-star party." A three-year marriage ensued, for Klement a long stretch. But still, the inevitable end. At some point, unspecified, post-Victor Vanessa had died from a rumored drug overdose at her home in Malibu.

I made a note: **At some time, VK lived in SoCal. Maybe still here?**

Onward.

Klement and Vanessa had created a son, incorrectly tagged by the paper as "Danny, a photographer."

After divorcing Donny's mother, Klement had taken a glacial break from marriage lasting twenty-five years. The article cited rumors of a "gypsy life" for the "shy billionaire."

But how, the writer wondered rhetorically, could any man, let alone one of Klement's "appetites," be expected not to seek the company of women?

Hence the punch line for the piece:

No "emotional entanglements" had surfaced until a year ago when the billionaire had purchased a "massive and magnificent" château / grand cru vineyard / fruit orchard / sheep farm in Bordeaux and hired a twenty-seven-year-old landscape designer named Nicole Aumont to refresh the gardens.

Finally a photo, but not of Klement.

Zoom-lens capture of a young, pretty, obviously pregnant blond woman kneeling as she weeded a rose bed.

The caption: "The young bride-to-be tends her flowers while awaiting her own blossoming."

I added to my notes: **SoCal/France?** and went into the kitchen for more coffee.

Because of my training, my instinct when introduced to murder is to look at the family. But it's more than academic interest; a large percentage of homicides are committed by alleged loved ones.

I sat at the kitchen table mentally untangling this victim's family.

Donny had been Victor Klement's youngest child for two and a half decades, soon to be displaced by a newborn.

What had caused Klement's change of heart after long bachelorhood? A need for companionship in old age? Doubtful; a billion and a half could buy you plenty of companionship without the need for a legal contract.

Robin and I had lived together without a legal contract. Hadn't talked about that for years.

The same went for Milo and Rick, choosing not to cash in on new freedom for gay people.

Nicole Aumont-Klement, younger than her new fiancé's children, had to know what she was getting herself into. Did she figure she'd hooked herself an aging gamefish and expect a brief but filling shore dinner?

What expectations had any of Klement's wives brought to marriage?

Interesting questions but no relevance I could see to a dead man in a bed.

Still, money was a combustible fuel and one less share of $1.5 billion could be explosive.

No forced entry, no struggle, could mean someone with whom Donny Klement had been comfortable.

A lover seething over a relationship ended badly? Someone Donny Klement had trusted enough to offer a key?

In any event, a shooter comfortable enough to break in after dark, confidence kicked up by a firearm in one hand.

Maybe a penlight, as well, for highlighting the target?

Getting up close but not so near as to be within arm's reach.

Bang.

The Wishers project had set Milo thinking about a homeless suspect, but how would any of them know the photographer's sleep habits?

Unless they'd been invited back after the shoot.

A social call follow-up instigated by a naive man convinced he'd made himself some new friends?

The Wishers project itself—bringing strangers with troubled histories into his home—seemed potentially explosive. Even assuming the best of intentions, Donny Klement had run the risk of being resented for toying with the emotions of people on the edge.

Dressing them up like full-sized marionettes and coaxing them to talk about their fantasies.

Then what? Back to the streets and slap-in-the-face reality?

So maybe he had tried to fill in some blank spaces with follow-up visits.

Or the man dubbed Adonis by his mother had bought into her adulation and thought himself an invulnerable demi-god.

I finished the coffee, shifting back to romance gone rotten. The bed had shown no signs of anyone sharing with Donny Klement. But beds can be straightened.

If Milo was lucky, the techs would pull up probative prints, hairs, or fluids.

But even if it turned out that Donny had slept alone, the crime scene could point to someone he hadn't been intimate with but still trusted.

Like a half sib. At least one of whom worked twenty minutes away from the blue building, in Beverly Hills.

The more I thought about Victor Klement's frequent domestic shuffles, the more chaotic the billionaire's life seemed.

Intentional turmoil, concocted by a man with no taste for durable relationships?

An only child who'd created five other solo acts?

No apparent craving for company, yet he'd propagated with abandon.

Out for self-replication?

The ultimate ego trip.

I phoned Milo to discuss all of that, got voicemail on his cell and his office phone. Crossing the kitchen, I left the house through the back door, walked the stone path that enters the garden, and stopped by the pond to feed the koi.

I've had most of the fish for twenty or so years and when my head's knotted up, their beauty and gregariousness help untangle it. As always, my footsteps brought them storming up to the rock rim, frothing and bubbling and leaping as I tossed in a handful of pellets. Nice to be appreciated.

I sat there for a while on a Japanese stone bench worn smooth, before continuing toward the far end of the property where Robin works in a mini-me of the house. Machine noise filtered from inside. One of her power saws—a high-pitched whine said the band saw. She'd spent the last couple of days creating jigs and shaping guitar backs and sides from old seasoned rosewood planks bought from a ninety-year-old cabinetmaker who'd finally decided to retire.

Not wanting to distract her when her hands were inches from the whirring oval of fangs, I sat back down and hung with the koi. Hearing sounds that had been there all along. The scuttle of unseen squirrels. A symphony of birdsong.

Eventually, the squirrels went mute and the birds kicked it up. Raven-rasps, cheeps and tweets from sparrows and finches and wrens. The bee-like buzz of hummingbirds, the surprisingly delicate peeps of hawks.

Last year, a Cooper's hawk had tended a nest of three newborns in one of our pine trees. Raptors get to adult size quickly but their brains lag way behind, so for a few months, you end up with a bunch of airborne goofs. For a full week, Robin and I had sat on the terrace and watched the comedy that resulted from young ones learning to fly. Including one horrifying direct hit of a studio window that we initially thought was fatal.

Just as we reached the inert body, the hawk shook itself off and flew away.

At some point you leave the nest.

Unless your dad's mega-rich and chooses to keep you juvenile.

Five, soon to be six, only children.

In Donny Klement's case, the additional complication of a drug-addicted mother.

Adonis. That could be a tough one out on the playground.

Vanessa Charles, blasted on dope, watching her idealized child frolic in soft, Malibu sand before overdosing?

If she'd owned her residence, Donny Klement had likely inherited it. Meaning the blue building could be an auxiliary residence and Milo had another place to list on his victim's warrant.

I made a mental note.

Check for an address in 90265.

The sawing stopped. When the quiet lingered, I saluted the fish and walked to the studio.

7

Robin was at her bench, goggles dangling loose, wearing black overalls and a red T-shirt, her mass of auburn curls tied up high. A stack of guitar-shaped slices of brilliantly hued purplish-chocolate wood sat in front of her, minus the one in her hands that she flexed and tapped.

Blanche, blond, sweet-faced, built like a fire hydrant, waddled toward me for a neck rub.

Robin said, "Quick on the uptake, girlfriend." Big smile. "Hi, handsome. Finished for the day?"

"You bet."

"Me, too, perfect timing." She placed the single board atop the others and trued the edges of the pile.

I looked at the wood. "Nice."

"Seasoned Brazilian, great resonance. Helmut told me he bought it sixty years ago in Spain and it was already aged."

Removing the goggles and hanging them up, she

brushed her bench spotless, kissed my cheek, then my lips, standing on tiptoes to reach me. Blanche, rubbing against my pant leg, began snuffling.

"Chill, dear, we need to share him. So what're we doing for dinner?"

"Up to you."

"I've been way too precise all day, hon. Please be masterly and make a decision."

"That place up at the top of the Glen."

"Great, let me clean up."

We entered the house, continued to the bedroom where she ran a bath and stripped naked.

I said, "Cleanliness can wait."

Later, after catching my breath, I showered and called the restaurant for a reservation.

text from Milo arrived between my two
morning patients.

Got a meet with Colin Klement at 2,
hope you can make it, here's where.

Followed by an address.

See you there.

The building was on Olympic Boulevard, the
south end of Beverly Hills where Beverly Drive and
Beverwil nudge each other. Three-story brick structure with a glass bow-front. The glass showcased
vintage Ferraris, Porsches, Lamborghinis, and such;
a dealer called The Real Wheels of Beverly Hills.

I was two minutes early but no sign of Milo.
He's never late. Most likely he'd gotten there even

earlier and, itchy for a lead, had gone in. I entered the lobby.

CMK Wealth Management was listed on the third floor. I took the stairs and ended up on a plum-carpeted landing. The bow-glass streamed sunlight from the north. Nice view of the Beverly Hills shopping district.

Four offices, the one I was looking for a corner suite.

Inside, soft lighting from a brass chandelier and music from an unknown source worked at enhancing a windowless waiting room. Walls were papered in green-and-red tartan. A cream-colored rug lay diagonally over hardwood. A brown leather Chesterfield trimmed with bronze nail-heads faced two tapestry-covered chairs.

Everything orchestrated to say **Your Money Is Safe with Us.**

On a side table, magazines were splayed precisely, as if never read. From **American Yachtsman** to **People,** with business periodicals in between. I looked for **Forbes,** found it. Wondered what Colin Klement had thought about the piece on his father.

Behind a demi-lune desk at the far end sat a beautiful young brunette in charcoal cashmere whose smile supplied additional wattage.

She consulted an iPad. "Hi, Dr. . . . Delaware. The lieutenant and Colin have started, I'll see you in, here's some water." Holding out a bottle of Dasani.

I checked my watch. Right on time.

She laughed. "Yes, I know. He got here before you did and Colin said why not. Colin's always busy."

She brandished the water. "This way, please."

A right turn took us down a plaid hallway hung with hunting and fishing prints and broken by two open doorways. Both offered views of good-sized but bare-bones white rooms. Three people in each, everyone fixed on computer monitors. One of them looked up.

Cashmere said, "Hi, Evan."

"Marie." Back to columns of numbers.

The final doorway was sealed by unmarked double doors. Marie knocked lightly and twisted a heavy brass knob.

This office shouted **The Boss's Lair.**

Honey-colored, linenfold oak paneling surrounded a massive, spit-shined mahogany desk backed by a wall chocked with enlarged, gilt-framed color photos and certificates. On the desk, two twenty-four-inch screens and three cellphones. A gilt Tiffany desk set inlaid with abalone disks shared space with a burled humidor and a gold cigar lighter. Across the room, a mahogany-and-glass bar on wheels hosted premium booze and crystal glassware.

Not a whiff of tobacco. Were the humidor and lighter props? Everything, from the moment I'd walked in, including Marie, felt choreographed.

The director of that grand production rose from an ergonomic chair behind the desk, leaned over, and extended a firm hand. Milo watched, expressionless, as we shook.

"Doctor? Colin. Make yourself comfortable."

As I settled next to Milo, Colin Klement laced his hands over his abdomen and studied me.

Melissande Gornick had dismissed Donny's brother as a "corporate," and Colin Klement looked every bit the L.A. moneyman. Broad-shouldered, slightly thickset, hair graying strategically at the temples. He wore authoritative steel-framed glasses, an earpiece, a tailored navy suit, and an open-necked blue-and-white-striped shirt. No tie, but the shirt had French cuffs from which onyx cuff links glinted.

He was also Black, hair cut close to the scalp and razor-shaped at the borders. His eyes remained on me. Waiting for me to register surprise? I supposed that happened fairly often.

Case in point: Mel Gornick's qualifier: "Corporate . . . even though . . ."

When I didn't react, Colin shifted his attention to Milo. "Okay, where were we—oh yes, Donny's mom. As I said, she's deceased, don't know the details, laid eyes on her only once . . . had to be over twenty years ago. Dad had flown in, we were heading to Santa Barbara for him to look at some paintings, and he stopped in Malibu without saying why and told me to wait in the car. A few minutes later, she came out with Donny—he was a little kid—Dad got back in and we continued. I asked him who that was and he told me. Then he changed the subject."

His resigned smile said, **You learn the rules and stick with them.**

Milo said, "What about Donny's other relatives? Any cousins on his mother's side?"

Colin shook his head. "Not a clue."

"So not much contact among the sibs."

"That's an understatement, Lieutenant." Opening the cigar box, Colin pulled out two Cohibas and offered them to us.

No temptation for me but Milo displayed ethical courage. "No, thanks, sir."

"Don't smoke, huh?" said Colin, eyeing the cigars and returning them to the humidor. "Probably smart. I started when I was on Wall Street, we used to celebrate deals with boxes of the stuff. I barely indulge anymore. Obviously, never in here, a lot of clients would hate the smell. And now, not at home, either." Fleeting smile. "For two days afterward, my wife refuses to kiss me."

The photos behind him showcased a pretty redheaded woman, six kids under twelve, and three well-fed Labrador retrievers. Blond, black, brown. The largest shot was the happy family posed in front of a panoramic lake, probably Tahoe.

An only child who **had** craved company.

Milo said, "Exactly how many sibs do you and Donny have?"

"Half sibs. Four, soon to be five in a few months," said Colin. "Dad surprised us and found himself a new amour in France." Tossing that out breezily.

His eyes clenched shut and reopened. "Sorry, it's wrong to be flippant but I'm still processing this . . . poor Donny. Why in the world would anyone want to do that to him?"

His chest heaved. "I misspoke re: sibs, it's actually three, soon to be four. We lost a sister years ago. Don't know the details, just that it was accidental."

"How did you learn Donny's mother was deceased?"

"He told me."

"When?"

"When we got together."

"When was that, sir?"

"The first time was . . . around a year ago. Since then, we've gotten together three, four times, the last was around a month ago. Why after all these years? Wish I could claim credit but it was my wife's idea. She comes from a big Irish family, has always prevailed on me to get to know my sibs. I've resisted because my family's situation is . . . unconventional but it's what I'm used to. I didn't see any reason to rock the boat. What finally happened is Sheila read an art magazine—she's a giant art fan—and it was a small notice of an exhibit Donny had in Europe.

It said that his home base was L.A. and that got Sheila going. 'Don't you think it's crazy that you don't even know him?' I said I'd think about it. That was two years ago. I finally made the move."

He wheeled back and crossed his legs. "Sheila doesn't nag but she can be gently persistent. When I called Donny, I expected it would go nowhere. But he sounded genuinely happy to hear from me and we arranged to have coffee. After that, we'd get together for lunch or dinner, every few months."

His lips curled inward. "Three, four times, total. Doesn't amount to much, does it? And now he's gone. I enjoyed being with him, he was a very pleasant guy." Sharp intake of breath. "My brother."

Another eye clench. When gray-green irises reappeared they were moist. "Anyway, I'm sure our eccentric family isn't what you're interested in, Lieutenant. You're looking for something relevant to what happened. You say it was a gunshot?"

"Yes, sir."

"A robbery?"

"Too early to tell."

"Did he suffer?"

"No, it was quick."

Colin Klement breathed in and out. "That's good. Poor Donny. He was a gentle soul. A little naive, I thought. Maybe too trusting. Are you aware of his latest project?"

"The Wishers."

Colin removed his glasses, held them up to the

light, wiped both lenses, and put them back on. "Bringing homeless head-cases into your home and dressing them up in costumes? Obviously, I thought it was poorly advised but of course I said nothing."

"Why of course?"

"My style, Lieutenant, is not to make waves." A manicured finger tapped the humidor. "Discretion is the core of my approach to life as well as to investment."

Milo said, "You do wealth management."

"With an emphasis on preservation. If you want get-rich-quick, I'm not your man. I start off with successful people and depending on their priorities, either I exercise damage control—it's not what you earn, it's what you keep—or get a mite more adventurous and grow their holdings slowly and gradually."

He wheeled back to the desk. "This is a boutique business, we oversee just short of a billion dollars. I know that sounds huge but in the investment world it's a blip on the screen."

"Got it, sir. So you think the Wishers might have something to do with your brother's murder."

"I don't have anything to base that on, Lieutenant. But logically, if you let mentally ill drug addicts into your life, you're being reckless, no?"

"Makes sense, sir. Do you know of any specific threats from those people?"

"No, but I wouldn't because as I said, we never discussed it beyond the basics. And Donny seemed so pleased with himself, I didn't have the heart to be a wet blanket."

"Pleased how?"

"He'd convinced himself he was actually helping them. And he'd gotten a nice write-up in some magazine, to boot."

"Is there anyone else you can think of who'd want to harm your brother?"

"No, but I'm not the person to ask, Lieutenant. As I said, our family structure is unusual."

I said, "Did your father set that up intentionally?"

Colin gave a start. Worked to produce a smile and ended up with something more like dyspepsia. "Spoken like a true psychologist. Yes, I know who you are. Lieutenant Sturgis explained your presence in terms of it being a case with possible psychological ramifications. I took that to mean analyzing the psychotics Donny chose to involve himself with."

He hadn't answered the question. Milo and I kept the silence going.

Colin blinked. "What was that you asked— oh, Dad. Was it intentional? I suppose on some level it would have to be. You don't just keep marrying and divorcing without expecting some sort of disconnect. On the other hand, keeping our issues separate could be explained in terms of Dad's desire to keep the peace."

I said, "Familiarity breeds problems."

"Exactly. Which isn't to say we don't get along when we do have contact. Which is admittedly rare. Take my older brother, Hugh, for example. He's John Wayne redux, invests in cattle, bison, elk, and ostriches for meat, has ranches in Montana and Wyoming and a fabulous house near Jackson Hole."

"Sounds like you saw him more often than Donny."

"Hugh reached out to me when I was on Wall Street, has had us to Jackson every couple of years. Last year it was Christmas, we had a marvelous time with his brood—he's got five. When he's here for business, we try to have dinner. We exchange holiday and birthday cards."

"Did Hugh have any contact with Donny?"

"None. When I told him I'd met with Donny, he said great, but showed no interest in joining in . . . but I should probably tell him, anyway." Head shake. Off came the glasses again. He rubbed his eyes. "This is surreal. Someone's here one day, gone the next."

I said, "What about the third sib?"

"My sister Bianca is based on the East Coast, does high-end home and commercial design that takes her to Europe and Asia. If she's been to L.A., she's never informed me and I doubt she has because she calls it La La Land—that typical New York thing. In the past few years, I've seen her maybe . . . three times when I was in New York for meetings. Drinks at the Carlyle. Again, cordial. But nothing beyond that. Now you're going to ask me if she ever met with

Donny and I'm going to profess ignorance. Which this conversation is really driving home." His forehead wrinkled. "On top of everything else, there's a generational thing. Hugh, Bianca, and I are all in our forties and Donny is—was twenty-nine. Whole different consciousness."

The gap soon to be widened by the arrival of a newborn in Bordeaux.

Milo said, "How did Donny support himself?"

"I don't know the details," said Colin. "But Dad's always been generous. And fair."

He blinked, looked away. "Yes, that means trust funds, we've all been lucky. Or as the kids say nowadays, privileged. Hugh, Bianca, and I have used our autonomy to develop successful careers. Would Donny have done that? I'd like to think so."

He shrugged. "On top of that, he owns at least one piece of prime real estate. The house he grew up in, right on the sand in Broad Beach."

"Do you have an address?"

"No, as I said I only saw it once. Not a huge place but the land value's got to be phenomenal and if he rented it out, the income would be substantial."

"As far as you know the building on Venice was his main residence?"

"He never mentioned another one," said Colin. "Mostly I'd ask him about photography and he'd ask about my kids. The plan was to have him over this Thanksgiving."

He threw up his hands. "So much for that."

I said, "Did the two of you meet near the studio?"

"Yup. I'd come to him, and we'd either walk or drive, depending."

He frowned. "To be honest, at first it was challenging. Getting to know each other. Finding common ground. It's hitting me now. How much more there was to learn—hold on, I just thought of something. He had an assistant, clearly head over heels about him. She might know more than I do."

"Melissande Gornick."

"You've met her?"

"We have."

"My impression was no Einstein, but she certainly seemed devoted to Donny."

Milo said, "One more thing. We found a white card with nothing but Donny's name on it in his wallet."

News to me. I stayed impassive.

Colin Klement's smile seemed to curdle around the edges. "Did you? The old carte blanche, huh? Literally. It's a major perk we all get because Dad's a huge client of U.S. Surety. When I was in college, I was a showy prick and had major fun waltzing into the Philadelphia branch, asking for money and walking out with it. My frat brothers, waiting outside, were immensely impressed. Especially when we blew it on beer. Carte blanche—can't think of the last time I used mine. Don't even know where it is. But Donny had his, huh?"

Milo said, "Along with his credit cards."

"So that might answer your question, Lieutenant. When Donny wanted money, he could go to the L.A. branch—which is downtown on Seventh, but don't try to find it. It's not a bank the way you'd think of it. Just a suite in a building that you can't enter until they scan your iris. And don't bother trying to talk to them. They'll stonewall you worse than the CIA. That's the whole point. Exclusion."

Milo said, "So theoretically, your brother could've kept serious cash in his studio."

"Theoretically, yes," said Colin. "You're thinking robbery."

"Now that we know about the white card, sure."

"On the other hand, Lieutenant, I can't see Donny hoarding money or anything else. At one of our lunches he told me he was aiming for simplicity in all things material. Or something along those lines. I thought it sounded sophomoric—a phase. But of course I said nothing."

He poked the humidor. "This is driving home how little I have to contribute. Because of the way we were distanced from each other."

His eyes hardened. "I'm sure Dad had no intentions along those lines. But . . . what's the difference? What's done is done."

He shot a French cuff, exposing a wafer-thin gold watch. "Feel free to contact me should other questions come up. Though I really don't think I'm going to be able to help you much."

Milo said, "Appreciate the time, sir. Just a few more questions, please?"

Quick glance at the watch. "I've got a client in ten, would like to compose myself before."

"We'll be quick." Out came the pad. "How can we get in contact with your father?"

"That's a tough one. He changes phone numbers regularly." He clicked on the earpiece. "Marie, could you please scare up my father's most recent number and give it to the lieutenant? Thanks."

"Any reason for all that secrecy?" said Milo.

"Dad likes his privacy and a man in his position needs to work at that."

"How often do you see your father?"

"When he's here, he calls. Not for a while." Steely eyes, now. Unwelcome territory.

Milo said, "Got it. Reason I'm asking is if we can't reach him, someone else will need to make arrangements."

"For the funeral?"

"For collection of the body and the funeral. Would you be willing to do it?"

"I suppose I'd have to," said Colin. "Scratch that, of course I would. And so as not to be evasive, I believe I last saw my father six years ago. I invited him to the christening of one of my daughters. He flew in, left right after the ceremony."

He got to his feet, braced on the desktop for a second, straightened, walked to the door and opened it.

Silent, plaid corridor. Wealth managed discreetly.

Milo said, "Just one more question, Mr. Klement, and please don't take offense."

"Let me guess. Where was I when it happened." Half smile. "Sheila watches a lot of true-crime shows. She told me you'd be asking that and not to get upset."

"Appreciate your understanding, sir."

"Thank Sheila," said Colin. "Well, before I answer, I'm going to need to know when it happened."

"Yesterday, most likely during the early-morning hours."

"That's an easy one. I was at our place in Tahoe with Sheila. Just us and our Tahoe caretaker, we left the kids with our housekeepers. It was a makeup anniversary celebration, we missed the actual day because our eldest came down with mono. We got back this morning at six and I was here by seven."

"Thank you, sir."

"If you'd like to speak to Jed—the caretaker— feel free."

"If you don't mind."

Colin Klement frowned. "Jed Stein. Marie will get you his number."

He walked us toward the waiting room. Stopped and let out a strange, dry laugh. "Sheila's going to want to know the details—what did they ask you, what did you tell them. She said you'd want to know about our travel itinerary so here it is: We have a jet card with Sentient, flew in and out privately. If you'd like, I can have Marie scare up the flight manifesto."

"Great, thanks."

"You really want it?" said Colin Klement.

Milo smiled. "For your wife's sake, sir."

"Ha . . . or maybe you're finessing. I suppose I should be thankful you're being meticulous. My approach as well. Pay attention to details."

He pivoted, returned to his office, and left us to make our own exit.

Moments later, Marie came forward with a number on a small piece of paper. "This is all I've got. The Dorchester hotel in London. Apparently Mr. Klement, Senior, stayed there six years ago."

As we left the building, Milo said, "Where're you parked?"

"Beverwil."

"Me, too."

We walked west and rounded the corner. Milo looked at my old green Seville, stationed a few yards south. "I got stuck with two blocks up. What's the secret?"

I said, "Maybe the gods like relics."

"Or you're just one of the popular kids."

We continued toward his unmarked. He said, "So what did you think of brother Colin?"

"Not much of a relationship with Donny but other than that, nothing jumped out."

"Little Mel made a little pissy face when she called him a money guy, so obviously in her book that's a character flaw. Then she added 'even though . . .' which I'm thinking meant even though he's Black."

"That's how I interpreted it."

"Like melanin's incompatible with a career in finance? Jesus, I thought this was the woke generation."

I said, "Youth has nothing to do with mental flexibility."

"What does?"

"Temperament and upbringing."

A few steps later, I said, "You knew how many sibs there were but asked Colin anyway."

"Works for lawyers in court and ace detectives hunting evaders and outright liars."

"You sense either in Colin?"

"Not so far, but I am gonna check out the jet company and the caretaker. Whole different world, this family. Daddy marries women, impregnates 'em, leaves 'em, and moves on. So far I haven't found any reports of the divorces getting nasty, so maybe Klement lets 'em down easy with huge settlements. Plus, as we just heard, trust funds and white cards for the kids. That came up a couple of hours ago, got a call from the lab. Who knew carte blanche was a real thing?"

I said, "Being able to walk into a private bank and get cash on demand would explain why Donny doesn't seem to have done much recently besides the Wishers project."

"It also explains why his wallet wasn't touched. With big bucks lying around, why bother?"

I said, "Given Donny's approach to personal security, lying around could be literal."

"He leaves a wad of cash in plain sight, brings the Wishers upstairs, and someone sees it. Beyond naive, but who knows? Anything else?"

I told him my theory about Klement trying to replicate his only-child persona.

He said, "Guy's out to clone himself?"

"Psychologically."

"Sounds like a massive ego," he said.

"It's also consistent," I said, "with putting each child in a separate compartment in order to maintain control."

"Hmm. You'd think controlling the dough would be enough power, so maybe he's a **major-league** megalomaniac. I guess that fits with the billionaire thing, he probably never hears the word no. Meanwhile, I've got a victim and no parent I can easily notify. You believe Colin about not being able to reach Daddy at will? No contact since six **years** ago?"

"I did some research, too, and Klement does come across obsessed with privacy. Haven't found a single picture of him. You?"

"Not so far," he said. "What were your sources?"

"**Forbes** and a French paper."

He grinned and slapped my back. "Great minds.

Did you also slog through a bunch of conspiracy theory bullshit?"

"Oh yeah."

He mimed brushing his hands off. "Putting the homeless aside, what do you think of two of Klement's kids meeting untimely ends? So far."

I said, "Someone aiming for a bigger slice of the pie?"

"It's a humongous pie, Alex. I'm gonna see what I can learn about the dead sister. I'd also like to know more about Donny's mom. The article said she O.D.'d but didn't specify on what. Before I got here, I looked for her death record, only found the summary. Manner is listed as accidental."

I said, "Colin's mom is also deceased."

"Her I found an obit on, **New York Times**, placed by the company she worked for."

He stopped, pulled out his pad, flipped a page, and showed it to me.

Sharleen Bostock Klement, born in Harlem, had started as a receptionist at the company where her future husband "the financier" Victor Klement was interning. They got married, he worked his way up to broker, she to executive secretary. Then she earned her own broker's license and moved to a larger company where she ended up as vice president in charge of government securities. Her death, ten years ago, had been due to diabetes.

I said, "He climbs the corporate ladder while

she's stuck making appointments. Eventually, she manages to better herself."

"The old glass ceiling. On top of that, a Black woman working on Wall Street forty years ago? When she got hitched to Klement he wasn't big-rich yet, so I'm thinking maybe true love. But obviously not enduring love. What's the thing you guys have for, when someone can't keep a relationship going?"

"There are all kinds of reasons."

"Yeah, yeah, but the **thing**?"

"Borderline personality?"

"Bingo. Goes with nuclear narcissism, right?"

"It can," I said. "Also with lousy self-esteem and the inability to maintain a consistent identity."

He laughed. "Fine, so I can't be a shrink, yet. It's probably irrelevant, anyway."

We resumed walking.

I said, "Colin didn't seem resentful of his father so I'm thinking when Klement's fortune did grow, he took care of Sharleen retroactively."

He said, "Controlling by doling the goodies, everyone falls in line. But maybe that didn't extend to the kids not resenting each other, Alex. Like you said, they were raised to be strangers. A billion and a half worth of pie coulda also made them competitors. Cut it four ways, instead of five. Which brings me right back to the sib who recently cultivated a relationship with Donny."

"Any evidence Colin's having money problems?"

"Not so far and nothing in his past is remotely iffy. But you don't need problems to want more."

He stopped again, checked his pad. "Here are his basics, per Who's Who. Phi Beta Kappa at Penn, played second base on the baseball team. Stayed at Penn, earned an M.B.A. at Wharton, worked for a few banks and hedge funds before starting his own firm ten years ago."

I said, "Sounds like Smart Person 101."

"It also sounds like someone with a **deep** appreciation for the benefits of dough. And the wherewithal to hire someone to do his dirty work while he's enjoying breakfast crepes lakeside or on a private jet. Come to think of it, what if he connected with Donny not because of his wife like he told us, but to fish out more about him? Like Donny's vulnerabilities. The layout of Donny's pad. Like where to lift a key."

We resumed walking, didn't speak before reaching his unmarked.

"Or," he said, "I'm just resentful because of the croissants."

I said, "All of a sudden, you're a class warrior?"

"Nah, just basic jealousy, anyone can achieve it. Nasty emotion, the green monster."

That made me think of street people dressed in fancy costumes by a rich kid, then tossed back into their realities.

I said so.

He said, "That, too. Some case, huh? Encompasses

the whole damn universe. Of which I am **not** a master."

We reached his Impala where he thanked me and continued to the driver's door. I'd covered twenty yards when I heard him call out my name.

Standing by the unmarked, waving his cellphone. I walked back.

"Just got a text from Deandra Sparrow, the one who reviewed the project. Willing to meet if we come to her. Still have time?"

CHAPTER

10

He dropped an LAPD card on the Impala's dash that might or might not avert a parking ticket and we took the Seville.

I'd worked on the leather for hours over the weekend with saddle soap. He sat back, sniffed. "Pretty nice relic, kiddo. What number engine is this?"

"Three."

"When's the fourth coming?"

"When it's necessary."

"Loyalty," he said. "Always been one of your strong points."

Meeting Deandra Sparrow took us to a surprise destination: chicken take-out place on a dreary stretch of Pico east of La Cienega. Two of four parking slots out front were occupied by delivery cars with rubber cockscombs on their roofs, the third was devoted to handicapped parking, the fourth vacant.

Milo said, "Another open slot, you were **definitely** one of the popular kids. Ever run for student council?"

"God forbid."

The interior of Prime Cluck was bright yellow, too-warm, with a full-width counter and a single eat-in table. Smells jog my memory more than any other sensation and the whiff I caught of stale oil mixed with poultry reminded me of childhood Mondays.

My aunt Eleanor's bare-bones kitchen recuperating from her solitary Sunday "broiler" suppers.

Not much of a cook but a sweet lady, my maiden aunt. Her old frame bungalow near the freight tracks had been a sanctuary for me. When I was able to sneak over there.

I recalled the whisper she'd place in my ear when my father glared at me.

You're a good boy, Alexander. Don't ever forget that.

This kitchen wasn't much bigger than Eleanor's. A fry cook lolled at the back, entranced by his phone. Out in front, a teenage boy with dual man-buns that evoked hippo horns swept the floor in lazy circles. A young woman behind the counter was also waxing cellular. She glanced at us and returned to thumb-work.

Milo walked up to her. "Deandra?"

She flinched, as if her name was a burden. Pocketing the phone, she pushed open low saloon doors to the left of the counter and stepped out.

Deandra Sparrow was twenty or so, five-four, squarely built, now blond, with a rolling walk and small, squinting eyes behind tiger-framed glasses. No more page-bob; her hair was long, luxuriant, and layered, reminiscent of eighties TV.

A Prime Cluck apron cut for someone with NBA proportions covered her from neck to ankle. She untied it and tossed it on a chair, revealing a baggy gray T-shirt and blue jeans held up by red suspenders. The shirt memorialized a twenty-year-old celebration of banned books.

Dropping onto one of three chairs at the single table, she tightened her shoulders and stared straight ahead.

We sat down facing her. Milo said, "Thanks for meeting with us, Ms. Sparrow."

"Soon as I texted you, I said, shit, that was a mistake." A baby-doll voice and a hard tone combined to create something oddly metallic. A computerized toy gone awry.

Milo said, "Oh? How come?"

"I've got nothing to tell you re Donny and I don't like talking to cops."

"Have you had bad experiences with cops?"

"Not yet," she said. "Just on general principles."

"Well, we hope to make this easy for you."

Deandra Sparrow played with her hair. Looking

up at a **No Smoking** sign, she shot us a dare-you smirk and pulled out a pack of Camels.

When we didn't react to her lighting up, she stopped puffing.

Milo said, "This isn't sucking up. Your review of Donny's project was interesting."

Squinty eyes hyphened. "Yeah, right."

He said. "That part about class consciousness."

She jammed the cigarette in her mouth, inhaled, and kept the smoke in her lungs for a long time. When she breathed out, a cloud of toxin filled the space between us.

Milo said, "So you freelance."

"If I had a permanent gig, would I be the fuck here?"

I said, "Know what you mean."

"About what?"

"Going from job to job. I paid my way through college gigging with a wedding–bar mitzvah band."

"Haven't experienced either rite of passage," she said. Her stony stare lasted a few seconds before giving way to curiosity. "What kind of music?"

"Whatever the client wanted."

"That doesn't tell me shit."

"Dances, lots of ethnic stuff—Greek, Hungarian, Latino, Israeli. Europop when they asked for it."

"Sounds profoundly fascinating," she said, aiming for a smoke ring but creating a flimsy semicircle.

I said, "Have you written other stuff for **Angel City**?"

"What is this, Wikipedia research? The only reason I got it was connections, okay? And if that sounds like pulling privilege, I don't give a flying shit because I'm good and I deserve what I get."

"Whatever it takes," said Milo.

"Whatever it takes that doesn't leave people **bleeding**." She formed a finger-gun. "Pow."

A cloud of flush rose on the back of Milo's neck. The color snaked its way up and across to his jawline. He worked hard not to grind his teeth. Put in even more effort and produced a smile.

"Someone," he said, in an unsettlingly soft voice, "left Donny Klement bleeding."

The change in his tone made Deandra Sparrow flinch harder. She blocked her face by smoking some more, reduced the cigarette to a half inch of limp paper before dropping it onto the floor and stubbing it out.

Hippo Horn, now behind the counter and drinking from a giant red cup, said, "Hey."

Deandra Sparrow said, "I'll clean it."

"Better."

She whipped her head toward him, glared, lit up a second cigarette, flung the match on the floor.

He said, "C'mon."

She said, "You deaf, dude? I'll take care of it."

He returned to his drink. She smiled like a victorious gladiator.

Milo said, "Did you know Donny before you wrote about him?"

"Nope."

"How'd you connect?"

"I heard about him from someone I knew and her mother's an editor so I got the idea and basically begged the shit out of her. The mother. First she said no, then she said, okay, they'd been having slow months, could spare a few inches."

She rotated a finger in the air. "Whoop-de-doo, they even paid me. Want to guess how much?"

Milo said, "Five hundred?"

"Try eighty and I had to rewrite like five times. I didn't give a shit, it was a credit."

I said, "How'd your friend hear about Donny?"

"She works for him. Calls herself a P.A. but she's basically a gofer. When she posted about this thing he was doing, I thought **Rolling Stone** or **The Atlantic**. But try getting through to them."

"We're talking about Mel Gornick."

"You know her?"

"She discovered the body."

"Fuck. Her head must be exploding, she's not exactly Zeno of Citium."

I laughed. "Definitely not a Stoic."

She stared at me, then smirked. "Oh yeah, college." She mimed frantic air guitar. "She's actually who **found** him?"

"Afraid so."

"**Is** she freaking out?" More of a clinical inquiry than caring about a friend.

I said, "She was pretty upset at the scene."

"The scene," she said. "Hey, good title for something, maybe I'll write **this** up. Cops trying to be cool in order to crack someone open."

Milo said, "You might want to wait."

"For what?"

"Until we actually know something."

"Like you'd tell me."

"Why not, if you helped us."

"Yeah, well, like I said, **I've** got nothing to tell **you.**"

"How about some general impressions of Donny."

"Hot looking. Nice person."

I said, "Did you watch him photograph the Wishers?"

"You want to pin it on them?"

Milo said, "We don't want anything, Deandra. It's a matter of where the evidence leads."

"Yeah, right. Like if it was a white privileged dude you'd go for that."

She smirked. Milo drew himself higher and leaned forward, maximizing his bulk. It generally works and this time was no exception. Deandra Sparrow shrank back reflexively. As if there was only so much space to go around and he'd just taken a second helping.

"I don't know what you want," she said, feebly. Two puffs did nothing to settle her.

"You don't know anything about us but you don't like us. Fine, there's nothing we can do about that. But how about you try to cut through at least some of the attitude so we can do our job and find out who murdered someone you say was a nice person."

He formed his own finger-gun. "Pow pow pow, while he was helpless in bed."

Deandra Sparrow shuddered and smoked.

Milo said, "A person who'd do that shouldn't be out on the street, Deandra, and equally important, a grieving family deserves justice. So whatever you think of us, you might wanna help."

"Touchy, touchy, touchy," she said, but her voice faltered. "Fine, ask what you want." Then, a dry bray. "Just don't pow pow pow **me**."

"Let's start with what you were just asked. Did you ever observe Donny photograph the Wishers? Or anyone else."

"Just one of them, a woman, don't remember her name. Or if I even heard it . . . no, I didn't. For sure. Just a woman—real skinny."

I said, "What costume did Donny put her in?"

"Blond wig, white satin dress, tiara on her head. Like a Jean Harlow thing—if you have any idea who she was."

That reminded me of a teenage patient I'd seen a few years ago. Astonished because I knew the names of the Beatles.

I said, "I was thinking more Mae West."

Frown. Not a clue. She covered her ignorance by smoking manically.

Milo took out his pad and scanned. "Donny called that person Beverly."

"You say so."

I said, "What was the interaction between them like?"

"She didn't look murderous if that's what you're getting at."

"Was the atmosphere friendly?"

We waited.

Deandra Sparrow said, "Nothing weird happened, no hassles. He was extremely sweet to her. I thought that was cool. Treating her like anyone else." Quick eye-shift. "Maybe it was even real."

I said, "Any reason to think Donny wasn't being sincere?"

"Nope, just general principles, I'm a cynical bitch," she said. "Haven't met a lot of sweet people. Don't guess that's your thing, either."

"Good point," I said.

"But yeah, he seemed to really be sweet."

"Can you describe the session?"

"I got there in the middle. He told me she wanted to be an actress from the glamour age and showed me the clothing they'd picked out together. She seemed a little . . . spacy. But smiling. She started to take off her regular clothes right there in front of us but he stopped her and walked her upstairs and came down by himself. A few minutes later, she came down all dressed and he met her at the bottom of the stairs, took her hand, and led her to the chair. Like a gentleman thing. Old-fashioned. She sat down, he told her she looked gorgeous and began fiddling. Getting rid of wrinkles in the dress, straightening the wig. Then he got some makeup and put it on her and started clicking away with a big boxy camera."

I said, "Donny did his own makeup."

"Why wouldn't he? 'Cause he was a guy?"

"A lot of photographers use stylists."

Milo frowned. Loss of a potential source.

"Well, he didn't," she said. The tremolo had returned to her voice and intensified. She removed her glasses, wiped eyes that had suddenly turned dewy.

"What I said before was fucked, he was **totally** sincere. He didn't deserve what happened. I'm sorry, okay? Okay?" Her voice cracked. "Since you texted I've been working on the hard-ass thing because what I **felt** like doing was bawling my fucking head off."

Giggles from the rear of the restaurant. She looked over her shoulder at the cook and Hippo Horn, both of them leering at phone images.

She glared and leaned forward and stage-whispered, "If I'm gonna freak, it won't be in front of **those** fuckheads."

"Got it," said Milo.

She tugged at her hair and squinted at him. "How do **you** do it? Looking at death shit all the time."

"You don't get used to it, Deandra, but you remind yourself you're trying to help someone."

"That's it?"

"It's the price you pay."

Suddenly, she was looking at him differently. Smooth-faced as a child. As wide-eyed as her genetics permitted. "Sounds fucking insane."

"It can be."

"Whatever—I'm sure it takes all types in any job."

"Indeed it does."

She looked away and smoked.

"Deandra, speaking of insane, a lot of homeless people have mental problems. Did Beverly show any signs of that?"

"Besides being ready to strip right there? Nope, but I never heard her say a word."

I said, "Did Donny talk to you about any of the Wishers being tough to work with?"

"Nope and I didn't ask him about it because that felt biased. I did ask him what it was like working with the unhomed community in general. He said they were prisoners of circumstances and that created unnatural histories for them. So the goal of the project was to restore a real history."

"Real in what sense?"

"He didn't get into that."

And she'd never asked.

I said, "Maybe what it would've been like if they were luckier?"

"Probably," she said. "A liberation thing, that's what I emphasized in my review. The healing aspect. Art isn't about making pretty shit. It needs to be transformative."

Milo took enough time to imply he was thinking about that. "Getting back to the Wishers, Deandra, we are not assuming any of them are suspects. But we'd be pretty sloppy if we didn't try to contact them, right?"

Long pause. "You say so."

"Any suggestion how to find them?"

"How the—how would I know?"

"You never asked Donny for contact information."

"Actually." She let the word hang there and shifted in her chair. "Before I came over, I did ask if I could interview a couple of them. To get the subjective side of the process. He said that would be a betrayal of trust and I thought I'd fucked the whole thing up, he'd change his mind. But he didn't and I was grateful."

The age of investigative journalism.

I said, "So Donny thought the project would bring them long-term change?"

Her lips pursed. "Not gonna lie, I thought it was sweet but not exactly realistic. But he's letting me into his world, you think I'm going to argue with him? Also—and here's where I know he was being open and honest—he said the core of the project was for their sakes but if he had to be totally honest, it was also for him."

"How so?"

"I thought it was brave so I didn't push it. I took it to mean that he was filling a hole in his own soul.

Everyone needs metamorphosis and he opened his up to me."

"Good point," said Milo. Sounding as if he meant it.

Deandra Sparrow edged closer to him, placing both her hands flat on the table.

"Like me, I changed my name, okay?" she said. "Not with paperwork but when I was a senior at Cross Lane, I told everyone to call me Sparrow and the administration backed me up. I did it because of my real name—who the fuck wants to be Starkly? I picked Sparrow because they dominate other birds and eat pests."

She stubbed out the second cigarette and chomped air.

I said, "They also flock to urban areas."

"So?"

I smiled. "Tough, like you said." Not telling her sparrow populations had declined massively in cities.

"Exactly. Yeah."

Milo said, "Anything else you can think of that might help?"

"What I **think** is you should talk to Gornick. I mean I was there for what, an hour and a half? She basically lived there. I think she had the hots for him."

"Why's that?"

"She was there when I was there and she was

like . . ." Her head bobbed to the side and back. "He **was** a hot guy."

Milo said, "What kinds of things did Gornick tell you about the project that got you interested?"

"Just that he was reaching out to the unhomed and it was heroic. And BTW, she didn't actually tell me. I read it on her social and contacted her."

"After you contacted her, did the two of you discuss it?"

"We're not like that."

"Like what?"

"Confiders. What actually happened is I begged her and she put me off and I kept begging and finally she hooked me up with her mom and then I begged **her**. Meanwhile, she's still posting about how what she's doing is going to change the world."

She opened her mouth and inserted a gag-me finger.

Milo and I laughed.

"Exactly. No surprise she freaked, she was always a total pussy. I only know her because we both went to Cross Lane. I was on scholarship, she lives in Brentwood and besides her mother being an editor, her father's some sort of big-ass lawyer."

She held out a hand, palm up. "**My** father's dead from alcohol-related liver disease and **my** maternal unit's hooked up to an oxygen tank because she's got COPD."

She looked down at the dead cigarettes. "What

the fuck, it helps me convince myself I'm immortal. And like the Doors said, hope I die before I get old."

Quote from the Who. No sense correcting her.

A phone rang behind the counter. Deandra Sparrow said, "Shit, here we go," trudged back and picked up the receiver. "Yeah . . . yeah . . . hold on . . . where . . . then it's around thirty . . . okay, give me your magic plastic."

Hanging up, she turned to the cook. "Basic box, separate wings, extra sauce."

We got up and Milo asked her if there was anything else she remembered.

"Nope."

Hippo approached the saloon doors and looked at the butts on the floor. "Hey, you said."

"I say a lot of things." To us: "Gotta deliver some breasts and thighs."

Looking straight at Hippo, she ignited a third cigarette and grinned. "Feel the burn."

CHAPTER

11

As I maneuvered out of the Prime Cluck lot, Milo said, "Angry kid. Sounds like she's had it rough." A moment later: "Were we like that at her age?"

"For me," I said, "it was a day-to-day thing."

"For me it was weeks at a time feeling like I wanted to smash someone in the face."

I said nothing.

"Hey," he said. "Congratulate me for all the personal growth."

"I'm beyond impressed."

He laughed. "So did we just learn anything?"

"Donny was passionate about the project."

"That's important because . . ."

"Passion can lead to carelessness."

"He let one of them get too close and paid for it?"

"Or it has nothing to do with the Wishers," I said. "Like you said, there's a big slice of pie at stake."

"Back to the family," he said. "I've got Alicia looking at his social pages, maybe she'll spot some conflict. Or romance present or past. The money angle's gonna be a helluva lot tougher to crack. I tried calling the downtown bank. No answer. Iris scanners? Anything else come to mind?"

"Like you said, Mel Gornick's worth recontacting."

He called the assistant's cell. A woman, not Mel Gornick, said, "Hello?"

"This is Lieutenant Sturgis from LAPD, for Melissande Gornick."

"This is Christine." Low, cool voice. A beat. "Her mother."

"Hello, ma'am. I'm working the homicide that Melissande had the misfortune to discover. I spoke to her yesterday under horrendous circumstances."

"Indeed."

"How's she doing, Ms. Gornick?"

"Ms. **Coolidge.** Mel's therapist has been made aware of the situation."

"Great," he said. "Could I speak with Mel, please?"

"She's indisposed."

"When she is available, could you please ask when we can talk to her again? We'd be happy to come to her."

"Why," said Christine Coolidge, "would you need to do that?"

"To get more background on Mr. Klement."

"Mel was a part-time gofer. Not exactly the executive suite."

"We understand, but still—"

"This has been extremely traumatic for her."

"Of course, how could it not be? But if you don't mind giving her the message."

"And if I do mind?"

"Mel isn't a minor."

"What're you saying? You'll subpoena her? Or whatever it is you people do?"

"Nothing like that, ma'am, but we will keep trying to contact her."

"You're saying you'll harass me until I comply."

"With all due respect, ma'am," double eye-roll, "we're not asking anything unusual. Melissande's boss was murdered and we're trying to get some justice for him and his family."

Silence.

"Ms. Coolidge?"

"I'll need to talk to her therapist."

"Sure," said Milo. "Though as an adult, doesn't she have confidentiality?"

"We've got an arrangement," said Christine Coolidge. "Mel, Dr. Framus, and I."

"An arrangement for—"

"Free exchange of information. Mel may not be a minor but I remain the gatekeeper."

"Got it, Ms. Coolidge, but please do get back to me. And by the way, just to show you how seriously we're taking emotional issues, we've consulted a psychologist on this case. In fact, he happened to be there when your daughter was feeling anxious and he helped her."

"The breathing thing? When she told me, I figured that was an EMT."

"The EMTs were long gone because Mr. Klement was deceased at the scene. It was Dr. Alex Delaware who helped Mel."

"And you're telling me this because . . ."

"I want to reassure you that every measure has been and will be taken to treat your daughter with sensitivity."

"You may actually believe that," said Christine Coolidge, "but Mel's an extremely vulnerable girl and these are extremely stressful circumstances."

"Understood, ma'am. When do you think you'll have a chance to confer with Dr. Framus?"

"You **are** persistent."

"In my job, ma'am, you have to be."

"Your job doesn't concern me."

"In terms of Dr. Framus—"

"I happen to be in Dr. Framus's waiting room right now, Mel's having her session. She leaves me her phone when she's in there."

"Great. So if—"

"If," said Christine Coolidge. "Longest word in the English language."

She cut off the call.

Milo said, "Vulnerable kid or helicopter parent?"

"Maybe both," I said. "I know Helen Framus. She was in the class below mine and we've cross-referred."

"Any good?"

"First-rate."

"Does that include cooperating with the gendarmerie?"

"That never came up," I said. "In the end, she'll do what's right for her patient."

"Meaning?"

"I'll try to talk to her."

After leaving a message at Helen Framus's number, I drove us east on Pico as he called Alicia Bogomil, one of the three younger detectives his captain sometimes loans him.

"Hey, Loo," she said. "Nothing much in Klement's social, just a little on the project—the basics, no bragging—plus the kind of music he likes."

"No love life?"

"Not that he's posted. There are posts from the girl Alex therapized yesterday. She does Face and Snap and Insta and a few others, just posted a bunch of sad-face selfies. She also emoted on the homepage of a school in Brentwood—Cross Lane. Looks like she went there for high school and is doing the auld lang syne bit spiced up with murder."

"What's she saying?"

"Quote: 'I found the body and it was profound and disgusting and beyond horrible, I'm feeling mega-PTSD.' Sixty-three responses, so far, all basically 'poor baby.'"

He grunted. "Just got off the phone with her mother, trying to set up a reinterview."

"No luck?" said Alicia.

"Apparently, the kid's fragile."

"Not so much that she wasn't letting the world know about her 'profound experience' at six thirty this morning. I couldn't help think she was milking it for attention but maybe I'm being too judgy. Alex observed her, you could ask his opinion."

I said, "Hi, Alicia."

"Oh, hey. What do you think?"

"She did come across a bit theatric but it was a terrifying event so let's give her the benefit of the doubt."

"Your job description, not mine," she said. "Too bad no one gave Klement the benefit. What do you need me to do, Loo? And by the way, it's just me until tomorrow. I know you wanted the three of us to start looking for homeless but Moe and Sean are both finishing up with that La Cienega shooting. I figured I'd start myself, maybe with Westside freeway underpasses 'cause they're the closest to the crime scene. Also, that shit-dump near the V.A. in Westwood."

"Makes sense, kid," said Milo, "but first check out real estate records and see if Klement owned a house in Malibu."

"Address?"

"Broad Beach, that's all I know."

"Starting at the beginning," said Alicia. "Time to have some detective fun."

As I neared the station, my phone lit up. **Helen Framus.**

I pulled over and answered.

"Hi, Helen. Thanks for getting back."

"No sense delaying," she said, chuckling. "Seriously, nice to talk to you and I won't drag this out. Whatever factors mitigate for or against Mel having contact with the police aren't new, nor are they going to change quickly."

I said, "Long-standing issues."

"To say the least, Alex, but no sense getting into it. The question in my mind is will the cops really be sensitive?"

"The cop I'm working with will be. Plus I'll be there."

"Your involvement is at that level? Wow. I know you've worked with them but we've never really talked about it."

"They call me in when things get strange."

"If APA ever goes corporate, that could be our slogan. Okay, then sure, I know you'll handle it appropriately."

"Any tips before speaking to her?"

"We're talking an immature, high-strung girl, no genius, lacks self-esteem, and is utterly dominated by an older sister studying microbiology at Oxford and two successful overbearing parents. The father, by the way, is out of the house. Divorce a couple of years ago. Mel says she and her dad were once close but he sees her infrequently and when he does it often deteriorates to tears. The times I've met him, he seems nice enough but she describes him as hypercritical. My goal is to toughen her up and get some resilience going."

"Her mother said she agreed to drop confidentiality so you could include her."

"Did she?" Soft laughter. "No, not quite, Alex. What I agreed to—on a session-by-session basis—was if Mel gave explicit consent, Christine could participate on a limited basis. And by explicit, I mean written consent every single time. So far, she's been allowed to come in at the tail end of a few sessions to hear what Mel has to say. Guess what usually happens."

"Christine talks instead of listening."

"She certainly tries. I run interference and Mel ends up with a commitment from Christine not to continue the discussion once they leave the office."

"Written commitment?"

"Written and signed, Alex. Yeah, it's a hassle but you know the board, never spelling out proper procedure. Her chart's starting to look like a dictionary."

"No notary?"

She laughed again. "I'm sure one day it'll get to that point."

I said, "Is there anything you can tell me about Mel's relationship with Donny Klement?"

"Without a notarized document? Okay, entre nous, she had a crush on him. Told me his real name was Adonis and it fit him perfectly. Anytime she talked about him, her eyes lit up, and that's about the only time they did. So obviously, the loss is going to be profound, one step forward, a couple dozen back. Speaking of which, thanks for handling her anxiety attack. We've been doing the same things here—breathing, imagery, mindfulness, CBT exercises. I'd hoped she'd learned enough to self-help. Was she pretty much freaking out?"

"I got active when she started hyperventilating."

"Wonderful," said Helen Framus, sighing. "I've seen that a couple of times, myself. We seem to be doing okay suppressing her anxiety, then she'll come back the next week with scratches all over her arms. Poor kid, she's just wired tight. Great talking to you, Alex. I'm sure you'll do right by her."

I thanked her, hung up, resumed driving.

"Kid's a potential basket case," said Milo. "How exactly do I go about doing right by her?"

"Now that we know she had a thing for Donny, don't push the love-life angle too hard."

"So I can't get into one of the main things I'm after."

"Bring it up but be aware of her feelings."

"Meaning?"

"Go slow, keep it low-key, embed it as one question of many, and don't push it."

He grimaced, wiped his face like washing without water, slid forward in the passenger seat and stretched his long legs.

"Tell you what," he said. "How about you run the show? You're the one with the malpractice insurance."

12

His call came just before two o'clock the following afternoon.

"Donny was the legal owner of the Malibu house. Broad Beach on the sand, so we're talking a serious chunk of change in addition to his trust fund."

I said, "Second home or did he rent it out?"

"Don't know yet, just that the fund pays the property taxes and the utilities."

"Who manages the trust?"

"Same outfit as the eye-scanners downtown but the main New York office. Finally reached the manager, some vice president, got a call into her. I took another look at the studio. Interesting fellow, young Adonis. All that dough but he kept it pretty bare-bones. On top of that, no obvious social life, didn't hold on to a single text or incoming call and his outgoings were boring except for one number that I haven't identified. Most of it was ordering food and groceries and materials from a couple of photographic supply houses plus lots of calls for pickup by a dry cleaner. I got through to them and they said they were always taking care of costumes, assumed he was some sort of director."

"In a sense, he was," I said.

"Short-running show, poor guy. The other weird thing was when I checked those two cameras in the studio. The digital was clean, the old-school one wasn't loaded and I can't find any other film, or prints, real-life or online. His generation lives on their phones. It's like he isolated himself. Maybe nuances of Daddy?"

"No call list?"

"Nope. No photos or videos, either. And he's a **photographer.** Little Ms. Gornick's gotta know something about him but she's avoiding me. I put in a subpoena to his phone carrier. If God loves me, that'll kick up a bunch of juicy deleted stuff. If not, all I've got to work with is that one call I can't identify. And it's the last one he made, just after seven p.m., unattributed recipient and the reverse directory has no match. I asked Nguyen for a warrant, he said lacking evidence that the number belongs to someone naughty, there are too many privacy issues. I bugged him and he said maybe. If I stopped bugging him. I'm praying it isn't a no-trace prepaid."

I said, "Maybe the killer cleaned the phone before leaving."

"I thought about that, but why not just take it and trash it, Alex? Either way, the shooter couldn't assume the carrier wouldn't give up the data."

"Could be someone impulsive and not a criminal mastermind."

"Hope you're right," he said. "Stupidity is the fertile soil I farm."

"Any chance Donny had a second phone?"

"If he did, I haven't found it. We'll see once the private banker calls back. Nothing pans out from her, I'm taking a long hike back to Square One. Like I said, different species, my victim."

"Keeping it simple," I said.

"There's simple and there's monastic," he said. "With looks like that and plenty of dough—hell, with a name like **Adonis**—why no girlfriend or boyfriend or whatever?"

"If the Malibu house was his main residence, you might find the answer there."

"Once I verify it **was** his crib and not a rental, I'll get a victim's warrant and give the place a total toss. Hell, even if he's got a tenant, I might head over there and see what they can tell me about him."

I said, "Nothing like a day at the beach."

"Who's more deserving than **moi**?"

"Bring sunscreen, Big Guy."

"First, though, I want to talk to Gornick, but my emotionally sensitive texts to her **and** her mother remain unanswered. If they keep stonewalling, I'll do a drop-in. What else . . . after Alicia got hold of the Malibu tax stuff, she went around to homeless encampments. No sign of any of the Wishers and no one admits knowing them. But we're talking four places out of God knows how many. On a positive note, Sean and Moe just finished playing Trivial Pursuit and are ready to do some real work. You free at four?"

To him, Trivial Pursuit is anything short of murder. In this case a robbery/shooting at a liquor store that had left three people wounded.

I said, "Sure."

The civilian clerk at the West L.A. station smiled. "Hi, Doctor. You know where to go."

I knew what she meant. Milo always tries to commandeer the same space for meetings: the largest of three interview rooms lining the second-floor corridor. Short walk from his closet-sized office and set up with a whiteboard on an easel, ample tables and chairs.

I was five minutes early but the last to arrive.

Another thing you can count on when Milo gathers the troops is catering by way of a bakery near the house he and Rick Silverman share in West Hollywood. I've noticed a correlation between his anxiety level and quantity. This afternoon, four pink boxes brimming with caloric overdrive topped a table pushed to the left wall of the room.

The culinary mood ring reading: **moderately edgy.**

A flanking table held a bubbling coffeepot and a

carafe of hot water for tea. Milo's green vinyl attaché case sat near a pair of whiteboards arranged side by side. One was blank, the other filled with erasable blue as Milo scrawled. Without looking back, he said, "Hey."

From behind a long table, three hands rose in greeting. I smiled and saluted.

Alicia Bogomil, aquiline and trim in a fitted black blazer and top over black leggings, sat to the left, enjoying something monumental and chocolate-coated.

To her left, Sean Binchy, freckled, lanky, his ginger hair gel-spiked, coped with a glazed donut wrought monstrous, patting his lips with a napkin after every bite. Per usual, he wore a blue suit, a white dress shirt, a bright necktie, this one patterned with turquoise palm fronds, and Doc Martens. The shoes are a reminder of a previous life. Before marrying and finding religion, Sean had been a ska-punk bassist.

Between Sean and my empty chair, Moses Reed abstained from everything but a bottle of something called Muscle Milk. Pink-skinned, baby-faced, and enduringly blond, Moe, always a weight lifter, seems to grow progressively larger every time I see him. Last year he'd won a strength competition by overhead-pressing two ninety and deadlifting six forty-five. That lifestyle means conventional clothes never fit right and Moe's duds always seem to be grappling with him. Recently he'd discovered an online supplier of garments for pumpers, attire that stretched but didn't look like plastic. Today that meant an unstructured tweed jacket, black jeans, and a black shirt worn open-necked. But the arm seams of the jacket still strained.

He said, "Hey, Doc," and offered a handshake. Gentle clasp; like being gripped by a careful gorilla.

Milo stopped writing, retrieved the attaché case with one hand, and used the other to grab a bear claw nearly as large as his head. He headed back to the boards, biting off a chunk, chewing aerobically, and scattering crumbs. Swallowing just as he got there.

Placing the case on the ground, he said, "We've been through the basics of the crime scene, Alex. Just heard from the pathologist on the prelim. Mr. Klement is carrying three small bullets in his heart and lung, doc figures low-caliber and not high-quality because they're seriously misshapen. He also had a bit of THC in his system along with Lunesta. The guess is what you said: He'd likely be sleeping deeply, would be disoriented if he woke up."

He moved to the side, exposing the left-hand board. "Okay, kids, this is what we've got in terms of family values."

He began at the top, pointing to several death shots of Adonis "Donny" Klement, including the neat triangle of wounds, then moving down to his diagram of the Klement family tree.

Each name was accompanied by a photo.

Hugh Klement's image was polished and high-def, likely enlarged from a high-end magazine cutting. The oldest Klement child had a narrow, sun-burnished face shadowed by a beige Stetson and partly obscured by a rust-colored brush mustache. A mesh of lines around the eyes and uplifted cheeks suggested a smile below but lip hair blocked confirmation. In the distance, gorgeous blue sky and purple mountains. I'd been to Jackson, Wyoming, for a conference years ago and recognized the peaks. The Tetons, named by French explorers in tribute to female anatomy.

Next: Colin Klement's driver's license headshot. No one likes being at the DMV and license photos tend to stiffen and age their subjects. But Colin appeared exactly as he had in person: well fed, well groomed, smiling pleasantly as he faced the camera with steady eyes. Calm and confident; perfect for someone entrusted with other people's money.

Below him was Bianca Klement-Steen's soft, roundish face, the color of high-grade ivory. Delicate features, cherubic eyes. Her hair was jet black, earlobe length, with high bangs. A black collarless tunic was fastened with red Chinese pegs and loops. Nice smile, but unlike Colin, well shy of comfortable. The kind of smile you get after repeated requests to relax, still failing to pull off ease. Still, all in all, flattering, polished, and professional. Like Hugh's portrait, likely a clipping from a glossy.

Victor Klement avoided media exposure but at least two of his children had sought it out.

Milo's hand moved down to a big blue question mark where he'd written, "Danielle Klement, deceased, date unknown."

That made me wonder. Death certificates aren't hard to get but he'd moved on.

The final branch featured a blowup from the French tabloid. Nicole Aumont kneeling in the garden, gravid and apple-cheeked, carelessly tied back golden hair framing a lovely face. The unspoiled beauty of someone nourished by outdoor life.

Twenty-seven years old and prepared to spend her youth with a man old enough to be her grandfather with a personal history that argued against permanence.

"Motley crew," said Alicia.

Milo said, "And notice there's nothing on the guy who created it. Can't find a single image of ol' Victor."

"Billionaires can buy anything, Loo, including privacy."

"Apparently. For obvious reasons, I'd like to talk to him, if for no other reason than he deserves a normal notification. But nothing about this case is normal. Moe and I combed corporate databases all this morning and came up empty. I even tried stock exchanges. Nothing Klement owns is publically traded so he might as well be the janitor. I've also got a call in to the paper that ran this."

Tapping Aumont's photo. "No response so far and the same goes for Klement's gofer and her over-protective mommy. Them I can drop in on. A trip to Paris seems less likely."

He shrugged. Permission to chuckle. Everyone took the opportunity.

I said, "How come no death certificate on Danielle Klement?"

"Good question, Alex. Zilch in the county, state, and national databases so maybe she died overseas."

Sean said, "Makes sense, Loot. People like this can hop on jets like they're Ubers."

Milo's fingertip traveled to Colin's face. "Which is exactly what this guy did a couple of days before the murder until a few hours after. He authorized me to contact the FBO at Van Nuys Airport—that's a fixed base of operations for all of you commercial plebes. Alibi confirmed but that doesn't mean he didn't hire someone to bump off his brother."

Alicia said, "Any reason to suspect him?"

"No specific indication but we are talking a massive inheritance somewhere along the line. In terms of the dead sister, I suppose I could contact her mother, she's a doctor in Beverly Hills. But given the way this family's structured—unstructured—it's not likely she and Donny were connected so I can't see having Mom dredge up sad memories."

Alicia said, "Accidental death. I'm picturing some horsey thing. Jumping in Monaco, whatever."

Sean said, "Skiing in Switzerland."

"Racing at Le Mans."

Reed hadn't joined in, serious as usual. "They're technically a family, but really a collection of strangers."

"Well put, Moses."

"Why would someone do that?"

"Alex has a theory about it."

I summed up my only-child clone thoughts.

Sean said, "He wants to be Big Daddy in name but not for real."

Alicia said, "Playing God by replicating himself."

Sean frowned at the suggestion of heresy. "That never works."

Alicia said, "Doesn't stop egomaniacs from trying. Right, Doc?"

Moe had sat through the exchange, silent, one leg moving up and down. He had a half sib, a former LAPD detective turned high-end P.I. named Aaron Fox. The brothers were as different as two people could be and they'd had their issues. But they'd never lost touch.

Alicia said, "They don't even **look** like sibs. It's like a random scoop of the gene pool."

Moe turned to me. "Egotism I get, but I still don't see why a father would want to deny his kids any chance to relate."

I said, "Three guesses come to mind. First, by socially distancing each mother-and-child pair, he figured he could prevent collusion and maximize his control."

"Over the money?"

"The money, the relationships, everything."

Alicia said, "Like one of those palace intrigues, everyone plotting against everyone else."

"Exactly," I said. "Or I could be overthinking and he was simply trying to minimize conflict. Keeping what he considered the peace by creating an **un**blended family."

She said, "Guess in a weird way, that makes sense. Where do we always encounter the nastiest stuff?"

"Domestics," said Sean.

Moe remained silent.

Milo said, "What's the third possibility?"

I said, "Something in Victor's own past led him to protect people he cared about by isolating them."

"Like what?"

"Neglect, abuse—anything negative about family life that he didn't want to repeat."

He thought about that, said, "Onward," opened the case, and drew out a handful of papers that he began taping to the empty board.

Donny Klement's before-and-after photos of the homeless. Above them, Milo's back-slanted scrawl.

The Wishers.

Alicia shook her head. "That's supposed to be art? Dressing them up like creepy dolls? Yuck—maybe like father like son."

Sean said, "What do you mean?"

"The control thing, his version of an ego-trip exploitation. We're talking compromised people, maybe one of them realized they'd been used and went for payback."

Sean said, "I guess."

She said, "What?"

"What I've heard so far doesn't feel disorganized, like what you'd get from a compromised person. Someone figured out a way to get in, sneaked around in the dark, and managed to shoot him smoothly. The wound pattern—tight, controlled."

Alicia chewed her lip. "Okay, you're making sense. And when we do see homeless crimes it's usually blunt force or cutting, not guns. We've had them being shot but I can't remember any case where one of them instigated a calculated shooting. Anyone come across that?"

Head shakes.

Milo went and fetched himself another bear claw.

13

Twenty minutes later a plan was in place.

Milo would continue to concentrate on learning more about Donny Klement by persisting with Mel Gornick, paying a visit to the house on Broad Beach, and nudging Deputy D.A. John Nguyen to fast-track a warrant on the phone of the person Donny had last called. If that failed, he'd work at finding a friendly judge and deal with whatever that evoked in Nguyen.

First step would be a walk downstairs and asking Captain Sandra Delvecchio to pass along photos of the Wishers to all West L.A. watch commanders and to her peers at other divisions.

Meanwhile, Alicia, Sean, and Moe would talk to uniforms they knew and draw up a map of the major homeless encampments on the Westside. Then, dividing up the territory, they'd continue what Alicia had begun.

"Any questions?" said Milo.

Silence.

"Go in peace, my children." His phone rang. The number on the screen raised his eyebrows. He held up a finger that stilled us.

"Lieutenant Sturgis."

A cheerful male voice said, "Hello, Lieutenant. I am Andre Friederich calling from Paris? You wrote to me at **La Verité**?"

Perfect diction smoothed by Gallic inflections. A lilt at the end of statements turned them into questions.

Milo glanced at his Timex. I checked my watch. Five fifteen p.m. in California meant two fifteen a.m. in France.

"Thanks for calling, sir. Working late?"

Andre Friederich laughed. "**Blaireaux**—badgers—work in darkness. What do you want to tell me about Mr. Victor Klement?"

"I was hoping you had something to tell me."

"If only, Lieutenant Sturgis, if only." **Lyo-Ten-Non Stairjiss.** "The man is an enigma."

"You knew enough to write about him."

"Ah," said Friederich. "Everything contained in my article resulted from the gossip of gardeners, carpenters, and plumbers."

"People working on Klement's château."

"A few of the people working, Lieutenant. For many, there was hesitation. When it comes to discussing Monsieur Klement, he is not cl**em**ent."

"People are afraid to talk."

"People like to eat."

"The picture of his fiancée—"

"Don't ask how that was obtained," said Friederich. "A pretty young woman, no? She was not my big prize but she fills space nicely."

"Have you ever seen a picture of Klement?"

"Have you?"

"No."

"Then we have something in common, Lieutenant. Why are you asking about him from Los Angeles?"

"A family matter," said Milo, "and you seem to know about the family."

Silence.

"Sir?"

"Lieutenant, everything I know is what I wrote."

"Don't imagine a plumber could give you the family tree."

Andre Friederich laughed. "You are a detective but I am a journalist and that means confidential sources. What family matter concerns you? Something with money, I assume?"

"Why would you assume that?"

"Because money is like dirt, Lieutenant. When it is skimpy dust, no one cares. When it collects into a mountain, people do crazy things to climb it."

"Good point," said Milo. "It's important that we

contact Mr. Klement, so if you know how to do that—"

"If I had that level of authority and knowledge, Lieutenant, I would be editor in chief of **Le Monde**. As I said, the man is an enigma."

"Does he live at the château?"

"To my knowledge no one has seen him enter or exit," said Friederich. "But I'm not in your position to sit and watch all day and all night. My stories are like bad relationships. One finishes and moves on. My editor would be very unhappy if I neglected my current story."

"Got it."

"You're not going to ask what my current story is? I thought detectives were curious."

Milo laughed. "What is it?"

"I am profiling Kurvy Kay."

"Sounds like a pop star."

"Good deduction," said Friederich. "She is a nineteen-year-old prostitute from Marseilles who is now a hip-hop artist. Last year, she earned more than our president and the entire **Parlement fran-çais** in combination."

"Money talks," said Milo.

"And everyone listens, Lieutenant. Now you can tell me about the Klement family matter and perhaps I can try to talk to various people."

"How about you do more than try."

Friederich chuckled. "Like that little guy,

Yoda . . . all right, agreed. I will find out what I can and now you will tell me why you called."

"Fair enough," said Milo. "On condition you keep it to yourself until more facts come in."

"Why would I want to do that?"

Milo said, "What I know right now, sir, isn't enough to give you a story. At best, it's two or three lines. Once I learn more, your editor will be way happier."

"Way happier," said Andre Friederich, as if learning a new phrase. "Lieutenant, you are an interesting man."

"Far from it, sir."

"Oh, I think quite close to it. So, where are we? You are guaranteeing me first opportunity to obtain facts on a murder—yes, I googled you and learned you are a murder detective in western Los Angeles. I have been to Los Angeles for the Golden Globes, years ago. Big streets going nowhere, random spaces pretending to be a city. I liked it very much. The western side is for the rich, correct?"

"There are some affluent areas."

"So," said Friederich. "Regarding your murder, it's only a matter of time until I find out which member of Victor Klement's family has either killed someone or been killed."

"You should be a detective, sir."

"Oh no, Lieutenant. What we have in common is persistence but what separates us is you are interested in figuring out who is good and who is bad.

If I cared about that, I would not enjoy my job. So. Who are we talking about? The cowboy, the fancy decorator, the Black money guy, or the artist?"

"Photographer," said Milo.

"Ah." The shuffling of papers. "The young one, Daniel."

"Actually it's Donny."

"I was told Danny, which is short for Daniel, no?"

"D-O-N-N-Y," said Milo.

"One letter," said Friederich, sounding rueful. "You say he is a photographer . . . okay, photography can be art. Have you heard of Henri Cartier-Bresson? Art with a camera. So. Did D-O-N-N-Y murder or was he murdered?"

"He's the vic—"

"Who victimized him?"

"If I knew that, I wouldn't have called you. If what you produce helps me, you'll be the first to know."

"A new condition, Lieutenant? I must produce?"

"Seems fair to me."

Silence.

Andre Friederich's transcontinental sigh was prolonged and theatric.

"Lieutenant, if I ever kill someone, it will not be in western Los Angeles."

Milo kept him on the line a bit longer, trying to extract a theory about why Victor Klement had limited himself to one child per wife.

The question perplexed Friederich.

"In matters of the heart, Lieutenant, there is no . . . almanac. The greater puzzle is, why so many marriages in the first place? A man of his means, why the need to entangle himself legally?"

"Good question."

"Hopefully, you will find an answer," said Andre Friederich. "And I will benefit."

The detectives went to work and I went back home and took Robin to dinner at a Greek place in Beverly Hills. Dim, quiet, plush room, compassionate lighting, great food, inconspicuous service.

The following morning passed without my hearing from Milo. I spent it on my own paperwork, was preparing for a run when he phoned from his cell at eleven thirty-seven a.m.

"How's the rest of your day?"

"Open."

"What were you planning to do with all that time?"

"Run, play guitar. And of course, wait with bated breath for your summons."

"Hopefully not in that order. Ready for sand and surf?"

Malibu beaches often bear imaginative names.

El Matador, Las Tunas, Paradise Cove, Surfrider. The Colony with its intentional connotation of ruling-power exclusivity.

Out on the west end, Leo Carrillo, commemorating a comedic actor from the fifties.

Whoever had tagged Broad Beach had been suffering from the literal flu.

That stretch of sand thirty miles north of L.A. has surrendered a bit of accuracy as the Pacific gets hungrier and reclaims silica. Unlike other sections of Malibu, houses on Broad often look out on ancient dunes that block sea vistas.

Years ago, a famous actor, grown rich marketing eco-conscious merchandise, had brought in bulldozers and destroyed his chunk of natural habitat.

Shortly after, another built a Balinese palace augmented by tons of imported sand.

The residents are reflexively socially conscious, and virtue-signaling abounds in press releases. That hasn't stopped them from hiring an army of guards to patrol Broad on ATVs and restrict access to anyone wandering over from the adjoining public beach at Zuma.

Milo picked me up at twelve forty-five and drove with his usual heavy foot. That and a quiet PCH brought us to Donny Klement's allotment of Eden forty minutes later. We spent the ride not talking much and enjoying eyefuls of sapphire sky and even bluer water.

The address we were looking for matched a small, square cottage with cedar siding and a gray tile mansard roof. No garage; parking was an oil-stained strip hugging the front of the house.

Small place, unrestored, at least fifty years old and showing the effects of salt and wind. The weathered wooden walls reminded me of my original house. Some bucket of fuel that had turned out to be, and looking at this place made me wonder. Fires visit Malibu regularly and when winds and slovenly power lines don't cause conflagrations, human error does its bit.

Several years ago a famous director's place on Broad Beach had gone up in flames due to alleged negligence by a painting crew. Coastal Commission rules had somehow been vaulted and a massive pile of postmodern stucco had phoenixed at warp speed.

We'd veered from the highway onto Broad Beach Road and passed that angular palace, now blocked by twelve-foot white walls slathered with highly flammable vines and neighbored by other weekend Shangri-Las.

Donny Klement's modest bungalow was a way up from all that, at the advent of a truncated drive more alley than street. The lot was no wider than thirty feet, sitting high and looking down on a section of beach piled with jagged rocks that turned a visit to the surf perilous. To the right of the house, a steep staircase of crumbling planks, many of the steps missing, others studded with protruding nails, tottered dangerously.

Milo said, "Not what I expected. What do you think it would go for?"

"Probably seven, eight mil."

He whistled. "I was figuring five, but you'd know better."

"Why's that?"

"You and Gorgeous rented here when you were rebuilding."

"Long time ago and seven miles up," I said.

"So?"

"Less fashionable and a whole lot cheaper."

"Still," he said, "you always seem to know about the hoohah stuff."

He eyed the structure. "No garage and no wheels outside so if there is a tenant, they're probably out. I'll try anyway."

He pulled the unmarked onto the oily parking strip, got out and knocked. Returned shaking his head. "I'll leave a card and then we can find some good seafood."

Just as he started up the Impala, a black Suburban turned onto the street and wafted toward us, waxed and gleaming, wearing livery plates. SUVs are today's stretch limos, the wealthy edgy about inciting class envy.

The Suburban's bulk stopped next to the unmarked and idled. A black-suited chauffeur exited the driver's door, stared at us for a moment, then hustled to the right-hand passenger door.

The pause meant he didn't get there in time to open the door. A woman climbed out on her own, walked around the vehicle, and shot us her own stare.

Young, six feet tall, improbably slender, celestially beautiful, she had long, silky black hair and luminous blue eyes. Long legs managed not to be bulked by gray sweatpants. Same for an upper body covered by a baggy white sweatshirt. Pale, spidery fingers wiggled impatiently. Sculpted eyebrows rose.

As the driver popped the Suburban's rear hatch and unloaded two brown composite suitcases, she said, "Can I help you guys?" Husky voice, somewhat flat, low volume.

Milo flashed the badge.

"What's the problem, Officer?"

"Do you live here, ma'am?"

"It's my boyfriend's place."

"Is your boyfriend Donny Klement?"

Cupid lips parted. "Is he . . . did something happen?"

Milo took a couple of steps closer to her. When he told her, she collapsed and he was there to catch her.

The chauffeur had stood there, addled and diverting his attention to the suitcases. I said, "I'll handle it," gave him a ten, and watched as he drove off.

Milo guided the gorgeous woman to the door. Shaking hands stopped her from unlocking so he took her key and did it. I followed them inside and laid the luggage down on a grubby, cracked tile floor.

That and the rest of the interior was as unimpressive as the exterior. Most of the house consisted of a single, stingy open space, sour with must, containing a sitting area, a card table with two folding chairs for dining, and a cubbyhole kitchen with plywood cabinets. The ceiling was raw wood and low. Furnishings were drab and old enough to pucker and sag, and that reminded me of the ground floor of Donny Klement's studio.

For all that, sliding glass doors leading to a high, narrow deck that faced the water transformed the place into more than a dump.

Milo and the young woman sat on a fuzzy gray

couch. She bent low and wept, shoulders shaking. I went to the kitchenette and pulled out a bottle of Evian from a chipped white fridge, then a clunky glass, one of six behind a warped cabinet door.

Low-rent anywhere else, a fortune in Malibu because of the views—and this view was spectacular, the elevated stance offering an unobstructed eyeful of the ocean. Blue water rippled like silk in a breeze. Seabirds bobbed, clumps of kelp floated. In the distance, a container ship seemed to glide atop the horizon.

Then a startling, kinetic burst as a trio of dolphins leaped in unison, no more than forty feet offshore. It's natural behavior for them and marine parks use that fact to look impressive.

By the time I got back with the water, the young woman was sitting upright. Exaggeratedly upright.

She took the glass, sipped once, then shook her head and held it out. I placed it on a splintering side table shaped like a giant hourglass and we waited as she cried some more.

Milo glanced at me and I knew what he was thinking. **Another one for on-site therapy?** But unlike Mel Gornick, she settled a couple of minutes later and he was able to get the basics.

She was twenty-five years old and her name was Alicia Lynn Dorfman but everyone called her Ali. "Pronounced like the boxer." A Montana driver's license confirmed where she'd come from "after I finished college and some scout saw me." Shrugging, as if it happened to everyone.

Where she'd gone to was a whole lot further, modeling across the country and internationally as Ali Dana and proof of that abounded.

Poster-sized blowups of magazine covers, runway walks, and fashion spreads hung on every wall of the tiny house, along with a series of black-and-white portraits that emphasized lithe limbs, limber movement, and a cameo face. The sole exception to The Temple of Ali was a single, amateurish color shot next to the fridge that I'd noticed when I fetched the water.

A skinny, tan, mop-headed boy in bathing trunks sitting on sun-splotched sand. Early teens, wide smile flashing a full set of braces, left hand resting on a purple boogie board. Next to him, a good-looking but hollow-cheeked blond woman in a white caftan struggled to smile for the camera. Her hair was long and knotted up carelessly, her hands rolled into white-knuckle fists. As if sitting still strained her.

Hollow eyes, focused elsewhere, suggested she was waiting for bad news.

Milo said, "So sorry to have to tell you, Ali, and so sorry for your loss."

Ali Dana sniffed and nodded.

"We know this is tough, but if there's any way you could answer some questions, it would be a giant help."

"A help in getting whoever . . ." She nodded, sniffed some more, accepted the tissue Milo offered her, sneezed into it, and crushed it with fine-boned fingers. "Help in getting justice? Yes, for sure. Of course. But I don't know how I can help."

"Can you think of anyone who'd want to hurt Donny?"

"Not specifically," she said. "By that I mean he brought people into his studio without knowing a lot about them." A beat. "Homeless people. Do you know about that?"

"The Wishers."

She frowned. "I told him he had a defective radar."

I said, "Not great at reading people?"

"Not great at realizing the way the world is," said Ali Dana. "I grew up on a ranch and on a ranch you're always watching for predators."

"Coyotes and wolves?"

"And grizzlies. And humans—humans are the worst kind. More than once my dad had to deal with people trying to rustle his stock. My folks raise Angus for meat and goats for cheese on three thousand acres and you can count on some lowlife sniffing around somewhere trying to freeload. Even foxes are the enemy, they're cute except if you keep chickens. Which we used to but don't, not worth the hassle."

I said, "Donny didn't see the world that way."

"Donny," she said, sighing, "was a man with

child-like aspects to his personality. Which I loved, he was so . . . he always saw the best in people. I admired that. Especially because of how he grew up. How much do you know about that?"

"Multiple marriages for his father, no full sibs just halves."

She rose gracefully, glided to the color shot near the fridge, and pointed. "This is Donny and his mom when they lived here. Vanessa was an actress in England, did a few horror films, then she married his dad and moved here and nothing happened for her career-wise. So she had Donny and got depressed and slid into dope. She O.D.'d on cocaine."

She rapped the photo. "It happened a few months after this was taken. Donny was the one who found her. He was fifteen."

She pointed to the closed door at the far end of the room. "It's our bedroom now but it was hers back then. Donny used to sleep out here."

I said, "In the living room?"

"On a futon. Rich Malibu kid, huh? He didn't care, he's like that, materialism means nothing to him. One day, he came home from school and found her in bed. He thought she was sleeping but she wouldn't rouse. He touched her." She winced. "He told me her skin felt like marble."

Milo said, "Poor kid."

"But still," said Ali Dana. "He had a crap childhood but it never got him down and the most wonderful thing was he never bitched about it.

Ever. Or tried to use it. That's the **main** reason I love him so much. There was nothing Montana about him but he still reminds me of my dad and my brothers. Being a true man. Sucking it up. On the ranch it's no wimps allowed, and let me tell you, that is **not** what I deal with on the **job.**"

She flounced, dangled her hands, spoke in a nasal singsong. "'My **hair's** bad,' 'I'm **bloated**,' 'My **ass** looks flabby.' Total nonstop narcissism and if I dare to tell anyone to quit milking it, I'm an insensitive fascist."

I said, "In his own way Donny was tough."

"I mean we're talking finding your mother dead at fifteen? Not only didn't he bitch, he always told me he felt lucky."

I said, "About . . ."

"Being alive," she said. More tears, silent and dignified.

She looked up and croaked something that could've been laughter. "He had a saying. 'Every day on this side of the dirt is a good one.' I told him he should aim a little higher, we used to laugh about it. Now it looks like he sensed . . . something. In here." Touching her belly. "Oh, God, I can't believe he's **gone!**"

She buckled again, reached for the fridge for support, fell short, and began to pitch forward.

Milo and I rushed toward her but she caught herself. Breathed in and out slowly, straightened her back, punched air with both hands.

Her jaw jutted. "I will **not** give in. I'm going to make Donny proud of me and pull it **together**."

She sat back down, took the water glass, and drained it. "Ask whatever you want."

Milo said, "How long have you and Donny been together?"

"Two years and three months." Lovely smile.

"Where'd you guys meet?"

"Here in L.A. It was basically a long-distance fix-up. Donny's oldest brother is a friend of my dad in Montana and Jackson Hole. They hunt and fish together and my dad told him I'd be in L.A. for a month doing some runways, a Guess shoot and maybe one for Max Mara, did he know anyone I could contact for information about living here."

Milo said, "We're talking Hugh Klement."

"Yup, Cowboy Hugh. Hard to believe he and Donny are related—Hugh's way older and . . . put it this way: He's pretty hard-core old school. My dad said Hugh reminded him of an old cigarette ad guy. Marlboro Man."

I said, "So Hugh set you up."

"Not a setup, he just gave my dad Donny's number and my dad called me. My initial reaction was 'You've got to be kidding, I don't need any help.' Being twenty-two and pretty much a pissy arrogant chick. But then the agency stuck me in a dorm-type situation with six other girls and soon I wanted to crawl out of my skin so I called the number and Donny was so nice over the phone. Not slick, like so many L.A. jerks. So we went out for pizza and it was like . . . I'm thinking this guy's too good to be true. Looks awesome, soft-spoken, not full of himself. And I could talk to him, you know? So we kept hanging out. Then that turned into **going** out. Then I moved in."

She looked around. "Now I'll be packing my bags. Not much to pack, when I'm not working, the last thing I want to think about is clothes so I live light. And to tell the truth, I don't like it here, only did it to be with Donny."

"The beach isn't for you."

"Nah. Boring. And I can't risk the sun trashing my skin."

She pointed to the glass doors. "Take away the ocean and it's pretty much a shitbox. But Donny doesn't care about things like that." Use of the present tense scrunched her eyes. She breathed a couple of times. "He really lived on another plane."

I said, "What plane is that?"

"Creativity. Ideas, inspirational stuff."

Milo said, "He was also sleeping at his studio."

Ali Dana nodded. "When I was out of town he'd do that rather than drive back."

"How often was that?"

"Most of the time," she said. "I'm gone at least two hundred days a year. Nothing supermodelly, but I do get a lot of print work and runways. My agent calls, I'm gone."

"Where'd you arrive from today?"

"New York, fashion expo at the Javits Center, then some ad work for a couple of boutiques in Soho." She smiled. "Was that like asking me for an alibi? If it was, I stayed at an Airbnb in Chelsea at a hundred a night charged to the agency."

She checked her phone and read off a number and an address on West 20th Street.

As Milo copied, she scrolled down the screen. Tears pooled in her eyes. "Sorry, this is hard."

"No reason to apologize, Ali."

"It's just hitting me in **waves**. Like seeing Donny's last call to me. The last time we spoke."

"When was that?"

"Three, four nights ago . . . nine forty-three New York time. I was already sleeping, didn't feel like a long conversation so I told him I loved him, we'd talk tomorrow."

Square shoulders moved up and down.

"Is this your number?" Milo opened his pad and recited.

"Yup," said Ali Dana.

One less mystery.

"What was Donny's mood like when he called?"

"The usual," she said. "Sweet, mellow— I should've talked to him longer. What a stupid bitch I was."

Milo said, "When we tried to find whose number it is, nothing came back."

She nodded. "It's issued by the agency, they've got some sort of security thing so the girls don't get harassed."

"Do you have your own line?"

"Long as they're paying for it, couldn't see a reason."

She stood again, swiped her eyes with the back of her hand, murmured, "No thanks," to Milo's offer of another tissue.

"Waves," she said. "Toxic waves—oh, **damn**, I can't **believe** this."

Blue eyes flashed. She made a low, grinding sound, clawed the perfectly formed hands. Grief morphing to anger.

"Can't believe what, Ali?"

"For some freakin' **reason**, I just got **hungry**!"

Striding to the kitchenette, she brought back a box of water crackers but made no move to open it. "I'm never a stress eater, just the opposite . . . crazy-time, total crazy-time."

Looking at the box, she shook her head. "Carbs, definitely going to bring on the water but who cares, I'm going to quit next week." She stood there, tapping the box. "Was planning to do it even before, now definitely."

Milo said, "Modeling."

"It's really not me, I always feel I'm wasting my time. Dad predicted it would be a waste of my time and he was right. But while you're doing it, you get into it. People telling you you're hot, you're perfect, exotic, sexy, the camera loves you. That's how it started with the scout. But I've always wanted to do something else, now's the time."

"Back to Montana?"

"Back to the best veterinary school I can get into. I'm going to specialize in big animals. Love 'em."

Milo said, "Can we get back to Hugh for a sec?"

"Sure."

"Were he and Donny in contact with each other?"

"Not that Donny ever mentioned," she said.

"Did Donny ever talk about Hugh?"

"You're not thinking Hugh could've hurt Donny. No way, sir, he's straight-up salt of the earth, my dad wouldn't waste time on him if he wasn't."

"We don't suspect him, Ali, we're just trying to get a sense of Donny's family. So, no bad blood between him and Hugh."

"Absolutely **not,** sir. And if I had to guess, I'd say the same goes for his other brother who lives here, and they **did** have contact. In fact, Hugh gave Dad **his** number, too, but Dad said he was married, better to call Donny."

Milo said, "Colin."

"Yup. Him, Donny talked about."

"What did he say?"

"Just that they'd reconnected around a year ago and he enjoyed getting to know Colin. Donny also has a sister, and when he lived in New York he spent a little time with her, she's some sort of high-end decorator. Her first name's Bianca. Hyphenated something. Donny liked her, too. Donny liked everyone."

"When did he live with Bianca?"

"I'm not sure about the exact time but it was after his mother died. First, he got shipped to a boarding school up near Palo Alto—a prep for Stanford. Not a good match, he's pretty severely dyslexic, words and numbers. So you can imagine how much fun a high-pressure place would be. So he transferred to a place in upstate New York that stressed the arts and he liked it. When school was out, he'd go to Bianca's place. Somewhere in New York but I have no idea where."

I said, "Who transferred him?"

"Hmm . . . you know, I haven't a clue. I suppose without his mom his dad would technically be in charge. But more likely someone working for his dad."

"Dad wasn't hands-on."

"Hardly. Donny told me he's this incredible loner, he doesn't even have a picture of him."

"Bad feelings?"

"Not that he said. But Donny was Mr. Positive. I figured maybe he just never developed any sort of relationship so there was nothing to miss. I mean a guy who gets married a bunch of times for a year or so? Crazy."

"Donny didn't complain about it."

"Never and why would I bring up anything

negative when our time together was so . . ." Biting her lip. "Precious."

She pincer-grasped a cracker from the box. "Actually, one of my fantasies was we'd both move back to Montana and I'd show him what a real, close-knit family was like. I told him there was plenty to photograph out there. But he never got to see it. God, this is horrible!"

She bent forward, grasped her knees, let go and slammed back.

I said, "Donny felt close enough to Bianca to live with her."

"Guess so—what he did say was she was nice but it got confusing because she kept switching boyfriends."

"Revolving door," said Milo. "Kinda like his dad."

"That's what I figured," said Ali Dana.

She twirled the cracker. "Maybe you think I should know more but you need to understand. With my travel schedule, we used our time wisely. Going places—museums, hiking trails, art galleries. The zoo because he knew how I feel about animals. Or just ordering some takeout and sitting out there on the deck and watching the tides roll in and out. We concentrated on quality of life, the present, not the past. And other than that stuff on the wall, he never took out his camera. Said he wanted to concentrate on me in real time. Quality time."

She sucked in breath. "Too bad there won't be quantity."

Nibbling the cracker to oblivion, she frowned. "Tastes like paper, I need to stop wasting calories— so who do you suspect?"

Milo said, "It's early in the investigation. Wish we had a suspect."

"You don't think one of those homeless did it?"

"They haven't been ruled out but first we have to identify them."

"Got it," she said. "It's not like they have addresses."

Another cracker heard from. "Far as I'm concerned, it's totally shameful. The homeless situation, here. Those people need help, not to be left on the street living in their own filth. If that makes me a fascist, fine. I mean sure, some of them had bad luck. Lost their jobs, got evicted. But from what I've seen in every city I've worked, most of them are mental or on drugs. Or both. That's what I mean by Donny not living in the real world. Why would you want to expose yourself to that?"

She put the box down. "I think you should look into one of them getting mad at Donny because of how Donny treated them. I don't mean he **mis**treated them. Just the opposite. He paid them each five hundred dollars, which is huge to a homeless person, right? Plus all the attention. I know he was sincerely trying to make their lives better with what he called 'guided imagination' but c'mon, they're not sane. All that money had to give them ideas."

I said, "Guided imagination as in leading them to positive fantasies."

Three emphatic nods. "Emphasis on **fantasy.** He said he was trying to raise their expectations by expanding their vistas."

I said, "Risky."

"You bet," said Ali Dana. "Like what if I thought I could be a supermodel and I couldn't? I'd be one of those bitter girls you see on the circuit who end up doing bad things to themselves. But I know my limitations so I'm a happy girl. It's like my dad says: when expectations grow faster than reality, watch out."

I said, "Donny might've led them to expect more than he was able to deliver."

"Exactly. But even if he didn't, even if he did nothing wrong, we're still talking **crazy** addicts."

"When did the project begin?"

"Hmm . . . less than a year . . . maybe six, seven months?"

"How did he find his subjects?"

"He paid some guy to find them."

Milo said, "Name?"

"All I heard was a nickname," said Ali Dana. "Cap. Maybe it's short for something."

"Cap. Like a hat."

"Guess so," said Ali Dana. "Only reason I know is once when we were out he got a call that he said he needed to take. Which was unusual, like I said, he respected our time together. I'll admit, I got a little irritated, so he said, 'Call you back later, Cap,' and hung up and apologized. I said, 'Is that a girl? Like Capistrana or something?' He cracked up. 'No, just a guy who's helping me find Wishers.'"

She shook her head. "Wishers. Like that's all it takes."

Milo said, "Donny got a nice review in a magazine."

Her eyes widened. "Did he? He never said." She pouted. "He was like that, no ego, never bragged."

I said, "In terms of his staff—"

"What staff? There was just that weird little girl—Melissandra whatever. I always felt he took her on out of pity."

"Why's that?"

"The few times I saw her she didn't seem to be doing much. Just sitting around on her phone. I asked Donny, what's up with that? He smiled and said when he needed her she was there."

"Any reason he'd keep her on if she wasn't?"

"He had a soft heart," said Ali Dana. She pressed her palms together. "Now **please** tell me honestly: My baby didn't suffer."

Milo said, "He didn't."

"For real?"

"For real. He was shot in his sleep."

She flinched. "Sleep was always a problem for him. He took meds and fell away like in a coma. **Please** tell me he never really woke up."

"Looks that way. Can you think of a way any of the homeless could've gotten into the studio?"

"Not legitimately but maybe during a shoot one of them stole a key?"

"Another thing, the alarm hadn't been set."

"That," said Ali Dana, "I can believe. Whenever I slept there I made sure to set it. When Donny was alone? Forget it. I know that because I'd come into town and we'd go to dinner and go back there and he'd turn the key and just walk in, no beeping. I got on his case for a while but gave up. You don't want to be that naggy girlfriend."

I said, "Donny wasn't security-conscious."

"If he was, would he have invited those **lunatics** in?"

She'd flushed, took several breaths. "Sorry . . . no, he wasn't security-conscious and on top of that he was super absentminded. Maybe that was the dyslexia, I don't know. Or maybe his head was just up in the clouds."

Milo's cell played Debussy. Ali Dana looked at him quizzically as he picked up, stood, walked a few feet away.

He listened for a few moments, said, "Got it," and clicked off.

In the interim, she'd devoured three stale crackers before slamming the box down. "Just ate like a ream of paper, now I'm totally disgusted with myself."

I said, "It's a tough time."

"No excuse," she said. "No excuses allowed. Ever."

Milo returned. "Anything else you want to tell us, Ali?"

"What I'd **love** to tell you is who killed my sweet, wonderful love. What I **can** tell you is nothing and that **hurts**." Massaging her chest.

Milo said, "We've learned about a white card Donny had."

"What kind of white card?"

"Enabled him to go to a private bank and get money for the asking."

"Okay, so that's how he did it," she said. "Was it like one of those rich-kid deals?"

"Carte blanche," said Milo. "That's where it came from. So you never saw it?"

"All I saw was he'd have cash. I assumed he got it from an ATM like anyone else."

"Lots of cash?"

"I mean . . . I never counted but it looked like . . . maybe hundreds? Once I asked him about it and he said he just found it easier to deal with than credit cards and checks. Checks I can understand. His handwriting was crap. Credit cards, what's the problem? But I didn't get into it. Like I said, our time was valuable, no sense wasting it on b.s."

Milo nodded. "Would you mind if we have a look at the bedroom and the bathroom?"

"You need to ask?"

"Actually we do. If you weren't here, we'd require a victim's warrant."

"That's stupid—sure, do your thing. I'll call Mom and Dad, tell them I'm finally doing the smart thing."

I said, "Vet school."

"Getting away from here," she said. "From empty minds and cold hearts."

She sprayed on sunblock, went out on the deck, and worked her phone as we searched. The bathroom medicine cabinet and much of the counter surrounding the sink was crowded with cosmetics. The stash spilled over to the rim of the tiny tub-shower combo and was joined by shampoos, conditioner, crème rinses, moisturizers.

The sole archaeology linking Donny Klement to the space was a tube of brushless shaving cream, a packet of disposable razors, and the same variety of sleep meds we'd seen in the loft.

The bedroom was ten by ten with a single window covered by a bamboo shade. Milo checked behind the shade then raised it. Small window. A hint of stunning view. The hum of the ocean, relentless, calming.

I said, "Hypnotic."

"And even with that he had trouble sleeping. Girlfriend makes him sound like an innocent space cadet but maybe there was more to him."

"Like what?"

"Guilt about having too much? Who the hell knows."

He gloved up and began exploring. A brief examination, because storage was limited to a pair of nightstands flanking a queen bed, a facing three-drawer dresser, and a narrow closet on the east wall.

The closet was crammed with women's sweats, jeans, and blouses, plus a full-length black leather duster tailored in Rome for a female. Eighteen inches of space remained for the same kind of basic male duds we'd seen in the studio loft.

On the closet floor, a couple dozen pairs of women's shoes bullied one pair each of men's Keds, hemp sandals, and well-worn Chelsea boots.

The only solo space reserved for Donny Klement was a single high shelf that hosted a purple Turbo Surf boogie board. Pristine condition; rarely used.

Milo moved on to the nightstands. One drawer each, empty space below. The one nearer to the closet held several still-wrapped eyeshades.

I said, "Business-class perks. She brought them back for him."

"No doubt." He squeezed himself along the beach side of the bed, pulled the drawer open, and inspected a stack of fashion magazines tagged with Post-its. A brief flip-through revealed Ali Dana vamping in clothing most people could never wear.

In some shots, she looked like the woman we'd just sat with. In others, makeup, lighting, and wigs turned her into a stranger.

A business card was paper-clipped to a copy of **W**, for a modeling agency on lower Park Avenue in New York. Milo camera-shot it and shifted to the dresser.

The two top drawers were devoted to lingerie, neatly folded jeans, additional sweats, and pajamas, ranging from size 0 to 4.

Milo said, "Maybe 4 is after a big feast of crackers," and tried the bottom drawer. Men's size medium T-shirts, sweats, a couple of bulk sweaters, three button-up plaid shirts.

Something white protruded from the breast pocket of one of the shirts.

Slip of paper. He read it and showed it to me.

Clumsy, ragged, barely legible handwriting, the slant shifting choppily between front and back. If I'd been asked to guess the age of the writer, I'd have said seven to nine. Knowing about Donny Klement's severe dyslexia reminded me about the peril of jumping to conclusions.

Lots of effort had been taken to lay down a single word, scrawled off center.

CAP

Below that, a 323 phone number.

Milo said, "Could be an early cell number from

back when they tried to sync area codes. Or I'll get lucky and it's a pardon-the-expression landline with a real-life location."

He placed the card into one of the small evidence envelopes he carries routinely, dropped it into a jacket pocket, and returned to the front room, muttering, "Show me the money."

Ali Dana wasn't there. The front door was open.

Milo worked in the kitchen, opening flimsy doors on a skimpy selection of foodstuffs: peanut butter, cereal claiming to be healthy, packets of dry fruit, an opened jar of tahini that had separated. On a low shelf next to a box of organic popcorn, a baggie of marijuana and a bottle of Chardonnay still wearing a six-dollar price tag.

We left the house and found Ali Dana standing just north of the door, wet-eyed and talking on her cell.

She said, "Later, Mom, love you," hung up, and forced a pitiful smile.

Milo said, "Didn't find a firearm in there but need to ask if you own one."

She looked at him, amused. "Why, because I'm from Montana?"

"When someone's shot it's a routine question."

"Oh," she said. "The answer is I don't have one here but you bet, back home I own a whole bunch. Twelve-gauge, ten-gauge, deer rifle, Colt revolver that I inherited from my grandfather, and a target pistol I use on the shooting range Dad built. I grew up popping cans and bottles."

"Got it," said Milo.

"Honestly, if it was up to me, I **would've** gotten a California permit but Donny wouldn't hear about it. We didn't fight, we joked about it. He called me Annie Oakley and I called him . . ." She choked up. "Little Prince Pacifist. We were totally different from each other but there was . . . something."

Milo thanked her and gave her his card. She ran inside the house, looking spindly and off balance as she rushed to the door.

None of the grace she'd displayed in her photos. A harried crane.

15

As we turned onto Broad Beach Road, I said, "What was the call about?"

"Lab came through and rushed everything. Unfortunately, a whole bunch of nada. Casings didn't match any firearm used for a crime, any prints on the first floor were too smudged and there weren't a lot. Upstairs, two clean sets, one of them Donny's. The other was mostly in the bathroom in expected places and didn't trace to AFIS and since our fashion model sometimes slept there, I'm figuring, hers. What'd you think of her?"

"Looks like **Vogue,** talks like **Guns and Ammo.**"

"If I verify she was in New York, she's off the radar."

He pulled over in front of a wood-and-glass citadel, called the modeling agency, spent more time than he would've liked ferreting out the info, and hung up. "Working all week, like she said. Now let's find Mr. Cap."

He drew out the evidence envelope, put on a fresh glove to hold the slip of paper, and dialed the number Donny Klement had scrawled.

Out of service.

"Cap as in Captain? Caspar? One of the Capulets?"

I said, "People who recruit for Medicare scams are called cappers."

"You think Donny went the sleazy route to get his subjects?"

"Maybe not intentionally, but if he met someone with experience roping in the homeless, he might've seen it as an opportunity."

His index finger tapped the number. "Let's grab some grub, then head back to base."

No pseudo discussion about where to eat. Milo had a lucid vision.

The Shack was a former bait stand on the land side of PCH, just a few miles south of Broad. We'd been there a couple of years ago, treated to lunch by a young couple whose wedding had been demolished by the vicious murder of a party-crasher.

At that time, ordering was at the counter; you received a bakery-type number on a plasticized card and waited until someone brought the food. Today, we got a little gizmo that beeped and flashed red when the meal was ready, and did our own pickup.

The basics hadn't changed, though. Good, reasonably priced seafood. Million-dollar ocean view if you ignored cars speeding by.

Milo asked for the extra-large portion of fried shrimp and curly fries. I went for fish tacos, today's fish, something called blue-faced sea bass. He waved off debate about payment, handed cash to the kid at the register, took charge of the gizmo. I toted napkins, utensils, and extra-large iced teas to a table far enough from the highway to muffle the din.

"Cappers," he said. "A law-abiding gent like you knows about that because . . ."

"When I was starting out, a guy offered me a job. His main thing was orchestrating expensive medical tests and treatment through a network of M.D.'s, physical therapists, psychologists, psychiatrists, and chiropractors. His targets were street people on Medicare and Medi-Cal. He had a squad of scouts driving around and scooping them up. He called them cappers."

"He just laid it out?"

"Oh, yeah," I said. "Quite proud. He didn't want me for any of that, though. He'd just branched out by buying a board-and-care facility for severely disabled teens and young adults. The alleged goal was to devise behavioral plans for them and creatively bill the county and the state."

"Alleged," he said. "The whole thing was bull?"

"Seeing as most of the patients were near-comatose, I'd say so."

The gizmo burped and flashed. I got to my feet before he did, fetched the food, and brought it back. My plate was round and conventionally sized, his an oval platter twice as wide.

He said, "Oh, man, that's a truckload of curlies, they got generous."

The heap looked identical to the one he'd enjoyed two years ago. He'd finished it.

He opened a packet of ketchup. "Feel free to take." A deep breath, as if prepping for an athletic event. "Here goes."

Ingestion as an Olympic event.

Several swallows later, he said: "That sleazeball, any way you could contact him?"

"Not without divine intervention," I said. "He was sentenced to federal prison, delayed it with appeals, and died before the decision came down."

"Unnatural death?"

"Stroke at his mansion in Hancock Park."

"You followed the case."

"Not at all. My name showed up in his notes so I got subpoenaed to testify at the trial. Which never happened. I tried to explain my situation to the prosecuting D.D.A. He apologized but said I still might be re-subpoenaed if there was a retrial because I was 'hard data.' No one called me to let me know the case was moot. I learned about the scammer's death in the paper."

He produced his pad and pen. "They didn't prosecute anyone else?"

"Not that I heard."

"Hmm." A dozen curly fries later: "Scammers are creatures of habit. Maybe I'll find this Cap's name in that indictment. Remember the guy's name?"

"Clearly," I said. "James Rourke, called himself Jimmy R. Disbarred lawyer but apparently that doesn't stop you from being a health broker."

"Remember the prosecutor's name?"

"Henry Gluck."

"Do you ever forget anything?"

"Sometimes why I've come into a room. I remember Gluck because it means happy in German and he always seemed to be in a good mood."

He phoned Sean Binchy, asked him to pull James Rourke's arrest record and contact info for Henry Gluck.

"On it, Loot."

When he hung up, I said, "Gluck would be in his sixties, likely retired."

"If he's breathing and able to converse, he interests me." He picked up a shrimp and bit it cleanly in half.

I said, "You're hoping Cap's still on the prowl."

"I aspire," he said, "to guided imagination."

Twenty minutes later, we got up from the table. My plate contained one of three tacos, his leavings consisted of two curly fries.

He said, "Wrap yours and take it to go."

"You have it."

"Full," he said, patting his midriff. "But no sense wasting." Swaddling the taco in a napkin, he dropped it into a jacket pocket.

I pointed to the fries.

He shook his head. "Discretion."

As we crossed the line between Malibu and Pacific Palisades, Sean called in.

"Rourke's arrest was in Rampart Division, Loot. The primary D was a guy named Obed Garcia. Retired and no one knows him."

"You get hold of the file?"

"Coming through the fax, right now, Loot. Eighty-three pages, so far."

"Take a read then put it on my desk. What about Gluck?"

"Also retired according to a civilian clerk at the D.A. She thinks he moved out of state but doesn't know where."

"See if Nguyen can find out."

"Sure," said Sean, sounding unsure.

Milo said, "John can get grumpy but he likes you."

"He said that?"

"No," said Milo, "but everyone likes you."

Ten minutes later, as we crossed into Santa Monica, Sean was back on the line.

"Caught John in a good mood and he called their

personnel office. They won't give out personal data but they did agree to email Gluck that you wanted to speak to him. I gave them your extension."

"Excellent. Any luck with the homeless canvass?"

"Not much of a canvass so far, Loot. These people are mostly sad and scared."

"No recognition of any of the Wishers."

"No, sir, and I don't think they're lying about it."

"Why's that?" said Milo.

"They just seem too . . . defeated to make something up. **Incredibly** sad." Soft sigh. "Gethsemane—my church—has an outreach program in Simi but we're talking a small number. What **we've** been seeing on this one is **neighborhoods** of homeless . . . I guess that would make it a canvass—sorry for going on, Loot."

"No apologies necessary, kiddo. It's a horrendous situation."

"Makes you wonder," said Sean. "God creates a wonderful world and we turn it into **that**."

We were on Santa Monica Boulevard, a mile west of the station, when Milo's cell abused something Baroque that I didn't recognize. No lute should ever be treated that way.

He pulled over to a red zone. "Sturgis."

"Lieutenant," said a cheerful voice, "this is Henry Gluck. I hear you want to talk to me."

"Yes, sir. Thanks for calling."

"First off," said Gluck, "I want to stress my inno-cence." Hoarse laughter.

"Got it, sir. I won't even Mirandize you."

"Heh heh heh. So what can I do for you?"

"I'm looking for information on a health-care scammer you prosecuted a while back named James Rourke. It's actually one of his cappers I'm trying to find."

"Good old Jimmy R. Charm personified. Are you aware that he's dead?"

"I am."

"Passed peacefully in a big bed in a big house," said Henry Gluck. "Unlike, I'm sure, some of the people he exploited."

That sounded like an opening statement.

Milo said, "Are we talking homeless folk?"

"Homeless, the working poor, addicts trying to get it together in halfway houses, mentally deficient people in a corrupt nursing facility he owned. Anyone he could offer up in sacrifice. Not only were the taxpayers defrauded, the people Rourke roped in were often put through painful, invasive proce-dures. I wanted to include assault in the charges but my boss said we were a white-collar unit, stick to white collar. Which capper are you looking for?"

"Someone who might be calling himself Cap."

"Mr. Literal," said Gluck. "If I had to bet, I'd say that's Abel Rodriguez because he was one of the most egregious operators. Pompous little twit, called himself El Capitan. I would've loved to prosecute him but once Rourke died, the scumbag doctors pled out and the case went **pffft**. It's one of the reasons I left the D.A. and transferred to the city attorney. At least there, I'd have no delusions of anything other than civil cases. But that turned out to be a bit of a yawn so I retired and moved to Dallas to be near my daughter."

"Good for you, sir."

"Sometimes I think it is," said Gluck. "Sometimes I'm bored out of my gourd. How come you're looking for Cap?"

Milo explained.

Gluck said, "Just photography? Nothing sketchy?"

"As far as I can tell."

"I suppose anything that put money in Rodriguez's pocket would be an incentive. At least no one got a spinal tap or a bone marrow aspiration."

We reached the station, climbed the stairs to Milo's office. He sat at his desk and I squeezed into a corner and tried not to cramp up.

His allocated space is closet-sized, well away from the bustle of the big detective room downstairs, devised as punishment years ago by a venal former chief of police. If the chief had done his homework, he'd have known his intended victim thrived in solitude.

Wheeling his abdomen closer to his monitor, Milo scanned the top page of the 102 Sean had left him. Brushing other papers into the wastebasket without examination, he junked a collection of departmental emails. Flipping pages and adding them to the circular file, he came to a list of names.

"Here he is but no number or address. Useless." The rest of the indictment got trashed.

I said, "Gluck's question was interesting. Was Donny's operation limited to photography?"

He frowned. "Donny's involved with a lowlife like Rodriguez, maybe not? Everyone describes him as a saint and doesn't look as if he needed the money. Though I'm still waiting for his financial person to call."

He looked at his watch. "Probably too late in New York." He tried anyway. Multiple-choice voicemail. The number one option **If You're a Surety Client,** the rest meant to discourage.

He logged the department's arrest files and key-worded **abel rodriguez.**

Four felons by that name, a twenty-eight-year-old gangster incarcerated at San Quentin for murder, an eighteen-year-old awaiting trial on an auto theft charge, a twenty-one-year-old out on bail for assault, and the likely Abel, fifty-four years old with an address on Alvarado and a three-decade his-tory of larceny, petty theft, narcotics with intention to sell, identity theft, and fraud.

No arrests for three years, the most recent charge defrauding an innkeeper.

Abel Rodriguez had skipped out on a motel bill on Sixth Street, less than half a mile from his resi-dence. Operating, like most criminals do, in familiar territory. He'd been nabbed walking away from the Starshine Inn in the company of an unnamed woman who was a "known prostitute."

I said, "He paid her but decided to trim his other expenses."

Milo said, "Ah, romance," and scrolled to the bottom of the page to learn the resolution.

Restitution, no jail time. No surprise.

The filing detective, William Allan Puente, still worked at Rampart but he was away from his desk. Milo left a message, then tried the day-shift lieutenant, Clive Barnsdale.

Barnsdale said, "West L.A.? You've got something on mine from all the way in Paradise?"

"What's yours?"

"The guy you're asking about, Rodriguez? Got himself murdered last week."

"You're kidding," said Milo.

"It's **not** about that?" said Barnsdale. "Then what?"

Milo explained.

"His name just came up on yours? Crazy."

"Mine was a gunshot."

"Then maybe nothing," said Barnsdale. "Or maybe, still. Rodriguez was blunt force, talk to my D working it. Sheila Folker."

"I know her," said Milo, giving me a thumbs-up.

"Good," said Barnsdale. "Then you can skip the small talk and try to make sense of this shit."

D II Sheila Folker and Milo made small talk about a conference they'd both attended last year in Desert

Hot Springs. Crap food but excellent cocktails at a local restaurant. The exchange seemed to cheer both of them.

Folker said, "So to what do I owe this?"

"A guy I was looking for on one of mine turned out to be one of yours. Abel Rodriguez."

"Him? You're kidding. That's a fresh one, six days ago. What's your interest?"

He told her.

She said, "Well, that could make sense because he did still call himself El Capitan. And for all I know he was still capping. Your victim had money, huh?"

"Lots."

"Then sure, why wouldn't a guy like Rodriguez get involved? He was a scumbag career criminal."

"I noticed recently he's been careful," said Milo. "No arrests in three years."

"Ha," said Sheila Folker. "I wouldn't assume careful or a new moral compass. More like we're short-staffed and don't go after bloodless stuff unless we get pressured from the D.A. for one of their P.R. things."

"Intrepid attorneys battling corruption."

Folker laughed. "Anyway, Rodriguez got his head bashed in a week ago behind a dark warehouse used to store imported nuts and fruit."

"Six days ago is three days before mine. What time did it happen?"

"Late," said Folker. "Best guess from the coroner is three, four in the morning."

"Around the same as mine."

"Some villain skulking in the wee hours?" said Folker. "Sure, that's when they skulk. And trust me, Milo, I'd love for there to be a link but I'm not hearing anything exciting. Yours got shot, mine got clobbered. Yours was an upright citizen, mine anything but. Plus the scenes are clear across the city from each other and for all we know my Cap isn't your Cap."

"Did he have a phone on him?"

"Nope, no wallet or I.D., either, and his pockets were turned inside out, seemed like an obvious robbery. No phone account I can find, so he probably used short-termers. His prints would've I.D.'d him but I got lucky and one of the patrol officers on the scene recognized Rodriguez from the neighborhood, Rodriguez basically a shifty hanger-on, when he'd see them he'd act friendly. You know cons, they always figure they've got **über**-charm."

"In Rodriguez's case, not the cleverest self-evaluation," said Milo.

"Good point," said Folker. "If he was a really good con, he'd be on the city council. Anyway, patrol dude was able to direct me to where Rodriguez lived. Rooming house not far from where he got brained. I pulled a V warrant and called in the techies. Pretty much a dump. We found a couple of handguns in pieces, all rusted out and inoperative, and the predictable dope—crank and pills—plus plenty of crap booze. But nothing that would indicate who did him. I've been assuming a robbery gone over the edge and that still seems logical."

"Any record of who Rodriguez associated with?"

"For the past few years he seems to have gone lone-wolf. A while back, he did get busted as part of a big Medi-Cal ring, working for some rich Hancock Park guy snagging patients for bullshit procedures. For some reason, the whole thing was dismissed."

Milo said, "That I can educate you on." He passed on what Henry Gluck had related.

Folker said, "Same old story. We do all the work, hand the lawyers what they need, they get lazy. Anyway, from what I saw at Rodriguez's place, he's slid down quite a way from big-time fraud. Your victim have any connection to drugs?"

"Not that I've found."

"He just took pictures?"

"So far, that's it."

"If he was legit, how would he hook up with a lowlife like Rodriguez?"

"Good question," said Milo.

"The homeless in costumes," said Folker. "Sounds twisted. Anything sexual going on?"

"Nope. My guy comes across as naive and trusting and out to do something noble."

"Noble and stupid," said Folker. "Anyone who lets a stranger in anywhere anytime is missing something upstairs. You're a rich kid with nothing to do and you hook up with people in the worst circumstances? You're brain-dead. Not to be judgmental."

Milo laughed and they agreed to touch base if anything interesting came up.

He hung up and half wheeled toward me. "What do you think?"

I said, "All those differences she pointed out could be relevant but to my mind, two murders three days apart outweighs that. What if Rodriguez had something to do with Donny's project and someone didn't want that known?"

"Like who?"

"At this point, the only thing I can think of is one of the homeless got enraged and decided to take it out on Donny. Expectations unmet, like Ali Dana said. Or planned to come back and rob Donny. Either way, if Rodriguez had put the two of them together, the killer knew he could point a finger."

"Homeless with a gun, shooting a nice clean triangle. Guess there's always a first time. Either way, I'm at the same place."

"I.D.'ing the Wishers."

"Digging up goddamn unnatural history."

He fished the Rourke indictment out of the trash can. "Maybe I was too hasty, gonna see what this masterpiece has to offer."

He lifted the prosecution tome, flipped a few pages, put it down. "The usual sprightly prose. Okay, now I'm gonna really exploit your good nature. Any way we can split this up, go through it faster? Save your buddy from O.D.'ing on jargon?"

I laughed. "Spread the risk? Why not."

"What a pal," he said. "And this time I'm not saying that lightly."

We transferred to an interview room where the light and space were more generous and began studying the case against James Elgin Rourke.

The prosecution summary was typical jawbreaking lawyerly pronouncement larded with repetition. Maybe attorneys attend schools where grades are based on how many words you put out.

I waded through a lot of thesaurus abuse before the basics took shape. Rourke's scheme had been far-reaching and monumental, stretching across several counties and resulting in an estimated nineteen million dollars of bogus billing. Way more than I'd imagined.

Twelve million of that had been recovered from a variety of accounts registered to Rourke, another five from the coffers of Rourke's corrupt partners. Leaving two million unaccounted for. The D.A.'s office suggested Rourke had stashed the money offshore but had failed to confirm the guess. Throw in foreign agencies and cooperation devolves to fantasy.

I'd ended up with the last fifty-four pages of the document and midway through, came across two pages of names. Abel Rodriguez and four other cappers under Rodriguez's supervision along with an army of health-care providers who'd participated

in the scam. Including two "neuro psychologists."
I knew a lot of the top neuro people in town but
recognized neither of them. I looked them up. A
pair of "counselors stripped of licensure."

What was missing from the document was
a witness list that might lead us to the exploited.
Meaning good luck connecting any of Rourke's
enlistees to the people Donny Klement had dolled
up and photographed.

I said so to Milo.

He said, "I thought your job was improving my
mental health."

"Okay, then here's some hope: Maybe there's
another list and Gluck knows how to access it."

He made the call.

Henry Gluck said, "How can I miss you if you
don't go away? What's up?"

Milo explained.

Gluck said, "Of course we had names. Hundreds
of them but they were expunged after the case
closed, don't even try."

Milo thanked him and hung up.

We walked back to his office where he said, "Gave
you a chance and you failed me," and dropped
the papers back in the can.

I said, "If Donny's Cap does turn out to be
Rodriguez, learning how he and Donny hooked up
could tell you something, and Mel Gornick might
know that."

"The delicate soul who's gone incommunicado."

"She lives in Brentwood."

"Meaning?"

"Stone's throw," I said. "If you're Reed."

When he finished laughing, he said, "Hell, why not?"

17

Gornick's driver's license put her residence on Girofle Court. GPS tagged that as a two-block loop north of San Vicente on the western edge of Brentwood. Just east of Twenty-Sixth Street, where the district melds with the higher-priced spreads of Santa Monica.

Traffic was a sour clot and we crawled, first on Wilshire, then on San Vicente.

Milo said, "Forget throwing stones, gimme a catapult."

Soon after he turned off Twenty-Sixth, the computer fouled the search with unlabeled dead ends. Good place to live if you didn't like visitors.

Supplementing with the Thomas Guide finally got us there.

The houses were a mix of low-slung, gravel-top ranches from the fifties and McMansions aiming for Mediterranean warmth and falling short. Nothing cleans the air like trees but for all the talk about climate change, L.A.'s criminally delinquent when it comes to planting them. Installation along the breezeway on Girofle Court was sparse and random, as if the neighborhood had been laid down and forgotten.

The house we were looking for was one of the redos, two blocky stories spreading to the legal limits of a narrow lot. Flat-faced but for curlicue appliqués above windows and a barely recessed doorway that would provide no sanctuary in the rain. The stucco was yellow sporting occasional orange undertones. The intention probably Tuscan patina, the outcome blotchiness that evoked citrus rind past its prime. A red BMW 3 sat in the driveway.

Milo's buzzer-push was followed seconds later by the door swinging open. A woman, ash blond, thin, wearing brown velvet sweats, tapped a foot, examined us, and gave a start.

"You're not the plumber."

Milo grinned. "Lieutenant Sturgis. But if it's something simple, I'm pretty handy."

The woman seemed to consider the offer, then shook her head violently. "Please, not now. This isn't a good time."

"There never really is a good time, Ms. Coolidge."

Waving a dismissive hand, she began closing the door.

Milo said, "I'm serious. What's the plumbing problem?"

"Clogged toilet, what else?" A thin, pinch-nostriled nose wrinkled. "Disgusting. The rooter people won't say how long before they get here."

"Do you have a plunger?"

"I think so . . . probably . . . yes, in the laundry room . . . I think."

"Let's give it a try."

She looked us over again. "Might as well get something for my taxes. Wait there."

When she passed out of sight, Milo clicked his heels and saluted.

I said, "Some people take 'civil servant' literally."

He snapped back to seriousness as Christine Coolidge reappeared carrying a red rubber plunger still tagged with a Home Depot label.

"In there," she said, pointing to a door on the right wall of the entry. "It's the powder room, no one uses it much, I have no idea how it happened."

Milo went in, closed the door, emerged a moment later, jacket slung atop a shoulder, shirtsleeves rolled to the elbows, hands scrubbed pink. "Done."

Christine Coolidge said, "You're kidding."

"If it was tree roots, you'd be out of luck. This was just someone using tissues instead of toilet paper."

"Oh, geez, I've **told** her."

Christine Coolidge's face took on what one of my professors called the you-got-me look. Red blotches sprang up behind her ears and on the sides of narrow nostrils. "She can be maddeningly stubborn."

Milo said, "It happens. I grew up with a bunch

of brothers. We each got lessons in Plunger 101. The hard way."

He tried smiling again. Despite herself, Coolidge reciprocated. "Now I suppose I owe you one."

"No big deal, ma'am. One way or the other, I'll have to persist in trying to talk to Mel."

"Why would you waste your time on her? Shouldn't you be looking for one of them?"

"Them?"

"The unhomed. Not that I'm assuming they're all criminals, at the root they're victims of the system, but still. Who else?"

She looked at me. "You're the psychologist?"

I nodded.

"You're here because you view Mel as still vulnerable?"

"I've been working on the case pretty steadily."

"I see," said Coolidge. "Actually, I don't, but never mind." Back to Milo. "Haven't you analyzed the situation and come to the same conclusion about the unhomed?"

Milo said, "Ms. Coolidge, we're not even close to making assumptions. That's why we need to talk to—"

"I get it, she worked with him, you're following your rulebook. The problem is, she has completely shut herself off so if you push her, there could be . . . consequences. Surely, you get that, Dr. . . . I forgot your name."

"Delaware."

"I knew it was a state. You see my point, right? About pushing."

I said, "Does Dr. Framus agree?"

"I have no idea how Dr. Framus feels because all of a sudden Mel has made me persona non grata with Dr. Framus. As in no contact whatsoever. And since she's an adult legally though far from adult in reality, I have no choice."

"Speaking of her being an adult," said Milo.

"I know, I know, I'm spinning my wheels trying to be a good mom and protect her. But wouldn't **you** feel terrible, Dr. Delaware, if something you did traumatized her further?"

I said, "In terms of Mel shutting herself off, she's actually discussed the murder extensively."

Christine Coolidge slapped her hands on her hips. "I find **that** hard to believe. Who are you claiming she's discussed it with?"

"Anyone with access to her social network."

As I began listing posts, she sagged. "The school site, too? Oh Lord. And of course, I'm the last to know. All right, now I feel like a total **idiot**. Fine, she's coming down right now and she'd better **cool** it with the drama."

Milo cleared his throat.

"What?" said Christine Coolidge.

"If you don't mind, ma'am, could you keep it low-key?"

"Now I'm getting parenting lessons from the cops?" She broke into crackling laughter, looked at the plunger and snatched it from Milo.

"Here's what going to happen: First, I'm going to wash and disinfect this disgusting thing. Second, I'm going to low-key my daughter down here. No worries, I'll not insinuate myself into whatever conversation you all end up having. Instead, I'll be informing the rooter people that they missed a golden opportunity to rip off another homeowner."

"Thank you, ma'am."

She pointed to a sunken living room. "Make yourselves comfortable. I'll even bring you drinks. And snacks. Once I've washed my hands."

The house was well kept, expensively but blandly furnished. Wall decoration consisted of a few abstract prints and half a dozen framed enlargements of **Angel City** covers. Editing Christine Coolidge was proud of.

An open doorway fed to a white kitchen large enough for a tribal dinner. There's a severe scarcity of tribes on the Westside of L.A. but warm and fuzzy fantasies persist.

Coolidge went in there and slipped from view. A few minutes of clatter and running water passed before she returned and laid down two cans of mandarin-flavored LaCroix water and a bowl of pretzel sticks.

Milo said, "Thanks, ma'am."

"You performed the royal flush, least I can do." She ran up the stairs to the second floor. Muffled voices began sounding from above. The maternal voice dominated. Two feeble rejoinders from the daughterly voice, then silence.

Moments later, Melissande Gornick trudged down the stairs followed by her mother. Only a leash was missing.

"**Go.** They won't bite you."

As Mother returned upstairs, Daughter entered with her head down and sat cater-corner to us. Mel Gornick's pink hair was tied up high and haphazardly, resembled an oversized radish. Her facial piercings remained except for the stud between lip and chin. In its place was a black-as-night pinhole that looked as if it might never close. She wore white fleecy sweats so grossly oversized they seemed to ingest her. Like an octopus wrapping itself around a sardine.

When she looked up, her eyes moved from Milo to me. My face evoked a violent flinch and she turned away quickly.

It can get like that when you help someone in acute stress. You remind them of how helpless they felt so they try to cancel you cognitively.

Milo took advantage of that and edged a bit closer. "Really appreciate this, Mel."

She shrugged. Scratched a forearm.

"First of all," he said, "is there anything you want to tell us? Something that might've occurred to you since we spoke the first time?"

"Uh-uh."

"No prob, Mel. The reason we're here is we consider you the expert on Donny."

Half smile. "Why?"

"You spent more time with Donny than anyone. Including his girlfriend Ali, who we just talked to."

"Her."

"Is there something we should know about Ali?"

Eye-roll. "She's okay."

"But?"

"She wasn't exactly there for him."

"She told us she travels extensively."

"Whatever."

"Ever observe any problems between her and Donny?"

"Nah . . . except for her not being there."

"Donny talked about that?"

Head shake. "It just makes sense. Someone's not there for you? Who wants that?"

"Donny was left alone a lot."

"He had me." Her hands began to shake and her face turned as pink as her hair. "I didn't mean it like that. Just that I spent more time with him. Like you said. That's all I meant."

"A hundred percent, Mel," said Milo. "If we're going to catch whoever killed Donny, we need information. So please tell us anything you can think of, even if you don't think it's important. Because, yeah, you really are an expert."

Mel Gornick allowed the smile to enlarge. That didn't sit right and she twisted her lips into a grimace.

"I mean," she said, "I don't know what you think I can tell you."

"Let's talk about the Wishers. Did Donny ever have any problems with them?"

"Never. He was so sweet to them. They appreciated it."

"They told him they appreciated him?"

"Not with words, but you could tell. I mean they never, ever got sassy at him. None of them, never. I know people are thinking one of them did it. My mother thinks that but trust me, there was nothing crazy going on, it was all peace."

She crossed her legs. "Like if they came in and they were hungry and thirsty, Donny would give them food and something to drink. And he always took his time with them."

I said, "He was patient."

"Totally. He never rushed them, he made sure they were always comfortable. As comfortable as they could get."

"Some of them had trouble getting comfortable?"

"No."

I waited.

She said, "What I meant was sometimes they could be restless. Jumping up. Walking around. Talking to themselves. Donny **never** rushed them and in the end, they all sat for him and had a good time."

He showed her the before-and-after shots. "Were these the only Wishers?"

"Yes."

"How many of them were restless?"

"I don't know. They're people like anyone else. Individuals. None of them were scary." She looked to the right. "I don't want to get anyone in trouble."

"No one will get in trouble unless they had something to do with Donny's murder."

She scratched her arm.

Milo said, "I'm sure you want the case solved."

Mel Gornick screwed up her lips and twisted them through several circuits. "The only one I remember who was **really** restless was Jean Harlow, I don't know her real name, Donny never told me."

Milo pulled the photo of the emaciated woman out of the mix.

He said, "Beverly."

"Never heard her name. Never heard any names."

"But this is the woman who was really restless."

"Yeah. Super skinny and jumpy. But not creepy restless, okay? She just kept walking back and forth. Moving her lips with no sound coming out. Waving her hands. Like she was talking to an invisible person. Donny was totally cool, he just brought out the dress and gave her time to look at it and she loved it right away and was totally happy. They're different, okay? But there's nothing wrong with being different, everyone's different if you just look enough, okay? Me and Donny respected that. There was never a problem. Never."

I said, "Beverly loved the dress."

"**Loved** it. Loved **posing** it. At the end she hugged and kissed Donny on the cheek and he was cool with that, too. Even though she smelled of booze."

"What happened then?"

"Nothing," she said, as if the question puzzled her. "Donny paid her and she left."

Milo said, "How much did the Wishers get paid?"

"A hundred dollars," said Mel Gornick. "Five twenties."

"We heard five hundred."

"From who?"

"Ali."

"She wouldn't know." Trying to sound confident but uncertain.

"So," said Milo, "how exactly did Donny hook up with the Wishers?"

"He used a guy."

"What guy?"

"Someone with connections to their community."

"The homeless community."

Her arms stiffened. "It **is** a community. Whatever you want to be a community is a community."

"Of course. Was this guy actually part of the homeless community?"

"No," she said. "He just . . . knew them. I guess. I'm not sure how. It wasn't my job to ask questions, just to make Donny—to be a good assistant."

"What's the guy's name?"

"I don't know his total name," said Mel Gornick.

"Whatever you know is fine."

"All I know is he called himself Cap. Donny said maybe it was short for Captain." She shrugged. "Maybe he worked on a boat. I don't **know**."

"Did you ever meet Cap?"

"Only one time."

"When was that?"

"When he came to Donny."

"Was that recently?"

"No," she said. "Months ago. After a couple of them had posed."

"Did Cap bring the homeless people to the studio?"

"Not that I saw."

"They found their own way."

"I guess. Or he drove them and waited outside. Or someone else did—I don't **know**, okay? I was just there when they came in and when they left. I keep saying I don't know but you don't believe me!"

"Of course we do, Mel. We're just trying to do our job."

"Whatever."

I said, "The time Cap did show up, what did he and Donny discuss?"

"No idea."

"Was it a long meeting?"

"Uh-uh, short." Another quick sidelong glance. Sensitive topic?

"Five minutes?"

"Something like that."

Milo said, "Maybe Cap came to get paid for finding the homeless?"

"Maybe."

"Any idea how much Donny paid Cap?"

"Nope. I only saw him once. In and out."

Milo produced Abel Rodriguez's most recent mugshot. "Is this Cap?"

Her face constricted. "**He** did it?"

No reason to mention the perfect alibi: three days dead. Milo said, "He absolutely did not."

"Then why are you **showing** me that?"

"We're trying to learn as much as we can about Donny. About the project, the homeless folk. Anything. So this is definitely Cap?"

"Yeah."

"Okay, thanks." Milo pocketed the photo. "So Cap hooked Donny up with the Wishers. Any idea how Donny found Cap?"

She looked to the side, yet again. Definitely a sensitive topic.

She caught my eye and swung back quickly in the other direction, speeding past Milo and fixing on one of her mother's framed covers. One leg began bouncing up and down. She bent forward, hugging her knees.

Milo said, "Mel?"

"Do I have to say?"

"Is there a problem with saying?"

"It's just . . ." She pivoted slowly, forced herself to look at both of us. "Okay." Deep sigh. "It's been totally . . . okay. It's this. Since he moved out, it's been for shit. Totally for shit. They want to hate on each other, fine, but why are they taking it out on **me**? I need things to stop being crazy. I can't mess it up even more by getting him pissed off at me."

I said, "We're talking about your parents."

Her nod was so violent it threatened whiplash.

"Your dad moved out recently?"

"Like . . . two months ago. They had a massive fight and the next day he was gone."

She turned back toward the second-story landing. Moved forward and half covered her mouth with a hand.

"**She's** been going all psycho bitch on me like it's **my** fault. And **he's** like sorry I can't talk to you. When I call his office, his secretary tells me he's in a meeting, when I call his landline, I get voicemail. Not his voicemail and not Heather's—his **girl**friend, she's like twenty-five. I get this robot voicemail. I mean, it's not like he's got to hide Heather, I know about her, I don't give a shit about her, he can do what he wants. But **talk** to me, dude, I'm still your daughter, okay?"

Milo said, "Tough situation."

"**Fucked** situation and that's what I'm trying to

say. I don't want to make it **more** fucked by pissing him off."

She rolled up a sleeve, resumed scratching her arm. Slowly at first, then steadily accelerating to allegro clawing. Welts rose; earthworms squirming beneath soft flesh.

Inspecting the blemishes, she muttered, "Fucking allergies," and slid her hands under her meager butt.

Maybe something she'd learned in therapy.

Milo looked at me. **Your ball.**

I said, "Your father knows Cap. We can see why you don't want your dad to know you told us. And he won't."

"Why not?"

"Because we wouldn't do that to you, we have no need to tell your dad. Lieutenant Sturgis just showed you a picture of Cap so we obviously knew about him before coming here. But any details you can fill in would be helpful. How your dad knows Cap, how Donny met him, anything."

"Like that matters?"

"It may not matter, Mel. But we can't know unless we try."

"Once I tell you, I can't stop you from telling him. Making me a snitch in a ditch."

"We don't do that, Mel."

She shook her head.

I said, "It's a promise: Your father will never know."

"You don't **understand**! **I'm** the one who **did** it!"

Milo said, "Did what?"

"Created it! Talked to Daddy about helping Donny! He's a lawyer and I remembered some dude he represented who did something with the homeless. He talked about the case, said it was a big one. He used to talk about work all the time but mostly it was DUIs, that's what he mostly does. When he talked work, it totally pissed **her** off, she'd give him the **look**. Like **You're boring me, dude.** Then she'd leave the room. But I stayed in the room, I didn't think he was boring. It made him feel good when I listened."

"Your dad does criminal defense."

"Yup."

"What did he tell you about defending Cap?"

"He didn't tell me a name, just one day said 'Want to know about one of my biggest ones, sweetie?' "

Her voice snagged on the last word. Scratch. Claw. Deep breath. "I said of course, Daddy, and he said he had a client who was on trial for doing something with the homeless. I'm like, what? And he's like, they were getting medicines and other stuff they didn't need. Hoses put up their butts, needle-sticks, really bad stuff. I said that's a hate crime, how can you defend someone like that? And he gave me his lawyer look."

She let out air in a long, sibilant puff. "The **You're a silly kid, we've been through this before, Mel,** look. And I'm like, 'I get it, people get defended, it's the Revolutionary War. But still.' So I'm like, 'Even if he hurt helpless people?' And he's like, 'He didn't actually hurt anyone, he just gave them rides to the people who did bad stuff, no one forced them to take the money.' I thought that was lame but he was getting a little pissed off so I didn't say anything more."

Freeing her hands, she laced them tightly around her torso. "Back then he was talking to me."

I said, "So when Donny talked about wanting to do the project, you remembered the conversation with your dad and thought about the driver he'd defended."

"Donny didn't know what to do," she said. "He had other projects that he talked about but didn't do. Maybe going out to Burning Man. Or taking pictures of places destroyed by fire and saying something about climate change. Or sick old people in nursing homes. Then he came up with it and liked it the best. Said it could be a vehicle for changing people's lives with constructive fantasy, how everyone needs fantasy. On an individual and on a world level. After that, it was **all** he talked about. Saying he craved—he used that word, **craved**—he craved showing them a side of life they wouldn't know without him. I told him that's beautiful, Donny, and he was like, now all I need to do is find them. He had no idea. Then he laughed and I'm like what's funny and he's like, 'Big ideas, as usual, but no clue how to put them into action because I'm too fucking privileged.'"

She reached for the pretzels, took one, twirled it, placed it atop the coffee table. "That really downed him. He got quiet for a long time. I felt so, so bad for him. Then I flashed on Daddy, his guy who knew the homeless, and it was like karma electricity and I'm like, 'Guess what?' I told Donny and he got **totally** excited so I called Daddy and Daddy said sure, baby, why not? Don't know if he's still around but I'll give it a try. Back then, he was like that, whatever I wanted. The next day, he calls, 'Here's the guy's number, your timing's good, he can use the money.' So I'm feeling like everyone's going to get helped, this is **masterful** karma. I give the number to Donny, Donny gives me a big hug and tells me I'm a lifesaver. I remember laughing inside. Thinking about being a **candy**."

Her hands came free and clamped around her chest. "A lifesaver. But I wasn't, huh?"

Milo questioned her awhile longer, got nothing new, thanked her and stood. She remained seated as we crossed the room toward the front door. Small, pale, fragile. I'd call Helen Framus and fill her in.

As Milo swung the door open, she called out, "Good luck."

We turned toward her.

Not fast enough. She'd begun running up the stairs.

18

Driving back to the station, Milo said, "Nothing iffy happened with the Wishers. You see her as credible on that?"

"She was enamored of him. If she really knew something about who killed him, she'd tell us."

"And post it on her social pages."

"That, too."

"Schoolgirl crush," he said. "Or whatever they're calling it nowadays. So put her aside and move on. The question is where."

"Don't know but at least you've got a fuller picture of your victim. Naive and trusting and inept to the point where it took Mel to get the process going. His learning disabilities may have played a role in it. Finding it hard to plan and organize. And having all that money didn't help, it just made him feel guilty. You saw the way he lived."

"The simple life with a trust fund and an ocean view."

I said, "I bet he would've said the same thing. But there are all sorts of poverties. This a guy whose brain didn't work optimally. Who was abandoned by his father and discovered his mother dead and as he approached thirty, hadn't accomplished much. Mel Gornick had a massive crush on him but even she described him as floundering. He finally settled on the Wishers project. The choice was as much for his sake as theirs. Searching for an easy solution to a complex problem. But he wasn't equipped to deal with what he'd started. Because if you feel you're unworthy, it's easy to get lax about protecting yourself."

"Screw the alarm."

"And let strangers with troubled backgrounds explore your living quarters. He preferred using cash, paid the Wishers that way. What if his carelessness extended to leaving a whole bunch of money around and someone got ideas."

"Fine, same question. Where do I go with it?"

"Keep trying to I.D. the Wishers. But also stay on the financial angle. We could be totally wrong about a homeless angle and it may turn out to be just another ugly family thing."

"No connection to Rodriguez."

I shrugged.

He said, "Silence ain't always golden." A beat. "You're right. Of course."

He made abrupt turns that took us out of the residential maze, idled at the light at Twenty-Sixth and San Vicente, and spoke briefly with each of the three young detectives.

Got three negative reports from the homeless search.

Moe and Sean clicked off without comment.

Alicia said, "What surprises me is that they're a lot less hostile than I expected. Not like when we deal with gangbangers. It's like they want to help but can't."

"Keep on it, kid."

"Of course," she said. "No choice."

19

We made it to Milo's office half an hour later. He plopped back down at his desk and phoned John Nguyen.

Before he could say a word, Nguyen said, "No, I do not have anything yet on that number your victim called."

"Forget it, John. Turns out he was calling his girlfriend in New York."

"You didn't think to tell me."

"I just found out. Sorry if you wasted time on it."

"Why does the girlfriend use a burner?"

Milo explained about the modeling agency's privacy concerns.

"A model? We're talking hot?" said Nguyen. "If you're able to think in hetero terms."

"I'm reporting you to the grievance committee, John."

Nguyen laughed. "I have no recollection of

anything anyhow anywhere at any time. Is the girlfriend smokin'?"

Milo said, "Exactly what you'd expect from
someone who walks the runway."

"Blond?"

"Brunette. Gorgeous face, legs that keep—"

"**Stop**," said Nguyen. "My brain hurts. And now
I'm thinking. There just might be an imminent need
to subject her to face-to-face prosecutorial scrutiny."

"She was in New York at the time of the murder
and there's no reason to suspect her of anything."

"Shucks," said Nguyen. "So why're you calling?"

Milo summed up the Rourke case, Abel
Rodriguez's involvement in the scam, and his recent
death. The importance of finding a witness list.

"Why?"

"Rodriguez may have gone back to the well. Got
the Wishers from the health-care homeless."

"And?"

"I.D.'ing the Wishers is the only way I can see
out of this one."

"I do crimes against people, not fraud. Talk to
the D.A.s who actually prosecuted it."

"Already did, John. Supposedly, it was trashed."

"Supposedly?"

"You know how it is, John. Stuff gets filed,
forgotten—"

"And I'm supposed to go digging randomly?"

"Okay, forget it. Sorry for wasting your time."

A beat.

Nguyen said, "Got a couple of interns from the U. Pretty much useless, wouldn't mind getting them out of my hair. Where was the trial going to be? That could help."

"Don't know."

"Big-time scam, homeless patients. Probably right here at Clara." Citing the main Superior Court Building on Temple Street, downtown. Named after Clara Foltz, the first female attorney on the West Coast.

Milo said, "So you'll check."

"With proper incentive," said Nguyen.

"That being?"

"Should the model require further investigation . . ."

"You'll be the first to know, John."

"How tall is she?"

"Six feet."

"Huh," said Nguyen. "Maybe she values brains over bulk."

Milo hung up, stood, stretched. I had an idea what was coming.

"You up for a walk?"

Bingo.

We'd begun to stroll south on Butler Avenue, opting for houses and apartments rather than the commercial din of Santa Monica Boulevard to the north of the station, when his cell chirped four bars of Dvořák's **New World Symphony**.

He read the screen. "Alicia again." Came to a halt without warning, like a ten-wheeler jamming an air brake.

"What's up, kid?"

"You're not going to believe this, Loo. Here I was bitching about making no progress and literally minutes later I go into another encampment, Pico, east end of Santa Monica, and the first person I speak to says, sure I know her and points to the skinny woman in the white dress. Says her street name is Jangles because she likes to wear jewelry. Like a dozen fake-type bracelets on each arm. According to my new pal, the Westside was an exception, she mostly hangs out downtown. Not Skid Row, farther south, near Thirteenth and Fourteenth, where it's supposedly safer."

"Who's the pal?"

"Woman who calls herself LaBelle. She talks a lot better than she looks, might know more than she's let on so far."

"Why do you think so?"

"I just get that feeling from her, Loo. Figured I should treat her gingerly so I didn't bug her about an I.D., just slipped her five bucks, circulated some more but no one else had anything to say. Moe's the closest to downtown so I let him know and he's following up."

"God bless you, Detective Bogomil."

"Ha. So should I try her again or go downtown and meet up with Moe? I can notify Sean, too, if you want, or he can stay in the Valley where he's checking out folk living under the 101."

"How long have you been working?"

"Not long," she said.

"Meaning?"

A beat. "Maybe twelve hours."

"Meaning more like fifteen," said Milo. "Notify both of them, talk to LaBelle some more, then go home and get some rest."

"With all due respect, Loo, I'd prefer not to. Al's out of town, it's just me and the streaming services, and I'd rather stay occupied."

"How about this, then: Can you incentivize LaBelle to come in for an interview?"

"Incentivize being . . ."

"A little more money, food, whatever works."

"Don't know, Loo, she's kind of squirrelly. Also, you may not want her indoors. There's a fragrance issue."

"Hmm," said Milo. "Okay, can you keep her occupied for another half hour so I can get there and talk to her myself?"

"Probably, I think she kind of likes me," said Alicia. "Said I reminded her of her daughter." Laughter. "Not sure that's a compliment."

"Take what you can get, kid. And God bless you."

"All this sacrament," said Alicia. "I could start to feel holy."

He took down directions to the Santa Monica

encampment and we walked back to the station. "Jean Harlow aka Jangles. It's a start."

I said, "The one Mel Gornick picked out as unusually restless."

"That mean something to you?"

"She might've been antsy because she was scoping out the studio. Maybe looking for a key."

He phoned Reed. "Where are you, Moses?"

"Where Alicia sent me to look for this Jangles. No sign of her but I just got confirmation from two other people. They don't know her real name but she definitely goes by Jangles. And guess what, she hasn't been seen since Klement's murder."

"They have anything interesting to say about her behavior?"

"All I got was a nervous type except when she drank and totally passed out."

"Her nerves cause problems?"

"Not that I heard, L.T., but it would take a lot down here to be considered abnormal."

"Good point, Moses. Anyone know about her posing for Klement?"

"Nope, she never told anyone," said Reed. "Didn't talk period, L.T. She's deaf and mute."

We'd gone inside for Milo to get his gun and his attaché case, were crossing to the staff parking lot when he said, "Deaf-mute but Little Ms. Mel didn't say anything."

I said, "Maybe she has no idea."

"How could she not, Alex?"

"Easily," I said. "Rigid thinking. She found Colin being a financial guy and Black dissonant. If she expected a homeless person to be intellectually dull, the lack of speech wouldn't have jumped out at her. Or, she's just not observant."

"Let's talk to her and see which."

He phoned as he cruised toward the parking lot gate. Mel Gornick's number rang four times before she said, "Yeah?"

"Milo Sturgis, got one more question for you: The woman in the white dress, did you notice anything unusual about her?"

"I already told you. She was like hyper."

"Did she ever say anything?"

"About what?"

"Did she talk, period?"

A beat.

"I'm not into being nosy."

"So, no."

"What's going on? Did **she** do it? Omigod!"

Milo said, "Nothing like that, Mel. We're just trying to locate the Wishers and we may have identified her. Apparently she calls herself Jangles."

"Okay."

"You never heard Donny call her that."

"Nope."

"She wears a lot of bracelets."

"That," said Mel Gornick, "I saw. Cheap shit, like from her wrist to her elbow."

Milo said, "We've also been told she's deaf and mute."

"So?" said Mel Gornick.

"You didn't notice any signs of that? Donny communicating to her in sign language or her reading lips?"

"No," she said. "He basically just . . . like he guided her. The way he did with all of them."

"He guided them physically?"

"No, no, not like creepy, no unwanted touching, never. He'd just like point to show her where to go and . . . maybe he'd have to touch her shoulder like to bring her there. **Guiding**. Like any photographer would do. It was that way with all of them. Not a lot of talking."

"Do you think the others were also mute?"

"Um . . . I don't think so, I think at least some of them said things but I couldn't tell you who . . . actually . . ." She trailed off.

"What, Mel?"

"Sometimes I wasn't there during the shoots." Making it sound like a confession. "Like when Donny would have me go get drinks and food. That happened a lot. I got them burgers and fries from McDonald's, they all wanted burgers and fries. She's really deaf, huh?"

"So we've been told."

"I guess I assumed she was like, you know."

"Know what?"

"Mentally challenged," she said. "We're not allowed to say retarded."

"Not allowed by who?"

"You know," she said. "People."

The gate opened, he turned right on Butler, then left onto Santa Monica.

I said, "Donny may have known her limitations, so he sent her on errands during the shoots. Or there were things he didn't want her to see."

"Like?"

"Additional payments. She knew about one hundred, he told Ali five hundred."

"Limitations," he said. "Wonder how she got the job in the first place."

"Probably Donny doing someone a favor."

"Why's that?"

"He sounds like that kind of guy."

He got caught at a red light, sighed and redialed. Mel Gornick said, "Now what?"

"Forgot to ask how you got the job with Donny."

"Why's that important?"

"It may not be but we need facts for the file. It's called doing background."

"Why?"

"To get justice for Donny."

"Fine. Whatever," said Mel Gornick. "I was

doing something for her, picking up P.R. stuff at a producer on Venice Boulevard—"

"Your mother."

"Ye-es. I stopped into a gelato place and he was waiting in line behind me and we started talking and then we sat down and he told me he was a photographer and was looking for an assistant. At first I was bummed but then I thought, great, I work for him, she can't send me on any of her bullshit errands."

"Bummed because—"

"A photographer? I thought he wanted to take my picture. But what the hey, a job was also okay. Now would you please stop calling me? I need to empty my head and enter a good space."

He muttered: "Shouldn't be that hard to empty."

"Huh?"

"You'll be fine, Mel. Bye."

He pulled out a panatela, jammed it between his lips but didn't light up. Afternoon was giving way to evening, the sky gray-blue streaked with copper, the setting sun fuzzy and lazy.

He reached into a jacket pocket and brought out a tiny tin of mentholated rub. He uses the stuff to coat his nasal passages when faced with serious decomp.

"Onward to fragrance, here, use it first," he said. "I know your personal habits, those guitarist hands are nice and clean."

20

Decades ago, Santa Monica decriminalized vagrancy and panhandling and began offering free food to the homeless. Combine that with balmy, ocean-cooled weather and it's no shock the beach town has become a magnet for people lacking a roof and four walls. Palisades Park, for ages an eyeful of beauty overlooking the Pacific, and newer Tongva Park, once lovely and a spot for children to play, have both become fetid homeless colonies. Smaller encampments sprout regularly throughout the city.

The official line is that a thousand or so of Santa Monica's ninety thousand residents are homeless. Speaking off the record, cops and social workers estimate it's nine times that amount.

The encampment we were looking for was on Pico a few blocks east of the beach but a world apart from glorious coastline. Tents and lean-tos dotted a half acre dimmed by the overhead 10 West freeway. The ground was a mixture of grit and mud, pocked by puddles of uncertain origin. Along with the improvised shelters, collections of worldly goods in shopping carts or piled in loose heaps marked territorial boundaries. Some people sat. Most were prone and appeared to be sleeping.

The smells reached us the moment we got out of the car, a combo of Sterno-seared food, unwashed clothing, stale piss and ripe shit, and wafts of vomit. Menthol did its best but fell short.

Alicia was waiting for us just outside the camp, gloved up and looking antsy. A woman stood next to her, rocking on her heels and waving at us with enthusiasm.

She was tall with body dimensions squared and obscured by a layered swaddle of gray-brown garments. Same for her hair, wrapped in a black bandanna printed with white dots but for a crackle of gray strands that had escaped. As we got close, the dots on the bandanna morphed into grinning skulls and I saw that her eyes were clear, bright blue, and active.

A high alertness could help you survive out here.

She stepped forward suddenly, surprising Alicia, who hurried to catch up. I'd braced myself for more stench but got a noseful of gardenia, sweet, cloying, unctuous. As if she'd bathed herself in perfume.

"Hello, Lieutenant Sturgis, LaBelle." Gleeful alto.

Milo squinted. "Do we know each other?"

"Nope, but we will, soon. Detective Bogomil told me your name and I filed it away." Tapping her forehead. "I use mnemonics to remember names because the short-term memory's gone. Know what mnemonics are?"

Machine-gun delivery.

Milo said, "Memory cues."

"A memory **technique**," said LaBelle. "You mentally tag what you want to remember with something mentally interesting. In your case, I thought, Sturgis? A **sturgeon.** If we meet again, I'll think of a big river fish and be able to greet you appropriately."

She put her palms together and made a wiggling, swimming motion. "Maybe I'll think of caviar. When you try to remember my name, picture a gala ball, as in LaBelle **of.**"

Milo grinned. "Great idea."

"I was taught mnemonics in school," said LaBelle. "Not Bryn Mawr, that place was all about being social. At the Agnes Irwin School in Philadelphia. Got a scholarship to study with the rich lassies. I was significantly smarter than them."

"Impressive."

"Not really. They shunned me anyway. Besides, it's what you do with your essence and your good luck and I screwed mine up with addiction and not treating my bipolar appropriately. Speaking of which, notice the pace of my speech?"

"A little fast," said Milo.

"A little?" she said. "Hahahaha. I call it my active period but the doctors call it manic. Euphemisms can be great comfort." LaBelle turned to me. "What's your name?"

"Alex Delaware."

"Easy-peasy. Your mnemonic is 'I'm in a state.'"

Everyone laughed, LaBelle the loudest. Her hands flexed nonstop. Her wide-open mouth revealed a few brown teeth but mostly empty space. The gardenia aroma seemed to intensify.

Alicia said, "LaBelle's been super helpful, and she was happy to talk to you, Lieutenant."

"Lieutenant," said LaBelle. "Rank has its privileges, huh?" She wrinkled her nose. "The privilege here is to **be** rank but I use White Shoulders. Not that my shoulders are white."

More laughter.

She said, "I will cooperate but you may not write anything down because tattling leads to battling and I don't want a paper trace coming back to indict me. Okay?"

"Sure."

"Okay-do**kay**, now that I've set the tone and the ground rules, I'll tell you what I know about Jangles. First off, she's not intelligent like me. Quite the opposite. Hard to say how much of that is her being deaf-mute, how much is lifestyle, how much is inborn brain weakness. But the end result is the same."

Another tap. "Not much going up here. That

said, if you're thinking she hurt someone you're mistaken. She's gentle, harmless, not a mean ossification in her corporeality that I ever saw."

I said, "When's the last time you saw her?"

"A month ago," said LaBelle. "Give or take, hard to say how much give, how much take, time takes on a different dimension here—be nice to have Albert Einstein spend some time with us and reformulate his theory. If you're asking if I've seen her recently, the answer is a resounding no. But I stand by my assessment, she's harmless. Also a bit bi-pole, in my assessment."

"Why's that?"

"Not in my league, of course, not even close, but when **she** got active she got fidgety, liked to pace. Skinny as a rail—which is a bird, did you know that? But never angry. That's my thing. Anger. I work on it constantly."

She glared exaggeratedly at all three of us in turn. Laughed, kept flexing. "Didn't scare you, huh? Back to Jangles. No anger issues. If anything, she was on the passive side. That's why she always had men around her."

Milo said, "Boyfriends?"

"She'd probably want to call them that if she was in a position to call anyone anything. I prefer hangers-on. Interested in one thing. Don't look so surprised, Detective Bogomil. We're a dissolute bunch but some of us are genitally functional. Not that **that** kind of function interests me." She winked, patted her pubis. "This vadjeela has long instituted a no-penis policy, Agnes Irwin and Bryn Mawr taught me more than reading and writing wink wink wink."

Her eyes bugged for an instant, then she turned serious. "In answer to your next question, absolutely not."

Milo said, "What was the question?"

"The one you were going to ask. Did I ever approach Jangles with **that** in mind and the answer is no, nein, non. I'm able to sense when my advances are welcome and when they're not. Which is something men seem incapable of grasping."

Milo said, "That wasn't going to be my next question."

"What was?"

"Who'd she hang with?"

"I don't believe you, you're a man and men are interested in one thing only," said LaBelle. "But I'll give you the doubt of the benefit and anyway if it wasn't the next it would have been your second or your third or whatever ordinal position in the series of questions. So let it be known: **Nothing** went on between Jangles and myself. Nor did I require a mnemonic to remember her name. She'd already arrived with a self-explanatory name."

I said, "The jewelry."

She rotated her own forearm. "You could hear her coming a mile away. Like a cowbell on a heifer."

I said, "Did her wearing jewelry pose a threat?"

"Did it attract thieves? All you had to do was to take a look and see that there was no point."

"Cheap junk."

"That, Mr. State, is redundant. But you are correct. She wore crap that couldn't be traded for drugs or alcohol and those are the currencies here and in places like here."

Milo said, "So who did she hang with—as in male friends?"

LaBelle shook her head. "When it comes to people like that, I don't waste my mental powers." She glanced back. "Like this bunch right here, transient, not worth relating to, I'll be moving on and don't ask to where because I don't know and even if I did I wouldn't tell you. That was Jangles, too, for that matter. She was here maybe two weeks and then she was gone and saying she was returning to a bigger place on Thirteenth Street. Not Santa Monica Thirteenth Street, downtown Los Angeles Thirteenth Street."

"Did she leave with anyone?"

"I thought you wanted to know about her boyfriends."

"Absolutely."

"A flock of penises."

Milo smiled. "Anonymous penises?"

"For the most part."

"Do you remember any names?"

"Are you going to write anything down?"

"You said no, so no."

"Then how're you going to remember?"

"Mnemonics."

She glared at him. Slapped her knee and burst into high-fidelity laughter, settled down gradually with a series of grunts that vibrated the swaddle.

Taking a few steps farther from the encampment, she looked back to study the residents, then back at us. "I remember two names. One called himself Sharky but he looked nothing like a shark. Quite the contrary, small and soft, more like an oyster out of its shell. After Jangles left, he stuck around and died a couple of weeks later and they took him away."

She half turned and motioned with her eyes. "His spot was where that blue tent is now. Someone found him in it, cold and stiff."

Milo said, "What'd he die of?"

"I'm not a doctor," she said. "Though I play one on TV." Giggling. "Natural causes, they said."

"They being . . ."

"The paramedics. Santa Monica EMTS, they came in their covered wagons. Someone called them, don't ask me who, they examined him and shook their heads and then a van came and they put him in a bag and hauled him away."

"Sharky," said Milo.

"R.I.P.," said LaBelle. "Oh, yeah, mea culpa, got it wrong. Not two, there were actually **three** of them she cozied up to. Before Sharky it was Milton, a man of color who played the harmonica. His son showed up one day and put him in a Mercedes. Said he'd been looking for his father for a long time."

She touched her left breast. "Touching scene. I can't see Milton being of interest to you. Old, feeble, tremors, two bottles of vodka a day, could barely walk. The third one? Now maybe you've got something there. Nasty piece of work and when Jangles left, it was with him. Called himself Butch. I mnemonocized him as one of my softball coaches at Bryn Mawr. We called **her** Butch."

Milo said, "Nasty piece of work, how?"

"Nasty piece of work," she repeated. "Mean. Mean eyes, mean mouth, mean head, mean scowl. Worst of all, he took himself seriously," said LaBelle. "You know the type, thinks he's better than everyone and wants you to know it."

I said, "Arrogant."

She looked at me as if I was the slow student. "Put it this way, State. If he took modesty lessons he might **achieve** arrogance. This was more like delusions of godliness." She walked her fingers horizontally. "He'd strut around, scowling, growling, trying to intimidate the rest of us. Pretending he didn't belong here."

I said, "A jerk."

"There you go."

"When did you last see Butch and Jangles here together?"

"She left with him about a month ago." She waved an arm. Layers of clothing beefed up the limb, like one of those pads used by attack-dog handlers. "Can't blame them, this place is on the way out, I'm already making plans to move on."

"Why's that?"

"Nature of the beast. Of us. The world goes blank and bland and blah. Unlike so-called normal, we survive because we're able to shift perspective, move on. We avoid psychological bedsores. We're superior to normals in that regard. Try asking some suburbanite to pick up and go just like that." Snapping her fingers. "Hah! Don't think so, there'd be major boo-hoo-hoos and plenty of shilly-shallying. We move. We **move.** And **don't** ask me where I'm heading. Even if I knew I wouldn't tell you because too many eyes on the back causes a crack."

Milo said, "Any idea where Jangles and Butch went?"

"Not at first, it's not like we threw them a bon voyage party," said LaBelle. "Sharky did tell me he'd met her before here, near MacArthur Park, there used to be a metropolis just south of the greenery. I myself resided in that metropolis eons ago. But that is irrelevant, someone heard Butch say Thirteenth Street downtown but don't ask who, don't know, they're gone, anyway. Know why? We **move.**"

She smiled. "I liked when Sharky told me MacArthur Park. It brought back nice memories. The water was nice, I liked the ducks, the trees . . . the entire setup wasn't bad if you avoided getting caught in gang crossfire and ignored the drug pushers. In the end, it got too quiet for me, which caused me problems regulating. When the outside's too quiet, the inside tries to compensate."

She pointed to the concrete mass of freeway overhead. "Here, I've got my own noise machine, the constancy helps achieve serenity, and once I get to my property—the yellow tent with the flowers— the drone lulls me into self-delusion."

Her eyes sparked. "Jangles has it easy. Closes her eyes and creates her own sounds."

Milo said, "She told you that?"

"She didn't have to, Lieutenant Caviar-donor. I'd see her sleeping and she looked like a happy baby."

Milo nodded. "With or without Butch."

"Butch never slept with her, he just **fucked** her and would go off by himself."

"Did he ever get aggressive with her?"

"Wish I could tell you yes but all I saw was the strutting and the look in his eyes. Sufficient to warn me, this one could be trouble."

"Jangles didn't mind any of that."

"Jangles doesn't **have** much of a mind," she said. "Once she drank, she was as pliable as pasta done way past al dente. Maybe it was one of those puzzle-piece things. Hooks and loops, dominant, submissive. It's all about fit, we operate the same here as in the so-called real world."

Tooth-deficient grin. "Only poorer, dirtier, and more addled."

Milo said, "What does Butch look like?"

"Mean. Tall, broad, mean eyes. When he first showed up he was doing the mountain-man thing: bushy beard, long hair. A couple of days later, all the hair's gone, face **and** head. Shape-shifting, made him look more demonic. Maybe that was the intention."

"When he had hair, what color was it?"

"Brown with plenty of gray. Unlike **this** endowment." Untying the bandanna, she shook loose a mass of wavy, platinum-blond hair.

Alicia said, "Nice." Meaning it.

"My original color restored," said LaBelle, swinging her tresses and giggling. "First time I got it done was at some government-funded thing in Palisades Park. Do-gooder beauty college students chirping away and feeling righteous. Got my nails done, too, one of those **get the homeless to develop self-esteem** deals. It didn't last long, those things never do, but when I saw how I turned out, I said, wow, you are gorgeous, girl. So I started to do it myself. Don't ask where I obtain my cosmetics."

She eyed Milo. "What do you think?"

"Excellent."

"Good for you, Beluga-Sevruga. Having taste."

He couldn't help laughing.

She said, "A man with a sense of humor. Women claim that's important. It is if there's also money and a functional penis. Enough money, eliminate the penis."

"Is there anything else you can tell us about Butch and Jangles?"

"Negative. Now how about you tell me about this photographic excursion."

Milo said, "I'll do better than that." Jogging to the car, he returned with his case and unsnapped it. Drawing out the side-by-side Wisher shots, he showed her Jangles before and after.

She stiffened, set her jaw. "**Fuck** her to hell."

"What's the matter?"

"She imitated me." Tugging at her hair. "Stupid fake-blond bitch."

New edge in her voice. She seemed to inflate and gain inches.

The same kind of changes Milo affects when he wants to intimidate; it's all about posture. He and Alicia shifted away from her, bodies tight.

She smiled. "Don't worry, I know how to focus my feelings, you're still okay in my book." She jabbed the photo with a filthy nail. "Look at that. Felonious."

Milo said, "They say imitation can be the highest form of flattery."

"**They**," said LaBelle, "are imbeciles. Imitation is nothing more than robbing the soul and I am not chuffed—that's a Britishism for being pleased. However, neither am I gutted—cast into despair. That would be turning the anger inward."

She took several breaths. Tucked her hair back in. Rocked on her feet. "The moment of ire has passed but I remain put off that she co-opted my tresses. Poorly. She looks like a failed trollop."

Milo put the shot on the bottom of the stack and showed her the other photos.

She shook her head. "Strangers in a strange land, don't know any of them. So what happened, this photographer got himself killed?"

"Yes, ma'am."

She beamed. "Ma'am. Haven't been called that in . . . probably never. And you were thinking Jangles had something to do with it?"

Milo said, "We're checking out everyone he photographed."

"Let me take another look . . . no, these others are utterly alien to me. How'd the now-dead-person find them?"

"Possibly through a capper."

"There was a health-care thing going on? The photographer had a crooked sideline?"

"Nothing like that," said Milo, "but it's possible someone who had capped for a health-care thing was involved."

Out of the case came Abel Rodriguez's mugshot.

Another head shake. "This one's got the look."

"What look is that?"

"Hunter-trapper. Like those coyotes who bring in the illegals and let them die in hot vans."

She stared at Rodriguez's image before pushing it away. "Been a long time since I was solicited for one of those. Something to do with endome-triosis, one of those paid research projects you see advertised on bus benches. The capper for that one looked like a college student. I'm sitting on the sand, enjoying the ocean, and she comes up to me all perky and telling me it's my lucky day. I told her my woman-parts were impeccable and untouchable. She said it didn't matter, I could be in a control group. I told her to control her skinny little ass out of my face."

Milo placed the photos in his case.

LaBelle remained in place, as if waiting to be served.

He said, "Is there anything else you want to tell us?"

"Negative."

"Okay, thanks."

"You're welcome." Turning her back on us, she began stomping back toward the yellow tent. A few steps in, she lost energy and ended up trudging awkwardly. Sliding into the tent with effort, she disappeared.

Alicia said, "Some temper, she didn't show me that side. Before I came across her, everyone I'd tried was drowsy and useless but she stood out because she was alert and friendly. Then she started talking and I'm thinking, whoa, this one's smart even if she is crazy. Then she tells me she knows Jangles and I'm thinking whoa, an actual lead. But now that I've heard her being really crazy, I'm wondering if any of it is true."

Milo said, "It's better than anything else we've

learned so I'm not gonna dismiss it out of hand. Let's see what we can learn about a homeless guy named Butch."

"A mean guy," she said, sounding doubtful.

I said, "A mean dominant guy would fit. Sending her in there to case the studio, waiting outside and quizzing her when she came out. If she told him Donny left big-time cash out in the open, that could've sealed the deal. At that point, he could've even sent her back in under some pretext—using the bathroom. Which is upstairs, in Donny's living quarters. Where she might've managed to lift a key."

"Robbery gone bad," said Alicia. Disappointed.

Milo said, "The classics endure for a reason."

I said, "What she said about Jangles also living in MacArthur Park was interesting. Not far from where Rodriguez lived and died."

He nodded. "You did good, Alicia."

"I hope so," she said. "This has been some experience, talking to so many of them. She also stood out because she could sound so intelligent. Or am I missing something?"

I said, "There's definitely education and smarts there."

"Then, what? Her brain blew up from within?"

I smiled. "Interesting way to put it."

"Can I ask you one more thing? The genius-insanity connection, is it real?"

I said, "There are brilliant psychotics and eccentrics but intelligence doesn't cause psychosis and, in fact, brighter people function better as a group."

"So without bipolar, someone like her would be even smarter?"

"She'd certainly have a better life."

"Got it," she said. "Okay, I'm off to downtown, Loo."

Milo said, "Can't convince you to take a breather?"

"I'll grab a bite and watch a short show on my phone while I eat, but no reason to idle," she said. "Devil's workshop and all that."

21

We walked Alicia to her unmarked Ford Fiesta, watched her drive away, looking grim.

I said, "Being with LaBelle ended up troubling her. Probably something personal."

Milo said, "Her mom was bipolar. She told me right at the beginning. When I encouraged her to apply to the department."

When we'd met Alicia, she'd been working private security at a dying hotel where a hundred-year-old woman got murdered. During the investigation, she told us she'd been a cop in New Mexico, had come to L.A. for a man, regretted it, and was thinking about returning to the real job. Milo, impressed by her acute eye and her work ethic, had helped fast-track her.

I said, "She told you out of some sort of due diligence?"

"It just kinda came up."

"Fifteen hour days and still going," I said. "Being high-energy means something different to her."

"Suppose so," he said, "but I've never seen anything but solid work out of her."

"Did her mother commit suicide?"

He stared at me. "How'd you guess?"

"Lucky grab," I said.

"Oh, sure."

Instead of returning to the station, he continued west and turned onto Ocean Front Boulevard, passing cafés and boutiques and luxury high-rises. He slowed down when he spotted a tall man pushing a shopping cart full of flotsam. Eyeing the guy then continuing until we were cruising east of the Palisades where he slowed to ten miles per and continued to look at people living tough.

I said, "Searching for Butch?"

"Total waste of time, but as long as we're here, why not."

I'd been searching also, on the lookout for large, hard-eyed men ranging from hirsute to skinhead. An arrogant strut would be another plus. The few males who fit the bill physically hunched and shuffled and emitted an air of defeat.

Assuming LaBelle had been accurate, I wondered if the man she called Butch had gone homeless recently. Or was he just another predator insinuating himself into a group of unfortunates, ready to squeeze what he could from the powerless.

Hooking up and dominating someone small, disabled, and impaired like Jangles fit that. Especially if he'd learned that she'd found sudden celebrity in a rich man's studio.

Milo said, "So much for that," drove to the end of the street, pulled a U-ey, and sped back to Santa Monica Boulevard.

We passed more stylish shopping and dining, along with scattered pockets of homelessness: mostly soloists choosing to live out their delusions without accompaniment.

Again, we searched. Again, we came up empty.

At Fourteenth Street, in front of a designer pizza joint, we passed a red-faced, obese man waving his fists and ranting at an elderly woman who sat motionless on a bus bench, hands in her lap, eyes frozen. Plenty of pedestrians around, but no one stopped to intervene, parting around the screamer and pretending to ignore the noise.

Milo pulled up, lowered the passenger window, and stared past me at the man, who went silent and glared back for a moment before hobbling off.

"You okay, ma'am?"

"Yes," she said, with strange resignation.

"You're sure."

"Yes. My son." She stood and went to follow the tormentor she'd birthed.

He'd turned a corner and slipped from view. Milo drove to the end of the block and watched as she tried to catch up to him without success.

Milo shook his head. "Only a matter of time." A block later: "Every year it gets worse. Any ideas?"

"Nothing I'd advertise," I said.

"Why?"

"Once things get political they turn toxic."

"Understood," he said. "Now tell your pal what the truth is."

"Don't claim to have the truth and at this point, there's no easy answer," I said. "In the seventies, some really horrible snake-pit mental hospitals were exposed. There were also good ones but crusaders decided every hospitalized psychotic was a political prisoner. The belief was that outpatient mental health centers would be a more humane approach, and tightwad politicians thought that was a great idea because it sounded cheaper. So down came the hospital walls. The problem was, mental illness is different from other diseases because sufferers don't think clearly, so it was naive to think patients would, or could, show up for outpatient treatment and forty, forty-five percent of discharged people ended up on the streets almost immediately. As time went on, that increased. Not all homeless people are actively psychotic but a significant minority is—maybe twenty-five, thirty percent—and there are other disorders and situations that make daily living a challenge. Severe alcoholism, addiction, abuse. Put it all together and you've got hordes of people banished to the streets."

"Baby–bathwater."

"The way it was done—wholesale, politicized, no serious planning—was baby plus draining a reservoir."

"And if you ran the world . . ."

"I would turn down the job."

"Seriously, Alex."

"If it was up to me, people unable to live independently would be cared for in small, humane hospitals subject to strong oversight and addicts would be offered clean beds, three squares, and serious detox, and if that didn't work, supervised dosage of drugs."

"What about folk who turned all that down?"

"There'll always be people who choose the streets and that's fine if they don't victimize others," I said. "But even impaired people can benefit from structure and when left alone, tend to create their own rules and regulations. What we just saw under the freeway: the staking out of territory, sad but not chaotic."

"Like with cons."

"These are people and they deserve care. There's no reason to sell anyone short and consign them to rotting on the streets. Years ago, a psychologist in South America was asked to run a failing mental hospital. We're talking utter bedlam. He asked his staff why meals weren't served on some sort of schedule. The answer was that psychotics were unable to deal with a schedule. He said, How do you know they're that psychotic? The answer: Because they can't deal with schedules. So he instituted schedules. A few patients didn't eat for a day or two but after that everyone got hungry and complied and meals were served on schedule. He followed that up with rules about grooming, making their beds, generally living a more organized life. It didn't cure them, far from it, but their quality of life improved. Everyone who's conscious deserves some level of expectation, not dismissal as a throwaway."

We drove in silence, were a block from the station before he said, "Yeah, you're right. Too much truth would get you in trouble."

When we reached the parking lot, he said, "Gonna be at the screen the rest of the day. After I talk to Folker again and see if she knows any Butches on her patch. If not, I'll ask her to check with her patrol guys and take a look at the moniker files. Though at his age, he's probably not a gangbanger or anything organized enough to get him into the moniker files. Any other suggestions?"

"Maybe go back to Culver City and if anyone matching Butch's description was seen hanging around nearby."

"Descriptions, plural. Hairy or hairless. If he's even real."

I said. "Need me for anything else?"

"Moral support." His card key activated the yard-arm. "Thanks for your time, Alex." He deepened his voice. "Should you think of anything else, sir, do not hesitate to make immediate contact."

I laughed. "Thinking of a transfer to Public Affairs?"

"Nah, it's just more diplomatic than telling you to go home and hang with your beauties and forget about my mess."

I got home thirty-five minutes later, still thinking about nothing but his mess. But when I unlocked my front door, I resolved to let it go.

Robin was in the living room, doing what she usually does when she's not working: sitting with Blanche curled next to her, reading, with music in the background. This afternoon's amusement was a Ruth Rendell novel and the Desert Rose Band. No obvious theme or link. Quality is quality.

I kissed the top of her head. She reached up and squeezed my hand and Blanche took the opportunity to plant her own slurpy smooch on my knuckles. I kneaded the folds of her neck. She purred like a cat.

Robin said, "Good move, girlfriend. Guys love that."

As I continued to my office, she said, "How'd your day go?"

I told her about the encampment, LaBelle, Jangles. The possibility of involvement by a hard-eyed man.

She said, "Hunter and prey. The poor guy opens his home and his heart and pays for it. Probably because he felt guilty."

"Why do you say that?"

"Some people seem to embrace guilt. I see it all the time with rock stars. They amass more money and stuff than they know what to do with but there's often a feeling they don't deserve it."

Her huge brown eyes fixed on mine. "Maybe that's not all bad, it helps some of them get it together morally—charity stuff."

I said, "The problem is people who should feel guilty never do."

She put down her book. "We're getting too weighty for day's end. Time to establish priorities: What're we doing for dinner?"

The following day was filled from nine to two with consults. Two child custodies, one traffic accident trauma / injury case involving an eight-year-old girl who'd endured seven facial surgeries.

At two fifteen, I sat down to chart and checked my phone. Lots of junk spewed by people wanting to sell me things or steal what I already had, plus a new referral from a judge and two "call-mes" from Milo. Fifty-three minutes ago and twenty minutes after that.

I punched the preset labeled **Big Guy.** He said, "Busy day?"

"Just got free."

"Feel like another drive to the beach?"

"Something new at Broad?"

"Closer in, up Rambla Pacifico."

"What's there?"

He told me.

I said, "Leaving right now."

I drove down the Glen to Sunset, took the boulevard through Brentwood and Palisades to its western terminus at PCH, swooped onto the highway, northbound.

Rambla Pacifica was seven and a half miles farther, an eastbound exit that roller-coastered just past Las Flores Beach. Back in my student days, I'd hiked there, enjoying the solitude of the road as it snaked through gorgeous, unoccupied hillside. Since then, houses had gone up, mostly flat-faced dream palaces perched on bluffs and graced with lusty eyefuls of emerald green relenting to sapphire blue.

But plenty of open land remains and it was on one of those patches, less than a mile from the highway and fronted by a growth of mature trees, where I spotted the yellow tape and the hubbub of crime scene investigation.

Stubbly earth rose steeply for a while before dropping down to a bowl-like depression in the dirt. Behind the pit stood more trees, then another rise-and-descend and another tree-barrier. Native sycamores and silver-dollar eucalyptus—visitors from Australia who'd renewed their visas for a century.

The growth created a natural blind, blocking the view of anyone driving past. As I got closer, I made out human movement through the branches.

Continued downward and spotted Milo standing just off center in another crater-like clearing. Next to him was a man, taller and wider than him, wearing a corduroy sport coat the color of single malt.

Malibu is County Sheriff territory and tan uniforms abounded, along with Sheriff's cruisers, vans from the crypt and the lab, and a wine-colored Chevy Volt that was today's drive for the coroner's investigator.

The deputies stood around looking bored, none of them bothering to guard the tape. I supposed it could get like that when you mostly worked open spaces with scant human intrusion. Or maybe they'd been given my description.

I slipped under the tape and met Milo's nod with one of my own. Corduroy joined in, bobbing his head twice and revealing a bald spot on the crown of a gray crew cut. He was fiftyish, wore black-framed specs and a perfect tan. When I got there, he shot out his hand. "Doctor, Ed Brophy, Malibu Sheriff's, but I'm a temp, eventually this will go downtown." Sounding pleased.

Milo said, "And from there it'll end up with me."

Brophy shot him a compassionate look. He had light-brown eyes that floated like bubbles in a carpenter's level. "Only psychologists we've got are the ones who screen deputies to determine who gets disability."

I said, "Popular folk."

"You don't want to know, Doctor." Brophy's

grin seamed his bronze face like leather upholstery overexposed to sunlight. "I was just telling Milo I was jealous, his having you. You ever have an itch to breathe some salt air? Maybe get curious and want to help out on one of our nasties?"

I smiled. "For me the beach is recreation."

He laughed. "Figured you might see it that way. And mostly it is pretty mellow out here in Mabiloo. Then you get stuff like this." He clicked his tongue. Laughed again.

Milo remained unamused. His pale, pitted face made more so by proximity to Brophy. His expression said life had just gotten way more complicated.

I said, "Can I take a look?"

He said, "Let's go."

Ed Brophy said, "Been there, done that," and remained in place. We'd taken three steps toward the eastern tree-blockade when he began leaving the scene.

The C.I., a woman in her thirties named Barnes, was busy on her cell, talking details with a pathologist at the crypt. Four techs sampled and scraped, their work zone the smaller, sunken area. Like a pup of the flat space on the other side of the trees.

The soil here was patched with clumps of viciously thorny, red-flowered creeping bougainvillea. The plant, bred to sprawl or to climb walls, has a high oil content that turns it easily to kindling, and despite its beauty and hardiness, decades of

Malibu fires have led smart homeowners to clear it. But this was county land with no one to oversee other than workers who commuted and the vines had been allowed to thrive. Same for the venerable eucalyptus, another potential tinder keg.

The secondary depression ended at a six-foot circular maw set below a low outcropping. Concrete culvert built decades ago to shunt rainwater from the heights. Despite years of drought, no attempt had been made to conserve the runoff, rendering the culvert a supersized drain expelling wasted water.

The effluence took with it dead vegetation, rocks, grit, and evidence of human transgression in the forms of bottles, cans, plastic sheeting, and Styrofoam take-out boxes. Detritus that hadn't found its way out remained dammed up on the floor of the culvert, a perpetual crust.

A foot or so in, human feet clad in sneakers were visible. Filthy rubber soles worn flat. Then, legs encased in filthy gray sweats climbing to the bottom hem of a torso wrapped in additional layers of clothing, and two mottled hands, the arms pressed parallel to the pants. The size of the sneakers suggested short stature.

Someone small, lying faceup.

The techs had worked the body and moved on. Milo hunched to clear the six-foot aperture and pigeon-walked into the culvert, continued until he was close enough to touch the body and, stooping slightly, pulled out his flashlight.

He aimed into the concrete tube, said, "Here you go."

I stepped in. The drain tube was surprisingly cool and dry.

The beam had landed on a face, turning it icy-white.

A woman, eyes shut, wearing the gray mask of death. A section of cord, white where it wasn't flecked with red—what looked to be a section of curtain pull—was knotted tightly around her neck.

Strangulation often leaves a victim bug-eyed and gaping. Someone had taken the time to close these lips and lower these lids.

Not wanting to see her stare back accusingly? Detectives usually assume that means a killer familiar with the victim. But human behavior's the greatest puzzle of all and sometimes even stranger-killers get curiously squeamish.

I examined the body. No sign of stiffness; rigor had likely come and gone. The timing of rigor is dependent on all sorts of variables so that didn't tell me much, but decomposition might.

I took the flashlight, kneeled, and had a closer look. No flies or maggots I could see; no cellular breakdown of any kind. That suggested a recent death but, again, it depends. The mild, dry air within the culvert combined with lovingly temperate Malibu ambience could've slowed the process of flesh surrendering to the earth.

The lack of damage made recognition easy.

The "before" image of the woman who called herself Jangles.

We retreated from the death hole. I asked Milo what he thought about the mouth and the eyes.

He said, "Who the hell knows, other than she's been staged. Sometimes gravity takes over with the lids but never seen it with the mouth and the way her arms are positioned has gotta be a pose. So maybe someone she had a relationship with or just an asshole who likes to choreograph."

"Didn't see signs of sexual assault."

"So far, no one has, but maybe we'll be surprised once the pathologists get to her."

"Anything under her nails?"

"Techs said just dirt."

"Any fecal discharge from the strangulation?"

"There are some stains on the back of her sweats but not as much as what you'd get if she lost control here. At this point, it's hard to be sure of anything because her clothes are filthy and all those layers could be hiding something. The only obvious blood is the small amount on the cord. I'm leaning toward it happening elsewhere, then she was taken here and dumped."

"Who found her?"

"County work crew stopping by to check the drainage at ten a.m."

I said, "Doesn't look as if they ever service the drainage."

He laughed. "I said check, not actually do anything—okay, let's be nice and say if they hadn't found her they would've cleaned up. Maybe. In any event, they're the ones who 911'd. Brophy drove over and took their statements, which didn't amount to anything. I found out because I always check the dailies and the death of a middle-aged white homeless female caught my attention. Not that far from where we talked to LaBelle, maybe someone found out she talked to the cops. I called Brophy, he emailed me a screenshot of the face, and I got a big surprise. I was here by one thirty."

"Brophy give you a hero's welcome?"

"Why?"

"You'll be doing the work instead of him."

"Can't blame him, he's retiring in three months, already bought his place in Idaho. The downtown tans could decide to hold on to it but probably not, they've got their hands full with a whole bunch of shootings in Westmont."

I said, "Any estimate how long she's been here?"

"C.I. peeked down the back of her blouse—blouses—and saw some moderate lividity. But so far, no body rot, so a fairly recent dump. I can't see someone risking it in broad daylight, so I'd guess before sunrise. C.I. has no problem with that, says humidity's been down in the thirties, that could've slowed down the germs. So would transporting her if a closed vehicle was used."

"Bad guy with a car."

"Yeah, I know, doesn't fit a homeless psychotic like the alleged Mr. Butch. Neither does how clean the scene is. Not a single fingerprint."

"Any footprints?"

"Nope, all the leaves and crap on the ground prevented that. Picking up casings fits a precision deal. So maybe the homeless thing won't pan out and we're dealing with a villain with an abode and wheels who wanted to wreak havoc on Donny and everyone associated with him."

I said, "A stolen car could've been used to bring her here."

"Sure, but how the hell do I find out which stolen car? A few days ago I got the GTA stats for last year in a general report. Thirty thousand plus change, and that's only L.A. city. Toss in the county and it's probably three times that amount."

"You could focus on Rampart Division stolens? Rodriguez was killed there and Jangles spent some time near the park."

He fished out his phone, logged onto a site, scrolled and studied. "Rampart, alone, had eleven hundred stolens. For argument's sake, let's narrow it to two, three weeks' worth. That comes to . . . sixty, seventy. Guess that's workable, okay, I'll text Alicia and have her check with the Rampart wheels squad."

When he finished typing, he looked at me and

churned air with one hand. "Keep going with the ideas."

I'd wondered early on about tunnel-visioning to a homeless suspect but he'd already raised that so I shook my head.

He said, "In that case, let's get away from here."

23

We reversed the up and down, getting past the westernmost tree-barrier and pausing as Milo checked for messages. None.

All but two of the deputies had left. The remaining duo sat in separate cruisers, engrossed with their phones.

I said, "Laid-back atmosphere."

"Guess sun and surf can do that to you," he said. "Speaking of which, when I got here I thought about Donny's house in Broad Beach. Not a hop-skip, but no huge trek, either. I mapped it. Fifteen-minute drive."

"A Malibu connection."

"Could be, if Adonis's naivete led him to hang with the local homeless. Or some evil Pacific Coast Mr. X."

"Any encampments nearby?"

"Brophy says from time to time you get squatters

in the hills, a year back they cleared away a bunch of tents up above Carbon using fire risk as the excuse. But nothing large-scale since then that he's aware of. Mostly they get what I saw coming over: loners trudging up and down the highway. A few were even hitchhiking. What if Donny picked someone up, maybe even figured he had himself a Wisher, and the guy ended up ripping him off."

I said, "How would that link to Jangles?"

"She and PCH Guy met at Donny's studio. Could've even showed up together. The guy killed her because of what you thought—she knew too much. Why here? He likes the salt air."

"Mel Gornick said the Wishers showed up one at a time."

"There could be plenty Mel Gornick doesn't know about, she herself told us she wasn't even there for some of the sessions," he said. "What if Donny held nighttime auditions using people Rodriguez snagged for him? What happens with auditions, Alex? Rejection. Someone takes great umbrage at being turned down, comes back for compensation. Why did he take care of Rodriguez before her? Maybe it took a while to find her."

"He posed her because he knew her."

"Or he just didn't want to feel like the goddamn barbarian he is."

I said, "Blunt force for Rodriguez, gunshots for Donny, strangulation for her."

"What are you saying? Multiple bad guys?"

"I was actually wondering about one bad guy able to adapt to circumstances. Let's go with the assumption that Rodriguez was lured behind a building to shut him up before the break-in at Donny's. The offender might've brought a gun but preferred to brain Rodriguez because it was quieter and ideal for a surprise blitz attack."

He nodded. "Also, he pulls out firepower, Rodriguez might make a run for it."

"Or produce his own weapon," I said. "Instead he cold-cocks Rodriguez without warning then stomps him once he's down."

"Why not do the same for Donny?"

"Donny asleep made a gun practical. Quick, clean, less chance of big-time blood. A few days later, it's time to clean the slate by taking care of Jangles."

"Because she couldn't be trusted to—" He shook his head. "I was gonna say keep her mouth shut. Poor thing. Talk about vulnerability."

I said, "Her size and disability made her pathetically easy to overpower and strangle so why risk the blood and mess of a bludgeoning or the noise of a gunshot? He stored the body then somehow got her here. Took her to a pretty obscure place, so you're right, there likely is some sort of Malibu link."

"Adapting to circumstances," he said. "Sounds like someone not very crazy. Should I put the homeless aside?"

"Nope. An untreated schizophrenic couldn't pull

it off but like I said, most homeless aren't actively psychotic."

"Joe Normal slumming?" he said.

"Or a psychopath embedded with the homeless. A relatively helpless population would be attractive to a certain type of predator."

"What type?"

"Someone willing to look the part."

He thought about that. Said, "What'd he figure, she'd rat on him using sign language? Poor thing—okay, let's go back and check with the science kids and see if anything's turned up in the last few minutes."

Neither the techs nor E. Barnes, the C.I., had anything to offer. At the request of the pathologist on North Mission Road, Barnes had just given the body a second frisk, probing layers of clothing but coming up with no identification papers.

"Sorry," she told Milo. "We'll get her printed. Okay to transport?"

"Go for it, Erin."

Erin Barnes got on her phone, eyes directed at the legs extending to the edge of the drain tunnel.

As Milo and I left the scene, I heard her sigh.

Getting back to the Seville meant a downward walk that amplified the ocean as it dipped, hurling a whole bunch of blue in our faces.

Milo didn't react to it. I fought back a stab of vertigo.

The ocean sometimes does that to me. Any vast manifestation of nature has the potential to do that to me.

Years back, while our house was being built, Robin and I rented a small place in western Malibu. I'd stand on the sand, watching as unmeasurable masses of roaring water spiked, curled, and spit spray.

Knowing that I was perched on the rim of a continent and feeling utterly insignificant.

Not always an unpleasant emotion.

When we reached the car, I said, "The bad guy could've been rejected for the project. On the other hand, he might've been one of the chosen few. Assuming a male, that winnows it down to four."

Milo loped ahead of me to his unmarked, returned with his case, and produced the Wisher photos.

We studied the men.

Closer examination revealed frail, narrow-shouldered Jack the Top Gun ace, coming across a bit cross-eyed and somewhat goofy. That assessment covered his snaggle-toothed grin, enhanced by the dental device Donny Klement had provided.

What led me away from him were his eyes—the soft, resigned orbs of a neutered ram put out to pasture.

I told all that to Milo.

He nodded. "Could be."

Next came Solomon the surgeon, wearing scholarly eyeglasses while pretending. His eyes were nearly obscured by drooping lids that fought gravity, the bits of sclera and iris visible, blank and dull in both photos

Milo flipped to the next shot.

Louis, before dress-up, was a bland-looking man, hard to characterize. His "after" had him sitting stiff and proper in an explorer uniform straight out of a thirties safari movie. That brought to mind one of the pompous foils the Marx Brothers had used to such good effect.

Louis had entered the shoot wearing a week's worth of patchy white stubble that coated his face like a rash, ended up shaven and graced with a glued-on handlebar mustache for his emergence as Dr. Livingston.

Toss in a monocle, safari shirt with epaulets, and pith helmet and the end result was comedic.

I wondered if Donny had sensed that. Or even intended it. Had the billionaire's son, for all his reputation for sensitivity, tried to create a bit of absurd theater at the expense of his subjects?

More important, had Louis—or Solomon or Jack—decided they'd been manipulated and ended up as punch lines?

More than enough to make a man resentful. To return for some spare cash and bloody revenge.

I studied Louis some more. Not a trace of menace

in surprisingly bright, dark eyes. Just the opposite. Enjoying himself, I had to admit.

In contrast, the pale-blues of Eugene, the aspiring corporate CEO, did betray a certain wariness.

Managing to scowl and smile conspiratorially at the same time.

I've got a secret and you'll never figure it out.

The breadth of these shoulders suggested bulk.

My finger poked the image at the same time Milo's sausage digit hit the paper.

He said, "Not gonna eliminate the others but I'll pay special attention to him, see if someone in Rampart—or anywhere else—knows him."

I said, "The CEO choice could be interesting, given who Donny's father is."

"How would this guy know about that?"

"Maybe Donny told him."

"Chitchatting like they're buddies," he said. "Donny would be dumb enough to let on that Pops had mega-dough?"

"Naive and guilty?" I said.

"True, bad combination. So he and Eugene, here"—poking hard—"developed something that went beyond the shoot? Donny's thinking he's made a friend, Eugene or whatever his real name knows he's snagged a pigeon."

He walked away, paced, returned, circled some more, came back.

"It's theoretical but a start. And who knows? On

the slim chance I haven't pissed Santa off too badly this year, I might get toys under the tree instead of coal."

"Coal being . . ."

"My evildoer's none of these individuals, just some random scary wanderer who could be any-where by now."

I said, "If he's a Malibu wanderer, maybe Ali Dana saw him with Donny."

"She didn't mention anything like that but I'll ask. She actually phoned right before I got here. Wanting to know how the investigation was going, sounding like she'd been crying nonstop."

He tried the number. It rang ten times before cutting off, so he sent a text. "She also wanted me to know she's going back to Montana in a few days, could I please keep in touch. She was the second interested party of the morning. At nine, brother Colin called, same deal, checking progress. When I told him there wasn't much, he seemed peeved, like I'd failed to meet his expectations. I asked if he'd connected with his father yet and that knocked him down a notch. Embarrassed to admit he hadn't. He did say he'd contacted his brother and sister and of course, they were shocked. But so far, not shocked enough to call me."

I said, "Interesting family."

He said, "More like an unreasonable facsimile of family. Thinking about **that** led me back to the French guy, Friederich, who I was schmoozing with just before you got here. Brophy listened in, thought it was hilarious. Nighttime in Paree, clinking glasses in the background, I'm picturing one of those sidewalk brasseries. Maybe accordion music and a mime risking a punch in the nose."

I laughed. "Friederich have anything to offer?"

He gave a thumbs-down. "**Rien.**"

"French is your new thing?"

"My line of work, it pays to know 'zilch' in multiple lingos. Like Swahili. They say **hakuna.**"

"You've been doing depth research."

"Nah, just got bored one night working a case that was logjammed. I'm at the home computer, immersed in self-pity and beer, figured why not go online and feel even worse? By the way, in Swedish, it's **ingenting.**"

"Did that case eventually work out?"

"Hell, yeah," he said, slapping my back. "Dorothy Swoboda, dead for thirty-six years, no apparent way to close it. I got you involved, the heavens parted, and hark, the angels sang."

"You're too kind."

"Not really. I'm telling you because I expect more of the same."

Just as I was about to leave, Ali Dana called him back. No, she'd never seen Donny with anyone homeless or otherwise sketchy.

I left Milo there and drove back home, paying more attention than usual to the nomads hauling their life's possessions up and down PCH. By the time I reached Sunset, I'd spotted five people trudging solo.

Four men, one woman, all young but aging fast. One emaciated guy hunched on a curb just north of the Sunset turnoff, holding a cardboard sign that said **Going to Salinas. Will share driving.**

Cars sped by. His mouth worked and his hands shook, wild eyes the only bright spots in skin darkened by grime and time.

Hard to imagine anyone taking him up on the offer. Had Donny Klement been the exception?

Had he paid for a trusting nature in the worst way possible?

Or, as I kept finding myself wondering, would the homeless angle turn out to be a distraction, the real motive based on getting a larger slice of the pie Victor Klement had baked?

One less heir left three living half sibs and an unborn child with a whole lot more money. And one of them had recently initiated contact with Donny.

Colin Klement had been to Donny's studio several times since meeting his half brother, giving him plenty of opportunity to scope the layout, get to know Donny's habits, even lift a key.

A solid alibi put him in Tahoe, but as Milo had mentioned early on, a man of Colin's resources could have easily hired someone. Had his call this morning been brotherly concern or trying to ferret details of the investigation?

On the other hand, there was mean-eyed "Butch." A real person? Or a fiction created by a self-admitted psychotic?

My head began to hurt so I switched the car radio to my KJazz preset. Miles Davis and John Coltrane doing **Kind of Blue.** That and the music that followed loosened my scalp muscles and sustained me all the way home. But by the time I was in my office, restlessness had taken over again.

◆

Coffee in hand, I took another look at the Wisher photos. Leaving the women in the mix this time, because why assume?

Trying to interpret the facial expressions of strangers ended up feeling as useful as reading tea leaves. That included the reexamination of Eugene the would-be executive, who I had to admit now showed no serious signs of hostility, just a curiously expressionless mien.

Mental illness? Boredom? Or retreating from the tension of trying to play a role convincingly?

How had he felt—how had any of them felt—when the play-acting in Donny Klement's studio was over and he was back on the street?

Wishing doing anything **but** making it so.

I had another go-round, gained nothing from staring at eight victims of unlucky biology, bad decisions, or some combination.

These were the people we pass by habitually, maybe tut-tutting, maybe feeling momentary pangs of compassion. Perhaps we give them change and feel virtuous. But for the most part, we take a wide berth, like the pedestrians I'd seen in Santa Monica, pretending a deranged man wasn't haranguing his mother.

The Invisibles.

Easy pickings for Abel Rodriguez's promise of a paid adventure.

But also for Donny Klement's altruism, egotism, or some strange combination seasoned by guilt.

The more I thought about it, the more convinced I became that three deaths tied to the photo shoots couldn't be ignored as a pattern. And that slingshotted me straight back to the Wishers.

Was one of them different from the others? Not a victim, not mad or merely manic. A psychopath, sane and amorally cold, who'd schemed to exploit Donny Klement's trusting heart by burglarizing the studio.

Then, money in pocket, what better place for a canny hustler to hide than in the pop-up shanties of the ill and helpless?

And a seasoned hustler would be sure to pick up the same qualities in Abel Rodriguez. To know Rodriguez would be a problem once news of the break-in surfaced.

So take care of him **before** the break-in.

I shuffled through the photos a third time, searching for any hint of cold, cruel clarity.

If psychological wisdom was there, I was missing it.

I sat back, closed my eyes. Kept coming back to the daily existence of the Wishers and people like them. Years ago, I'd come to California, penniless, not knowing where my escape would land me. But I'd had resources—intellectual, social, and most important, a clear sense that I was worthy of better.

If you lacked all that, what hope was there?

"Living off the grid" has taken on an air of glamour, presented by the media as the world of lean, clean-jawed, adventurous sorts opting to drop out and establish sustainable mini-worlds. But most people who lack an address, a paper trail, any documentation of their existence, don't choose to live that way, and searching for them was a detective's nightmare.

I imagined Milo's grunts, scowls, muttered curses. Heard his voice in my head.

"The one going really nuts is me."

It can be like that with long-term friends. You sense them even when they're not around.

He called the following afternoon and I prepared myself for a tale of woe.

But his voice was light when he said, "Finally heard from Donny's financial person in New York. Actually, Daddy's person, everything's in trust and guess who controls it? She wouldn't give me details of the grand total but she did say U.S. Surety pays all of Donny's bills. It threw her off that I knew about the white card and when I pushed her on it, she finally admitted he could use it to get cash on demand. The ultimate privilege, she called it, and she sounded kinda jealous."

I said, "Working for the rich doesn't make you rich. More like a modern-day palace servant."

"I asked how much cash Donny took out and she said she'd have to check with the L.A. branch. I told her I had plenty of time, she clicked off and came back a minute later. Meaning she had the numbers right there all along, was bullshitting, then decided why hassle. Over the past year, Donny took out fourteen monthly withdrawals, mostly two, three thou at a time, all cash. The grand total was just shy of thirty-seven K."

"Not much of a high-living playboy."

"No need to be, Alex, with Daddy paying for everything."

"Still," I said, "a lot of people in his position would exploit that level of freedom. Any idea what he used the thirty-seven for?"

"Seeing as it was cash, no way to know," he said. "But I'm figuring day-to-day stuff—Mel's salary, food for Mel to fetch, maybe taking in a movie. Or taking Ali out."

"Plus paying the Wishers five hundred bucks for sitting. To them a fortune. He probably had no perspective."

"Easy access to money plus a soft heart? I can see it. Either way, thirty-seven grand seems more than enough for occasional expenses so there could've been plenty stashed in the studio."

I said, "He let the wrong person see it. Wouldn't have to be thousands, motive-wise. Hundreds would do the trick. Maybe Abel Rodriguez spotted a cash wad and put together a burglary, partnering with someone. It backfired when the partner decided why split the proceeds."

"The partner being a street person. Like Eugene the CEO."

"Actually, I was thinking it could be any of them." I described my reassessment of the faux executive.

Milo said, "Funny you should say that. I also reexamined and decided I'd gotten carried away but figured maybe you'd spotted something I didn't. Okay, we'll keep looking for all of them and try to find who Rodriguez hung with. Now I've got a bunch of other info for you. First off, Jangles's real name is Corrine Mae Ballinger. Want to guess her age?"

"Fifty-five?"

"Forty-two. Her prints were on file but her arrest record isn't impressive—all misdemeanors, she didn't even make it to NCIC. Her last arrest was twelve years ago and even back then she had no address so I'm thinking long-term mental disability."

"What was the most recent charge?"

"Public drunkenness, she got a citation, never paid it," he said. "There was probably some sort of warrant out on her but paper gets lost."

I said, "No arrests since then is probably due to no more enforcement of the drunk laws. Where was she arrested?"

"Near Skid Row. I found a Social Security number on her but no evidence she's ever collected benefits. If anything's a sign of mental illness, that's it. Who doesn't put in claims for free dough?"

"It also suggests she had no steady companion getting her to claim."

"Mr. Butch as a boyfriend is a bust? Maybe a figment of LaBelle's fertile mind."

"Could be."

"This case is like running through a house of mirrors . . . back to Jangles. Can't find any family. Her birth certificate says she was born in Memphis but the woman listed as her mother is deceased and there's no father of record."

Nowhere Woman.

I said, "Anything new on cause of death?"

"Nope, the obvious, strangulation. Plus no evidence of recent sexual activity nor does it look as if she ever had a baby. What the X-ray showed was a hugely enlarged liver and a nasty-looking pancreas. The pathologist I spoke to said her body was ravaged by malnutrition, she weighed in at eighty-nine pounds. He's guessing booze for her drug of choice because several layers of her clothes reeked of it and she had no tracks or puncture marks or erosion of her nasal passages. Theoretically, he said, she could've also been a pill-dropper but between COD being obvious and their short-staffing, he didn't see any reason to go further. So no internal scheduled. In terms of TOD, best guess was what we figured yesterday: eight to twelve hours."

"Corrine, not Beverly," I said. "So either she chose a play-name or Donny dubbed her."

"Yeah, I thought about that, could make looking for the others using names a waste of time.

Onward to my privileged victim. He got an autopsy and they pulled out three highly deformed slugs. Other than that, Donny was a healthy young guy. His bloods showed plenty of cannabis and a whole lot of Lunesta. That pathologist said everyone reacts differently to sleep meds so he coulda been anything from slightly drowsy to out cold. When I told her he was found sitting up, she said, sounds like he mighta woken to the sound of an intruder but his reactions coulda been slowed, explaining no sign of a struggle."

"Trapped," I said, imagining seconds of horror before darkness returned forever.

"Maybe he was lucky not to know what hit him. That's all of it, so bottom line: **nič**. That's Slovak."

25

For the next two days, I kept busy with consults and report-writing. On the third day, shortly after I'd said goodbye to a five-year-old severely bitten by a neighbor's cat, Milo knocked on my door.

"Saw a mom and a tyke drive away, figured it might be a good time to intrude. But if you've got more tykes scheduled, no prob."

"I'm free. C'mon in."

"Actually, I'm wondering if you can come out."

"For?"

"Day in the park. We found Eugene."

The man Donny Klement had clad in pinstripes had been spotted by a pair of alert West L.A. patrol officers. With an oversized backpack weighing him down, he'd been conspicuous as he exited the massive building on Pico where the Department of Social Services, West L.A. branch, doles out money.

When the uniforms offered him coffee and donuts from a box they had in their cruiser and assured him he wasn't under arrest, he agreed to accompany them.

Cheviot Park, more commonly known as Rancho Park, consists of two hundred pretty acres in the midst of an upscale neighborhood. A few years back, Milo had called me in on a homicide—a young woman found on the park's southern edge. But that was the exception, likely forgotten by everyone but the victim's family. Overall, it's a pretty, pleasant place.

The sharp-eyed cops were waiting with their charge just inside the parking lot bordering Motor Avenue. The sound of tennis balls clopping on nearby courts evoked distant horses.

The man tagged Eugene wore a red Esprit sweatshirt, baggy jeans, and white sneakers turned to gray. His pack was olive drab and patched in several places.

Large man, broad-shouldered, long-limbed, barrel-chested.

The officers stood flanking him as he sat on a park bench, drinking from a cardboard cup and nibbling with surprising daintiness at a pink-glazed confection.

One of the officers came forward.

D. J. Munro, straw-colored hair ponytailed, firm jaw, appraising green eyes.

She took a quick look back, pivoted, and spoke softly. "He dumped five packets of sugar in the coffee and this is his third donut."

Milo said, "Junkie sweet tooth?"

"That would be my bet. There's plenty of heroin in his sheet but also meth. He started out a little fuzzy around the edges but then he started talking pretty fast, so who knows what he's running on? We figured you didn't want us to roll up his sleeves."

"You figured right. What else is on the sheet?"

"It's a long one," said Munro. "But nothing violent if that's what you're after. The usual addict stuff—shoplifting, petty larceny, skipping out on restaurant bills, a few forgeries. Also public intoxication back when that was considered a problem."

"Okay. Thanks for spotting him."

"I was driving, my partner's the one who saw him."

"What name did he give you?"

"The one on his Cal I.D.," said Munro. "Eugene Maxwell Cudahy. He says call him Gene."

"That's his real name?"

D. J. Munro was surprised by the question. "I.D. looks bona fide to me, Loo. DSS liked it, as well. They gave him a groceries voucher." She smiled. "Theoretically."

Milo said, "Forget the cereal and milk and trade it at one-quarter value for dope."

She shrugged. "Dope's a tough thing to beat."

Throughout the conversation, Gene Cudahy had remained fixed on the few inches of universe directly in front of him. That lasted until we were a few feet away, when he looked up and stared at us blankly.

Since his would-be CEO pose, he'd grown out his hair to a patchy, wild thatch, his beard to grizzle the color of iron filings. The face in between was square and sunburned with strong cheekbones and the suggestion of robust substructure. But the initial impression of well built ebbed upon close-up: Saffron-yellow eyes shouted jaundice; blackheads, scabs, and dark blotches were scattered over cheeks, forehead, and chin; and a once firm jawline bottomed in a dewlap of loose skin. The tops of his hands were splotched with larger, coal-black patches. The pinkie of his left hand was a stub.

As we got within a foot, his eyes fluttered and his lips began to quiver.

Milo said, "Mr. Cudahy? Milo Sturgis. Appreciate your talking to us."

"I guess." Gravel voice. "They wouldn't tell me what it was about."

The other cop, **A. Lomitas,** said, "We did tell you you're not in trouble, Gene."

"So you say. But he looks like a felony detective." A glance at me.

Milo said, "This is Alex. Good call, Gene, I am a detective. Okay if I sit down?"

"Do I have a choice?"

"Absolutely."

Cudahy peered up at Milo's bulk. "Yeah, sure." He slid to the right and Milo settled at the other end.

"Feel free to keep eating, Gene."

Cudahy looked at the donut as if it had turned rancid. "Maybe later."

A. Lomitas's radio squawked. Injury traffic accident on Overland and National, ambulances on the scene, backup requested.

Munro said, "We should take this, Loo."

"Go for it. We'll give Mr. Cudahy a ride to wherever he wants to go. Again, thanks."

"Pleasure," said Munro.

The two of them headed for their cruiser.

Milo said, "Any idea why we're here, Gene?"

"Nope."

"It's about Donny Klement."

I'd expected some hedging. Maybe a claim from Cudahy that he had no idea who that was. He rubbed the crook of his left arm and said, "The photographer. What's up with him?"

"Someone killed him, Gene."

Cudahy's mouth dropped open, showcasing pallid gums and blackened teeth. When he spoke next, his voice had weakened. Gravel turned to silt. "No effin' way."

"I'm afraid so."

"Oh man." Gene Cudahy's chin bobbed up and

down, bristling beard hairs. His back curved and his eyes filled. He wiped away tears. "That's wrong, man. That is so effin' wrong."

"Yes, it was, Gene."

"He was a great guy. Great, cool, great."

"You liked him," said Milo.

Cudahy held out a hand, palm up. Serious tremors. "He gave me a hundred in twenties to take my picture. Made me feel important. He had food there for me. Sandwiches and Coke, said as much as I wanted. Plus M&M's and Reese's Pieces, he had a bowl, said, 'Dip in, no worries.'"

"Generous."

"I took eight bags of M&M's. Started with three, he says, 'Go ahead, take more.' So I took eight, he says, 'Great.' He gave me the hundred in the beginning. I'd just took off those nice threads he borrowed me, they smelled good, like just-baked. I'm leaving and he says, 'Hold on,' and goes and hands me an effin' wad. Later I counted it."

Sallow eyes widened. "Five **hundred**. Four **more**. Twenty twenties. Like **this**."

He spread his thumb and index finger. "Like **this**. I walk out with five hundred effin' dollars."

"Really generous," said Milo.

"Crazy generous. He was like . . . a saint. Now you're saying . . . oh, man, that's not right, not right. **Not** right. Who the eff would do that?"

"That's what we're trying to figure out, Gene."

Cudahy shook his head. "Just **wrong**." Slumping

for a moment, he sat up sharply. "Hey. I thought of something. Maybe he gave money to some evil motherfucker and they ripped him off."

"Could be, Gene. Any idea who?"

"No, I'm just— you can give out shit to some people but you can't give it out to everyone. You just can't do that." He shook his head. "Killed. Where?"

"In his studio."

"There," said Cudahy. "Right there? That's just wrong."

"Agreed, Gene. So when's the last time you saw Donny?"

"There was only one time. That time."

"The photography sessions," said Milo.

"Yeah."

"What'd he tell you about that?"

"That he wanted to see what people wanted deep inside themselves. Their goals if they could have their way. I didn't get what he was getting at. Not gonna lie, I wasn't really listening, had one thing on my mind. Okay? A hundred bucks, that's what I thought, a hundred."

Milo nodded.

Cudahy said, "Not gonna lie, best offer I had in . . . probably ever. Definitely ever. He says, 'Anything you want to be, Gene.' So I think and feel it had to be cool to be a boss so I tell him. He says 'Like a CEO?' I say, sure. So we did that. He gave me a razor and shaving cream, then those fresh-baked clothes."

He rubbed the side of his face.

I said, "Did you enjoy the session?"

"Hell, yeah," said Cudahy. "Best time I had in a long time."

Milo said, "And this was how long ago?"

Cudahy's forehead knit, creating two vertical lines between his eyebrows. "Like . . . months ago." He shook his head. "I don't remember so good anymore. Whenever he took my picture is when."

I said, "So it was a positive experience. How about after?"

"What do you mean?"

"Did you feel good about it after you left?"

"Why the eff wouldn't I? Sandwiches, Coke, five hundred buck-os? Gave me a good feeling to dress up. Been a long time since I dressed up. Back when I was selling Bibles."

"When did you do that?"

"When I was out of the navy and doing nothing in Chicago," he said. "Got paid by a Bible outfit in Decatur. They'd print these Bibles and send you out to sell 'em. My region was Nebraska, Kansas, Wisconsin, not the cities, the farms. The farmers liked me. Even when they already had Bibles, they bought another one."

I said, "Generous, like Donny."

"No, no, not the same thing," said Cudahy. "Farm folk paid for their Bibles but they wanted every penny of their change back. Sometimes they gave me a little food. But not like Mr. Donny.

Not anything I wanted. Not five **hundred** I didn't ask for."

"Did you see where he got the money?"

He nodded. "This wooden thing near the camera—like a closet, but wood. Same place where he kept the clothes, he reaches in and out comes this effin' wad. I'm thinking this can't be real. Waited until I was outside and alone to count it. Twenty twenties tied up with this paper thing from a bank. I had to break it up into three sections so it wouldn't bulge my pockets, you know?"

"Pays to be careful," said Milo.

"Ain't that the truth."

"Unfortunately, Donny may not have been careful."

"That's what I'm thinking. He's giving me a wad, I'm grateful, I'm thinking good thoughts. What if there was an evil dude who wasn't and came back for more?"

"You never came back."

Yellow eyes bugged. "No-oooh. No, no, no, no, don't **go** there, sir. Do **not** go there. Please." Cudahy dropped the donut and folded his arms across his chest. "I'm thinking I should leave."

"Sorry, Gene. These are just questions we need to ask."

"You already asked, I already told. He gave me extra I never asked for. To me, he's like a god, you don't mess with a god. No way, sir. Don't go there, sir."

"We're not, Gene, but I do need to ask you another question to be thorough."

The arms tightened. **"What?"**

"Where were you two Mondays ago?"

Gene Cudahy's face screwed up. "Two ... Mondays ... how the eff am I ... like I said, I'm not real good with time ..." He brightened. **"Two** Mondays? The one before the last? Ha!" The arms dropped. A finger pointed at Milo, then over at me. "Gotcha! Two Mondays I was at Pitchess."

County Jail branch in Castaic. Intended as an honor farm before the number of inmates forced diversity.

Milo said, "How long were you in Pitchess?"

"Eighteen days, just got out three ago. That's why I was at DSS."

"What landed you in Pitchess, Gene?"

"The usual." Cudahy looked down at the bench, took hold of the donut, and raised it to his lips. Three quick bites; nothing left but crumbs.

Milo said, "The usual."

"I got found with paraphernalia. Usually they let me go with that but this time I also had a little extra dirt in there." Pointing to his left sneaker. "Trying to stretch it out so I could be healthy all day. Serves me right." Ragged grin. "Trying to be mature. So now it's paraphernalia plus the dirt and they could've still let me go but they didn't, that's how it is, you never know what's gonna happen. So my PD says plead out, you'll get minimum security—basically room and board for a couple. So I did. That proves it, right?"

"Proves what, Gene?"

"That I'm no criminal. It's effin' **Pitchess.** Know what they used to call it? The Drunk Farm. Now it's the stupid stuff farm. They put me in Fire Camp but they didn't try to teach me how to do fireman shit 'cause I was too old and wasn't staying long enough. You can look it up. That's where I was. Fire Camp."

He brushed crumbs from dirty jeans, sat back, and observed with amusement as Milo made a call, got transferred several times, finally confirmed the dates of incarceration.

"Okay, Gene."

Cudahy snickered. "Sometimes you should just believe folk."

Milo smiled at him. "Think so?"

"Nah. That would be effin' insane."

Milo showed him the shots of the other Wishers as well as Colin Klement's DMV shot. Cudahy took the time to study each photo before shaking his head. "Who's the Black guy? He doesn't look street."

"Someone Donny knew."

"You think he did it?"

"No evidence of that, Gene. How about this guy?"

Showing Cudahy a ten-year-old mugshot of Abel Rodriguez.

Cudahy tightened up. "**He** did it?"

"Nope. So you know him."

"Eff yeah, that's Cap. He's who hooked me up with Mr. Donny."

"How'd that happen?"

"I'm sitting in the park—Lafayette, near that courthouse."

Cudahy's eyes shot to the left and he rubbed his arm.

No mystery about the sudden edginess. Years ago, I'd testified as an expert in an injury case at the Civil West Courthouse on Commonwealth adjoining Lafayette Park. The bailiff had warned me, "Don't go in there, it's nothing but hypes, pushers, and other lowlifes happy to cut your throat."

Milo said, "We couldn't care less why you were there, Gene. Tell us about Cap."

"Nothing to tell. He's walking around, like he does."

I said, "When he's looking for someone."

Nod. "He sees me and comes over."

"He capped you before."

"Not for a while. Medical things, he drives me somewhere, they give me X-rays, measure my head, my teeth, my legs, put a thing across here and let it beep."

Rubbing his chest. "Sometimes they stick a needle in and take blood. Or shoot something in." Sudden smile. "Not a problem, right? Sometimes they put something up my you-know-what. Afterward, they pay me. But not like Mr. Donny. Twenty, thirty, I think the most was like . . . fifty a thing."

"How many things were there?"

"Couldn't say."

"More than twenty?"

"Maybe . . . I don't know. Not going to lie, don't know numbers."

"A few," I said. "But not for a while. How come?"

"I been traveling," said Cudahy. "Went back to Chicago to see my mom then she died. Came back here like . . . two years ago?"

"Got it. So Cap remembered you and came over. What'd he have to say?"

" 'Hey, man, got something sweet.' I'm thinking, **Here goes something up my you-know-what again** but I said 'What?' 'cause I needed to stay healthy. Then he told me some rich dude wants to take your picture. I say okay, just X-rays. He says, no, not X-rays, real pictures. Photography. I say naked? Something filthy? 'Cause I got my limits. He laughs and says, 'You're paranoid, dude. Normal photography and you get paid a hundred.' So I did it. And that's all I know."

Milo said, "Okay, thanks for your time, Gene. Where can we take you?"

"No place, sir. I'll just sit here, there's nice sun." He raised his face to heat and light, accenting every flaw in a once sturdy structure.

"If you think of anything, here's my card, Gene." Wrapping it in a ten.

Cudahy unfurled the bill. "What's this for?"

"Cooperation. Take care of yourself."

Milo held out his hand. Cudahy hesitated then shook it. Spreading the bill tight, he slipped it into a pocket and smiled. "Not a twenty like Mr. Donny used, but okay."

The smile wavered and died. "Shouldn't happen to him. Not right, not right at all."

We left Cudahy on the bench and returned to the unmarked. I got in but Milo went to the trunk and retrieved something. Bottle of liquid disinfectant that he squirted on the hand Gene Cudahy had touched. Rubbing both hands together for good measure.

Cudahy hadn't noticed. Hadn't followed us at all, as he remained peering upward. Enjoying a warm bath of L.A. sunlight.

Sooner or later, the comfort would pass and he'd experience chills and go searching for a remedy, ten-dollar bill in hand.

26

"Alibied by the penal system," said Milo, driving back to my house. "Theoretically, he coulda gotten a buddy to do a break-in but I believe him about liking Donny. You feel any different?"

"I don't."

"So for the time being, two Wishers down, six to go. If I include the women."

"I would," I said. "A woman could pull off a shooting and strangling an eighty-nine pounder. A bludgeoning, too, if she was strong enough and had the right weapon. But even without that, what's to stop one of them from getting a boyfriend to collaborate on a big-money break-in. Or to do it as a couple."

"Big easy money, kept in full view and shelled out freely," he said. "If he gave five hundred to Gene, no reason to think he skimped on the others." He shook his head. "Lottery time for people without a crumb to their names. Poor guy was a victim made to order. It's almost like he had a death wish, Alex. You talked about guilt. Think on some level he coulda been suicidal?"

"So far we haven't heard about any serious mood issues or desire to pack it in. Even if there was guilt, I still think he was primarily trying to be kind."

"Flash a little white card and every day's Christmas," he said. "You live like that, money takes on a whole new meaning."

I said, "More like lack of meaning."

"Too much, too soon warps you?"

"Satiation screws up perspective, especially when it's seen as undeserved. Animals know that intuitively and opt for something called contra-freeloading. When given a choice between a bowl full of food and one that requires some work, they choose work."

"Really," he said. "We talking your maze-rat buddies?"

"Rats, canines, birds, apes, even some fish."

"Hunh . . . so maybe ol' Victor didn't do his kids any favor. At least one kid, the others seem to have done some kind of work."

"The others are considerably older, it may have taken time. Or they brought more resources to the table. Colin certainly did. Smart, athletic, and his mother was a good role model. Working herself up the ladder when that wasn't easy."

"Adonis's mother, on the other hand, O.D.'d and left her golden boy to find her body."

"Toss in severe dyslexia and it couldn't have been easy."

We drove for a while, not speaking.

The conversation had brought to mind the comfortable life I enjoyed now, years after my escape from Missouri. Arriving in Oakland and lucking out with a kind aunt who prevented me from starving and bankrolled my application to the U. Entering college at sixteen, barely shaving, lying my way to pick up guitar gigs in places I was too young to enter legally.

Milo said, "Helluva noisy silence. What?"

No sense getting into ancient history.

I said, "There was a poster that circulated years ago. **I've been rich, I've been poor, rich is better.** Sure, thinking you have too much and you don't deserve it can be an issue but you're always free to give away as much as you want. Which is exactly what Donny may have been trying to accomplish. No way to know how far he would've taken it. In contrast, people like Jangles and Gene don't have much by way of choice. Maybe that really got to one of them."

"Encountering Mr. Generous." He sighed. "Then he gets encountered."

"Could be someone asked Donny for more than five hundred and got turned down."

"I can see him doing that," he said. "Not to pull rank. To be fair."

His phone abused Delibes's Lakmé "Flower Duet." He handed it over.

I read the screen. "Andre Friederich."

"After midnight in Paree—push the button." Click. "**Bonne nuit, monsieur.**"

Friederich said, "You speak French?" No bistro sounds in the background. I pictured a walk-up flat, shabby but elegant, in one of the moderate arrondissements.

Milo said, "Not much beyond that, Andre. What's up?"

"I am calling to inform you that Victor Klement was spotted at his château yesterday. He did not look happy but I cannot tell you why. How's your investigation going?"

"Not brilliantly."

"Ah, well, such is life. No suspects?"

Milo chuckled. "When it's resolved, you'll know. So who saw Klement?"

"My source," said Friederich. "I'm sorry, he— she—whoever—must remain confidential because good positions are hard to find. And this person knows nothing that could be of use to you, merely what I just told you."

"Victor showed up," said Milo. "Big stretch limo?"

Friederich laughed. "We don't do that in France. A Mini that he drove himself."

"Was he by himself?"

"With his bride-to-be. Neither of them looked happy. I doubt that has anything to do with your case, life offers many opportunities for **la grande tristesse.**"

A woman's voice filtered through. "Aahn-dre?" Soft, sultry.

Friederich said, "I must go. Be well, Lieutenant." Click.

Milo said, "No big sadness for him tonight. So Daddy's in a blue mood. Maybe he found out about Donny or maybe Friederich is right."

A moment later: "Probably nothing to do with Donny. If he'd heard, he'd likely get in touch with me, no? Or maybe not, since this isn't a real family and he isn't a real dad."

As I handed the phone back, it began to abuse another piece of music. The victim never to be known because I killed it after two notes.

Sean Binchy said, "Loot, I'm back in the shop and there's some people here to see you about Klement."

Milo said, "His father?"

"Couple of fathers but not his. Along with their kids. They just showed up, it's kind of interesting."

"Kind of?"

Sean summarized.

Milo said, "Give 'em something to drink. Offer them nibbles from the snack bin downstairs, be there in fifteen."

27

Larry Amundsen was fiftyish, heavyset, and pink-faced, with thinning gray hair.

Frank Cervantes was fiftyish, heavyset, and bronze, with thinning gray hair.

They lived within a hundred yards of each other but hadn't been aware of that until today.

Amundsen worked as a night security guard at an amorphously shaped new building on Washington Boulevard that housed a videogame unicorn.

Cervantes worked as a night clerk at a twenty-four-hour truck rental yard on Culver Boulevard.

Their homes were apartments on the street perpendicular to Donny Klement's studio, less than three blocks north of the crime scene. Neither man had anything to offer about the murder. Neither had heard of it. Until hours ago.

That insight had come from a series of terrified

texts exchanged between their respective oldest children, aged sixteen.

Frank Cervantes, a marine vet who viewed the world as inherently corrupt, more so since the inception of the internet, made a point of monitoring all his five kids' cyber-communications. Whether they liked it or not.

"My house, my rules," he told us, man-spreading on a folding chair in the big interview room with the twin whiteboards, now wiped clean. Milo and I sat facing him. Sean Binchy stood in a corner.

Next to Cervantes, positioned similarly, Larry Amundsen nodded appreciatively. "Smart. Should've done it, myself." He turned to glare at his son Aidan. That cued Cervantes to glare at his daughter Tiffany.

Both teens squirmed.

Aidan Amundsen was blond, gawky, a little weak in the chin, six-two, one forty after feasting. Tiffany Cervantes was a foot shorter, a hundred pounds, if that, and wore transparent-framed eyeglasses that magnified squinty brown eyes.

They both attended a charter high school for artistically gifted students, Tiffany's specialty being creative writing, Aidan's, computer graphics. The divergence in interest minimized the classes they attended together, but Honors English had seated them next to each other and that had sparked romance.

A year of covert romance, enabled by the fact that Aidan's father didn't check his three kids' texts and Tiffany had been conscientious about deleting anything to do with Aidan or any other boy.

Until this morning, when she'd slipped up. Insisting to Aidan that **we need to deal with it its seriously moral!!!**

Wrong morning to forget. Frank Cervantes, sleeping in on a rare day off, had come into the kitchen for breakfast, ready to kiss his wife and lecture his progeny about table manners. On the way, he passed the bedroom Tiffany shared with her two sisters and spotted her on her lower bunk, fingers racing and "looking like a scared rabbit."

Stomping in, he'd snatched the phone from her hand. Read. Bellowed.

"Serious? What's **serious**? You talking moral or **immoral**? Don't go telling me you've done something seriously stupid, girl. Don't go **telling** me that!"

Obviously, Tiffany had burst into tears and continued sobbing as she threw her arms around her father. His impulse was to hug her back but he stood there because this was no time to get mushy.

"Tell me you're not pregnant!"

At that, Tiffany drew back and planted her hands on her hips and glared at him. "I can't **believe** you said that! That is **shameful**!"

Frank, relieved and chastened, said, "Then what's immoral?"

"Not immoral." As if talking to a moron. "Moral. Like one of those choice things they teach us about."

"Fine, fine. What? Spit it out."

Taking a deep breath, Tiffany told him.

He sat down on the bunk next to her, shaking his head. "Too much, girl. You are complicating my life."

Then he texted Aidan. **This is Tiffany's dad. Get yours on the phone. Now.**

Milo looked to the leftmost chair where Aidan Amundsen sat, both knees pumping up and down, fidgeting with his cuticles. Poor kid already had nails bitten down to nubs.

In the rightmost chair, Tiffany Cervantes alternated between looking put-upon and sneaking glances at Aidan.

Between them, several hundred pounds of paternal bulk.

Milo tried smiling at the kids. Failed to catch their eyes. "First off, all of you, we really appreciate you coming in. We value the community's help."

Larry Amundsen said, "We hear about stuff from neighborhood watch, get once-a-month lists. How come this wasn't on it? Being so close?"

Frank Cervantes said, "Point eight miles, according to Google. Way too close."

Milo said, "This case, there are details we can't divulge, yet."

Frank said, "Then how can we help you?"

"By doing this, sir. Providing information."

"You say so." Burly arms crossed a convex chest. Larry Amundsen began to imitate the gesture, then changed his mind and sat still.

Aidan and Tiffany maintained deer/headlights stares.

"Gentlemen," said Milo, "do I have your permission to talk to Aidan and Tiffany by themselves?"

"Why can't we be there?" said Frank.

"You certainly can, sir, but from what I understand, any information you have comes from Aidan and Tiffany so they're really who we need to talk to."

The dads looked at each other. Larry shrugged. Frank said, "Fine, but you need to protect them, I don't want some lowlife coming after them."

"They're not in any sort of danger, sir."

"Better not be."

Tiffany's head whipped toward her dad. "Thanks, Papa."

"For what?"

"Caring."

"Of course I care, what do you think." Releasing his arms, he snaked one around his daughter's shoulders and squeezed briefly.

Milo turned on his ever-so-patient avuncular smile. "So, it's okay? Just briefly."

Frank Cervantes said, "Fine," and got up. Larry Amundsen did the same.

Milo said, "There's coffee and baked goods in the room next door. Detective Binchy will show you."

Another D might resent being used as a waiter. Sean, along with Moe Reed and Alicia, had learned an important lesson working with Milo: **Put your ego aside. Whatever it takes.**

The fathers' exits made the kids more nervous. As planned, I moved my chair closer and talked first.

"First of all, thanks so much for coming in. It took courage."

Tiffany Cervantes said, "I was kind of forced when he found out."

I said, "I've read your texts. This has been on your mind from the beginning."

"Aidan's, too," she said. "We both freaked out. After we found out."

"About what happened in the blue building."

"Yes, sir." On the verge of tears.

Aidan remained silent and continued to worry his fingers. Blood rimmed a cuticle. Tiffany got up and sat next to him and took hold of the picking hand, restraining it. His knee jacked higher and faster.

I said, "How about we start at the beginning and tell us what you saw."

The teens looked at each other. Aidan's wince begged Tiffany to take over. She stroked the hand she'd suppressed. Crossed a leg and said, "We really didn't see much."

"Whatever you did see. It was two Mondays ago, right?"

She nodded. "We arranged to . . . go outside."

"To meet."

"We don't do it a lot, just . . . sometimes. Our dads are working at night and our moms are sleeping so we . . . I live on the ground floor and one of my windows . . ." Glancing at Aidan.

He said, "I live on the second floor so I go through the front. My mom sleeps deeply and my brothers aren't snitches."

I said, "So Tiffany leaves through the window—"

"I get there first so I can help her get out."

"Two Mondays ago was one of those times."

"Yes, sir," said Tiffany. "We wanted to do it on Sunday night, like eleven, but we both had to go on family trips so we got home late and my dad was still up 'cause he wasn't working. I had to go to Long Beach to see the aquarium even though I've been there a ton of times." Sticking out her tongue. "Aidan visited his grandparents in Temple City."

I said, "So the schedule changed and everything got pushed up to early Monday morning."

Emphatic nods.

Tiffany said, "It was still dark."

"Do you remember what time you left through the window?"

"I remember exactly, sir. Three eighteen."

Aidan said, "I got up at three oh three. I was there by three fourteen and then she came out at three eighteen."

Tiffany said, "I'm short, even a first floor is scary. He always helps me out." Smiling at her amour.

He said, "Anything's high for her."

She cuffed his arm lightly. "You're making me sound like a baby."

Aidan's smile was wry. "You ain't center on the b-ball team."

She laughed. He laughed back. Their shoulders pressed together. I imagined their trysts. Stolen moments of joy.

I said, "So you were together outside by three eighteen. Then what?"

Tiffany said, "Then what we always do. Walk and talk." Squeezing Aidan's hand.

He said, "Walk and talk, that's it." Challenging me to doubt him.

I said, "Where'd you guys walk?"

"Where we always do," said Tiffany. "Like a few blocks either way. Sometimes away from Venice, sometimes to Venice. Then we do it again depending on how much time we have."

Aidan said, "Sometimes we get three times back and forth."

Tiffany said, "I bring snacks. I like granola bars, he's into Cheetos." She looked at him and giggled. "Orange lips."

I said, "So two Mondays ago, you walked to Venice and . . ."

"There was a car there. Near the place. But nobody was in it, so we just walked by. Then the second time, we saw someone come out of the place and get in the car and drive off really fast."

"Out of there being . . ."

"Where it happened," said Aidan.

"The blue building."

"Yeah. Where we saw the tape later, when we came home."

"From school?"

"Yup."

Tiffany said, "We both take the bus and get off at the same time."

Aidan said, "Line One, we walk from Washington."

Another opportunity to stroll and talk.

I said, "So you passed the blue building and saw the yellow tape."

"There was a cop there," said Aidan. "We said what's going on and she said something happened but she wouldn't say what. So we knew it was bad."

Tiffany said, "We went on social media and put in the address and it said a homicide. That freaked us out. We even checked the news sites but there was nothing."

"What social media outlet had the details?"

"Some rich-kid school," said Aidan. "The guy we saw, we thought what if?"

"Not **what** if," said Tiffany. "Definitely if. Who else would it be?"

Aidan said, "Right."

I said, "What did the guy look like?"

Tiffany shook her head. "It was dark and he was moving fast."

"Hurrying to the car?"

"Yes, sir."

"Tall, short?"

"Maybe somewhat tall," said Aidan. "But can't say for sure because he was running like this."

Standing, he rounded his shoulders and lowered his head.

I said, "Kind of hunched over."

"Yes, sir," said Tiffany. "So maybe a little tall but we're not sure. He was wearing a long coat."

"What color?"

Another head shake. "It was dark. The air, I mean, not his clothes. We think they were dark, too, but we can't be sure and we don't want to tell you something we're not sure of."

I said, "We appreciate that. Anything else about this guy stand out?"

"No, sir."

"White, Black . . ."

"Didn't see," said Aidan.

"Heavyset, thin?"

Head shake duet.

I said, "Okay, what about the car he drove away in?"

"White Hyundai Accent, the post-2018 model."

"Wow, that's precise, Aidan."

The boy grinned. "I'm a gearhead. Especially subcompacts. It had a chrome grille, which they added to the SE model after 2018."

"Excellent," I said. "You didn't happen to see the license tag numbers."

"There was none."

"No plate at all?"

"Nope. I noticed that the first time because it was weird."

Milo's pad and pen were out. "White Hyundai Accent, post-2018."

"Fifth generation," said Aidan. "It had dents."

Milo said, "Where?"

Tiffany said, "The passenger side is what we saw first because we were walking on that side."

Aidan said, "Both passenger-side doors. Like it got gouged along the whole side. Then coming back, we crossed the street and I saw one deep dent on the driver's side. Did you?"

Tiffany said, "Wasn't looking." Pride in her voice. Her man had eagle eyes.

He said, "Messed up bunch of metal. Lucky we crossed otherwise we would've been close to him when he ran out."

Tiffany shuddered. Aidan's left arm assumed the same position as her father's. This hug brought a smile to her face. Then both of them looked at the door and drew apart.

Afraid of being discovered. Again.

I said, "You guys have been really helpful. Is there anything else you want to tell us?"

"He was carrying a bag," said Tiffany. "Like a shopping bag."

"Plastic or paper?"

"Plastic. I think." Looking at Aidan.

He said, "White or whitish, so probably plastic. Kind of sagging? At the bottom? Like it had a lot of stuff in it."

Tiffany said, "We thought a burglar but we weren't going to say anything because what did we really know and burglaries happen all the time, my friend Brooklyn had one at her house and the cops didn't do anything." She flushed. "Sorry, but that's what happened."

Milo said, "That's what often happens."

Aidan said, "We figured the same thing would happen and we didn't want to get in trouble with our dads."

"Then we found out a homicide," said Tiffany. "I kept thinking about it. What if we'd walked on the other side? You can't have murderers running around, what if what we saw was important. So we discussed it."

Then you got nailed by Dad.

I said, "We're really glad you came forward."

"Well," said Aidan.

"We didn't really," said Tiffany. "My dad did. Then his. They dragged us here."

I said, "You were in a tough spot, we totally understand."

"No matter how it happened," said Milo. "Your information is really helpful."

"It is?" said Aidan.

"You bet."

"Are we going to have to testify?"

"We're a long way off from that, Aidan."

"But we could?"

"It's possible, but—"

"That would be cool," said Aidan. His knees stopped moving. Relaxed as he imagined a cameo role in court.

Tiffany singsonged, "Do you solemnly swear," and the two of them laughed simultaneously.

It sounded like something they'd done a lot of.

With both kids restored to their fathers, Milo, Sean, and I watched as the four of them left. Larry and Frank in front, talking about the Dodgers, Tiffany and Aidan lagging behind and daring occasional touches of their hands.

When they were gone, Sean said, "Good people. Any new details?"

"Just the car." Milo filled him in.

Sean said, "Beat up, no plate, sounds promising for a GTA. We find it, maybe we get prints."

"I'll check. Meanwhile, fill Moe and Alicia in, go back to the crime scene to recanvass neighbors about the car."

"On it, Loot."

As we headed to Milo's office, he said, "Ah, young love. You never know what leads to a lead."

He plugged the details of the car into the city-wide stolen list. Four Hyundais had been ripped off during the past month, including a black one in Rampart, still missing. The single white car had been lifted in the Wilshire district, a few miles west of Rampart, and returned to its owner.

Milo learned the name of the auto theft detective, Marcia Brandywine, and caught her at her desk.

She said, "No, that one was pristine and not really a GTA. Single mom, her fifteen-year-old bundle of joy decided to joyride with his buddies. How he managed not to wreck it was a miracle. We took it off the list but obviously something messed up."

He thanked her, hung up, turned to me. "Maybe the car Romeo and Juliet saw wasn't boosted and we do have a bad guy with wheels."

I said, "Someone living in his car. Or it's a junker no one bothered to report."

"Or register," he said. "Like those ghetto crates, get rented out, then they're allowed to die. For all I know, it's sitting in some gully in Angeles Crest. Bottom line, the kids didn't tell me much."

I said, "You've got a fix on the time of the murder and the burglary theory's been confirmed."

"Guy in a coat, holding a bag full of stuff. So I put aside the inheritance angle and go back to basics . . . unless one of the sibs hired a lowlife to get rid of Donny **and** make it look like a burglary . . . in a jalopy? Nah, too complicated, this has to be connected to the photo sessions."

"Agreed," I said. "Concentrate on the Wishers and anyone who wished along with them."

CHAPTER

28

Milo checked in with Moe and Alicia, heard a lot more about nothing and stood. "You see anything else I can do, right now?"

"Nope."

"So I either catch up on paperwork or go home and catch some snooze."

I said, "Let me guess."

"C'mon, I'll drive you home."

Back in my office, I thought about how different this case was.

In most homicides, loved ones usually stay in frequent touch with detectives. Unless they're the perpetrators. Sometimes, when they are. It's a source of stress for investigators, feeling the pressure to produce justice for the dead and their kin.

In **this** homicide, family contact had consisted of Colin Klement's single follow-up call.

In this homicide, the victim's closest relative remained a phantom.

The more I thought about Victor Klement's absence, the likelier it felt like a choice. His reach meant he'd been informed about his son's murder. If not by his surviving children, then via the people who did his bidding. Dispensed carte blanche.

Was Klement so cold he really didn't care? Was using enigma as a weapon in his personal and business affairs a habit he was unwilling to break even now?

I recalled the varying descriptions of Klement, all wrong. The man was essentially a human Rorschach blot upon which prejudices were projected. Had he been banking for years on **not** being available because that forced others to assume and assumption led to errors?

Still, this wasn't a business negotiation. What type of father wouldn't get in touch after the murderous loss of his flesh and blood?

The type who was a father in name only? Who didn't care much for human contact lest it grow durable and distracting?

That led me to wonder about Andre Friederich's report of the billionaire's sour mood during his recent visit to the château. Was Klement more sensitive than I was giving him credit for? Processing his loss in solitude before contacting Milo? Or would his unhappiness turn out to have nothing to do with Donny and end up being something far more mundane?

A tiff with his new pregnant bride-to-be?

A blip on one of what had to be multiple financial screens?

Then I remembered the Klement seeking the help of a Beverly Hills physician for treatment of an unspecified "disorder" and wondered if he suffered from some sort of chronic condition that raised his vulnerability to stress.

Unlikely, given enough energy to purchase a new palace and a much-younger Wife Number Six. Complete with baby on the way.

Nor had Klement been too infirm to deter that same doctor from becoming Wife Number Four. Exchanging her soon after for Wife Number Five, Donny's mother.

Klement's game seemed clear: shuffling women and children like playing cards.

I checked my notes for Four's name. Leona Gustafson. A few keystrokes showed her to still be practicing in B.H., on Camden Drive in the heart of the city's medical district.

Specialty: rheumatology.

I supposed discomfort from a joint disease could explain Klement not looking overjoyed in Bordeaux. Maybe an ailment that remitted and recurred, leading to an ebb/flow of energy.

But none of that explained why he hadn't picked up a phone.

I thought about it for a while, made no headway and wondered if learning more about Gustafson's specialties could tell me something about Klement.

Andre Friederich had described her as "glamorous and educated at the finest schools," and both assertions were backed up by her website. Probably where Friederich had gotten them.

The headshot Leona Gustafson, M.D., posted revealed a fine-boned, smooth-faced woman in her fifties with a swan neck, a warm but somewhat reluctant smile, and gleaming dark hair drawn back tight.

Top-level educational status came from a degree in biochemistry, with honors, from Stanford followed by med school, internship, residency, and rheum fellowship at the U., where she served as a clinical associate professor of medicine.

Specialties: lupus and arthritis. The former could fit a fluctuating pattern.

I read on. Leona Gustafson had received uniformly excellent patient ratings on several sites and was often singled out for her caring nature. The only exception was occasional carping about delays in the waiting room. An inconvenience one patient excused away as "she's busy because she's so great."

I looked for her social media pages but found none. Switched to an image search because sometimes photos are indeed worth a whole lot of words.

Leona Gustafson's photos weren't. Nothing but three identical versions of the website shot.

No record of her at fundraisers, Hollywood parties, or other attention-grabbing shebangs.

"Glamorous" but avoiding the public eye?

Another asocial one?

Had that formed the basis for the attraction between her and Victor Klement? For all the talk about opposites attracting, similarity was a far better predictor of marital rapport.

Not that this marriage had succeeded any more than Klement's previous couplings. Had Leona Gustafson been so smitten that she'd ignored an obvious pattern? Blurring professional boundaries to become the Other Woman. An apparently brilliant woman who'd not only ignored Moira's plight but those of Mary and Sharlene before her.

The result: eighteen months of less-than-blissful matrimony, producing a single child.

Who'd perished in an accident.

A death for which Milo had failed to find any record.

That had intrigued me at first. Then one of the young D's had suggested an out-of-jurisdiction incident, which made sense.

Now I found myself wondering what had happened to Danielle Klement and why she had slipped from official memory.

Websites are fine for self-promotion but they're

scant sources of reality. I went into the kitchen, brewed coffee, and brought it back to the office, thinking about who I could call about Leona Gustafson.

The only possibility that came to mind was a pediatric orthopedist with whom I'd worked on several injury cases.

Aliza Bat Dor was a whiz at knitting together tiny bones and a softhearted woman, to boot. Trained in Israel, she'd done her postdoc work at the U. around the same time as Leona Gustafson. And her office was on Bedford Drive, one street over from Gustafson's practice on Camden.

Lots of docs in B.H. but you never knew.

I called Aliza's office, was informed by a harried-sounding front-desk woman that, "Doctor's busy all day with office visits. What's this about, please?"

"A referral."

"I'll take down your name," she said, sounding unimpressed. "Hopefully she'll call you."

"I will cling to hope."

"Pardon? Oh yeah, haha. It really has been frantic—sorry, have to go."

Not expecting a callback anytime soon, I went to see Robin, learned she had another hour or so before leaving the studio. Returning to the house, I took my old Martin guitar out of the case and began tuning up. Had just finished and was ready to play when my cell began doing the jumping-bean thing on my desktop.

Aliza Bat Dor said, "Alex? How are you doing?"

"Well. You?"

"Busy," she said. "Too much, I need to find a way. The message I got says a referral. I'm afraid I'm booked up for three and a half months. Is it an emergency?"

"Actually," I said, "it's more of an information search."

A beat. "I don't understand."

"Do you know a rheumatologist named Leona Gustafson?"

"Lee? You want to refer to her?"

"Not exactly. Her name came up in a police case I'm working on because her stepson was murdered."

"Murdered? That's terrible. Does she know?"

"I doubt it, Aliza."

She laughed. "So you fibbed to get through to me."

"Your front desk is pretty formidable."

"You've encountered Yolanda," she said. "She can be a bit . . . still, a little naughty, Alex."

"No offense."

"Just the opposite, Alex. I'm flattered. A stepson? A child?"

"A young man." I gave her a capsule summary.

She said, "Six wives? Wow. Lee never mentioned anything about that, just that she was divorced. But she wouldn't, our relationship comes from serving on the resources committee at the med school. We sit and listen to foolishness, sometimes have time for coffee where we talk about the foolishness. Anyway, good luck to your policeman friend. This is the one you've talked about?"

"The same," I said. "What's Leona like?"

"Lovely," she said. "Really lovely."

"Did Leona ever mention the death of a daughter?"

"No," said Aliza. "That also happened? Oh my God, recently?"

"Years ago."

"Terrible," said Aliza. "You know, sometimes she does have a sadness about her. But as I said, she's lovely, very bright, very caring. Okay, you did me a favor by making me take a break. Now it's over and back to reality. Bye, Alex."

I retrieved the guitar and played Scott Joplin and a bit of gypsy jazz for a solid hour until Robin came in and kissed me and asked what my deep thoughts were.

I said, "About dinner?"

"About anything but dinner's an acceptable topic."

Blanche, tagging after her, had perked her bat-ears at the sound of "dinner" and began panting.

Robin said, "Be easier to have a stupid dog—hold on, Princess, I'll get you a menu."

I was up early next morning, had time to run, see two patients, and begin some report-writing. I'd just broken for a bagel when Milo phoned at one ten p.m. A clogged voice said peaceful slumber had eluded him.

"New development," he said.

"Great."

"New, not great. May turn out to be nothing. Or something. Sorry, you'd need to come here, you have time?"

When I stepped into his office, his eyelids were puffy. On his desk was a jumbo coffee and a glazed, raisin-studded bear claw. The raisins looked dry.

"Tough night?"

"Tossed like a guilty man from midnight to two, finally pulled off something like sleep, then Moses called me at six thirty. I sent him home to get some shut-eye, told him to be back here by two. He's young, has a body worth preserving. Once I was up, I was up."

He yawned, got up, yawned again, took hold of the coffee and the pastry, showering his desktop with crumbs that he didn't bother to brush off. "Let's go wait for him."

We walked down the hall to one of the smaller interview rooms. Once seated, Milo drank coffee and studied the bear claw for clues.

By the time Moe Reed strode in, ramrod-straight, Milo had explained why he'd called me.

The young D had worked the night shift fruitlessly, checking out homeless encampments in Rampart Division and finishing a couple of miles south of MacArthur Park in the parking lot of a long-shuttered strip mall. He'd spent his time approaching people either mentally incapable of responding to him or unwilling to cooperate because they feared or hated the police.

Reed had resigned himself to another shift ending in failure when, approaching the far end of the knock-up neighborhood, he passed a tiny, toothless, elfin person living in a ragged army-surplus tent who seemed to welcome him with alert eyes.

Reed introduced himself. The man said, "Pleased to meetcha. Cal."

When Reed showed him the pictures of the Wishers, Cal said, "This one was here."

Jabbing a child-sized finger at the "before" image of the woman Donny had tagged as Katie and dressed up like a pediatrician.

When Reed asked Cal if he knew her name, the man said, "Sure, Kathy," and suddenly Reed was interested.

Now he sat opposite us.

Milo said, "Get some shut-eye, kid?"

"Couple of hours."

Milo held up his coffee mug. "I'd offer you some but it's not green, sludgy, and strangely vegetative."

Reed's smiles are infrequent and tentative. No exception today. "Had a protein shake."

"What a shock."

Reed rolled his bull-neck and shoulders. Pulling out his pad, he scanned a couple of pages of neatly printed notes, slipped it back in his jacket pocket.

Milo said, "I caught Alex up to the point where you were impressed. Go."

Reed said, "I asked Cal if Kathy was still around and he said no, she left with a new boyfriend. No name or description, turns out he never actually saw the guy, was basing it on what she told him. My boyfriend's getting me out of here and taking me to Vegas or Reno. When I started writing stuff down, he got squirrelly so I stopped. Obviously having him come in for a formal statement was out of the question."

"Best we're gonna do with that crowd," said Milo.

"What's interesting is Eugene Cudahy used his real name and so did she. If that's true of most of them, it could end up helping us with I.D.'s. On the other hand, Corinne went by Jangles, so who knows?"

I said, "I can see Donny asking them what they wanted to be called. Jangles went for a street name, at least two others didn't."

"Mr. Democratic. Yeah, that sounds about right. What's your assessment of Cal's credibility, Moses?"

"I think pretty good, L.T. He didn't play games, told me straight out that he'd seen her, and did know her name. And when I gave him five bucks he told me why he was sure it was her."

A sheet folded in four emerged from another of Reed's pockets. He spread it flat and smoothed out the creases.

Katie's "before" shot. We'd paid scant attention to it.

Gray-haired woman with a ruddy, bloated face, liverish lips, and eyes that had long surrendered. Reed tapped a crescent of skin that filled the vee of her moth-eaten gray sweater.

Every visible inch was brocaded with blue, black, and crimson ink. A mass of interlocking tendrils and what looked like reptilian claws. A riot of dermal art climbing upward from the sternum, as if clawing for the throat.

"That's some load of ink," said Milo.

Reed said, "According to Cal, she's got no tats

anywhere else except for the front of her torso, which is totally covered. Like a fuckin' T-shirt was his way of putting it."

Milo peered. "Looks to be decent quality, not prison stuff."

"Cal said it was well done. Dragons, horses, castles, all kinds of 'insane stuff.' He also said she liked to pull up her top and show off her chest. Bragged about being a 'sexy doll' and having lots of boyfriends, including her 'new man' who was going to show up soon and take her away."

Milo said, "Sexualized, like Jangles."

Reed said, "I'm no expert, L.T., but I'd guess it's not rare in those places. Loose inhibitions and all that."

He looked at me.

I said, "People doing what it takes to get by. A whole lot of them ended up victims."

The liberation of political prisoners.

Milo said, "When's the last time Cal saw her?"

Reed said, "He was hazy on that, maybe two days ago, maybe three. Guy drinks heavily, there was a ton of empties in and around his tent. I asked him how long she'd been living there and he held out for another five bucks, then told me a week. But he didn't sound confident about that, like he did with her name. I asked where she'd slept and he showed me. I was hoping she'd left something behind but it was just bare asphalt. Then he told me he didn't actually see her leave, just that she wasn't there in the morning. Then he stopped talking to me and crawled in his tent. I circulated with her picture again, used her name, showed the tattoos, got nowhere with anyone else."

He shook his head. "So many of them were numbed out, it was like talking to statues. Once I was out of there, I caught Sean and Alicia up, then put in a call to Rampart Patrol. No bells rang but with the tattoos we might have some luck."

Milo said, "Normally, I'd say check out parlors but it's doubtful she could afford these now, so they're likely old. Any ideas, Alex?"

I said, "With that level of decoration, she might've once been a biker gal or the friend of an artist. Or one, herself."

"Even if we find her, she could turn out to know nothing, like Cudahy. But we've got nothing else, so let's get everyone looking for her."

He studied the photo. "Dragons and castles. Why'd she want to be a doctor and not a sorceress? Weird."

I thought: **The more remote, the better the fantasy.**

His pocket vibrated. He pulled out his phone. "Hey, Sean, not much to report since Moses told you . . . what? You're kidding . . . oh shit . . . okay, hold down the fort."

He shot to his feet.

"We're taking a drive, Moses."

"Why?"

Milo told him.

Reed's eyes rounded. "You're kidding. **Unbelievable.**"

"Wish it was."

CHAPTER

30

This yellow tape was strung along the trunks of a dozen red-barked cedars. Fifty-foot-high, heavily branched trees ringing a clearing heaped with conifer needles and dry leaves. One copse among many in a centuries-old grove.

The grove was tucked just above the southern rim of Griffith Park. Not far from East Hollywood but eerily quiet and worlds away from tourists and felons.

Which had probably been the point.

During the drive, I'd looked up the distance to the park from the camp where Katie had been seen last. Just over six miles.

All sorts of routes could get you here from the Westlake district, ranging from a northern drive up Alvarado Street then continuing along the 101 or maneuvering a maze of residential streets. Or simply veering west into Hollywood at any point along Alvarado and approaching from Los Feliz Boulevard.

In any case, a trip on wheels.

Man with a car.

The body had been discovered by a couple of Dutch tourists who'd hiked down from the park's upper reaches looking for a place to picnic. Those plans had been disrupted by an insistent, metallic buzz that grew louder as they approached. Blowflies rejoicing. Then the smell.

The dead woman lay flat on her back in the clearing, sheltered now by a pop-up assembled by the three techies who'd backed away to let us observe. They stood ten yards to the south, snacking, drinking, phoning.

The woman's toothless, agape mouth was the only discernible part of her face. The rest was a purplish-brown pulp that gripped my guts and twisted them hard and clamped my eyes shut.

I collected myself and took another look. Obliterated face but the rest of her was bizarrely untouched but for blood spatter on her clothes. Her arms dangled parallel to her body, identical to Jangles in the culvert. She wore soiled pink sweatpants, flimsy shower sandals, and a moth-eaten gray sweater. Tattoos filled the vee of the sweater. More of the same peeked from above the waistband of the pants where the sweater had risen three or four inches.

The exposed abdomen wasn't the flagrant, vicious exposure favored by sexual psychopaths. This shift had been accidental—the result of being moved.

Or exploration by a foraging animal.

What looked like crusted bites scattered among inky curlicues and fronds said some critter had tried. But the damage was superficial. Maybe a rodent already sated had begun but figured it wasn't worth the effort.

Sean Binchy stood to the left of the body looking pained. Next to him, a coroner's investigator I'd never seen before, a Black man wearing a navy crypt polo shirt and jeans, appeared just as troubled. Doesn't matter how often you confront it, normal human beings don't inure easily to cruelty.

Reed and I followed Milo over. Milo turned to the C.I. L. **Bostock.**

"New face. Milo Sturgis."

"Larry Bostock, just moved down from Portland."

"Welcome aboard. Anything interesting?"

Bostock's eyes shifted to the body. "Detective Binchy says a person you're looking for is and that's the way she looks to me. Best guess on TOD is a couple of days, maybe a bit longer but you know how it is, final determination is up to the docs. In terms of COD, not much guesswork. Her head's caved in, front and back, and so far I haven't found any sharp-edged defects, puncture wounds, or bullet holes and don't expect to. So unless she's been poisoned by someone into Agatha Christie, it's going to be blunt-force trauma."

Milo said, "Any idea what kind of weapon?"

"Again, not up to me to say," said Bostock. "Off the record? Not skinny like a pipe, looks wider, more like a baseball bat."

He pointed. "No I.D. or anything else in her pockets but the tattoos look pretty unique. It's a pretty intact body and the fingers look printable to me. There's plenty of livor where you'd expect it and some decomp, especially at the back of the head where the maggots are eating brain tissue."

He winced, looked away. "What else . . . okay, there looks to be some animal damage on her belly and chest but it's not extensive. More like tentative nibbles before the critters changed their mind. Can't tell you why it happens but I've seen it before. Anyway, the techs will resume once you give the okay and when they're through, they'll call the drivers. My boss told me they used to send the drivers straightaway but it's gotten too busy, we need to keep a tight schedule. Speaking of which, I just caught a call in Compton, so unless there's something else you need me to do, nice meeting you."

Milo said, "You've summed it up, Larry."

"Doesn't pay to be unclear," said Bostock. "Unclear leads to problems."

He smiled fleetingly and left looking burdened.

Milo said, "Blunt-force injuries front and back match the pics in Abel Rodriguez's murder book.

On Rodriguez the pathologist also said a weapon around the circumference of a baseball bat. How do you picture it unfolding, Alex? Won't hold you to it, just imagine."

I said, "She was looking forward to an adventure in Vegas or Reno with the new man in her life, packed up and left with him at night. From her camp to here is six-plus miles, so we're talking a vehicle. To my mind, the Hyundai those kids saw is a strong candidate."

"Why stop here to do it?"

"Because she expected a longer trip and he wanted to catch her off guard. 'Before we hit the road, we'll party in a place I know.' Maybe he brought food. Most likely he brought booze or dope to numb her senses. Once they were here, he waited until she turned her back and battered her. Then he did the same thing to the front of her face to obscure her identity or he just enjoyed it."

Sean said, "I just checked the BOLO on the Hyundai, nothing so far. I doubt he's traveling without plates, so he probably stole some and put them on. Some eagle-eye spots it, we're in luck."

"Or," said Reed, "he junked the car or stashed it somewhere out of view and got himself another ride."

Milo said, "Or he sold it to someone else who can give us a lead. We need to prioritize the car and not leave it up to patrol."

I said, "Bad guys usually stay close to home but he's ranged from Malibu to here, supporting someone who lives out of his car."

Sean said, "Or is a long-distance trucker."

"I'd say bite your tongue," said Milo, "but I like you." He looked at me.

I said, "A trucker with a semi would find it hard to keep his vehicle out of sight when hanging in the camps."

"So back to the Hyundai. Let's all do drive-bys between here and that parking lot the poor woman was camping in. We'll avoid the freeway, obviously, and concentrate on Alvarado and the parallel streets. Look for cameras along the way."

"What about the remaining Wishers?" said Sean.

"We keep looking for them, too, but we'll divide it up six hours on the car, two on the Wishers."

Both young D's smiled. Amused at the idea that their day lasted only eight hours.

Milo said, "When I say we, I mean me and Alicia, also. Alicia is involved. Where is she?"

Reed said, "This morning she recanvassed in Culver City, Mar Vista, and Palms, got nothing and said she was trying the Valley again for camps Sean and she hadn't covered yet."

"Have her come in, Moses. I'll begin here, the northern mouth of Alvarado starts, you guys do the parallels. Don't limit yourselves to streets. If there's a big parking lot or other open area that

twangs your antenna, check it out. You find nothing, rinse and repeat. None of that pays off, we'll
expand to other sections of Rampart unless some
hot lead comes up elsewhere. **That** goes nowhere,
we'll sit down and have a big group boo-hoo. Now,
before we get going, let's step back and try to figure
out why she died in the first place."

Another glance at me.

I said, "I don't see the basics changing. Whoever
shot Donny is eliminating anyone he thinks can
connect him to Donny."

Reed said, "He's worried about one murder so he
commits others?"

"He considers the Wishers throwaways no one
will care about but knows Donny is anything but."

"Okay . . . but let me ask you this, Doc. Seeing
as it's only female Wishers he's killed, you don't
think it could be a sexual thing? What we were saying before about both of their behavioral patterns."

Sean said, "What were you saying before?"

I said, "Both Jangles and Katie were sexually
active and let everyone know about it. Despite
that, no, I don't see it as a sex murder. Donny and
Rodriguez certainly weren't, and neither Katie nor
Jangles was posed sexually."

Three sets of eyes swung to the body.

Milo said, "The arms are positioned the same
as Jangles. I'm not gonna say he was trying to give
them dignity. You don't do this to someone unless
you're a goddamn savage. But it's almost like he

tried to keep the scenes low-key. To me that says he had some kinda relationship with them."

Clatter from the south drew our attention. The trio of techs toting their gear in hard cases that clacked after each footstep.

Two women, one man, all in their early thirties. One of the women said, "Any idea when we can resume, Lieutenant?"

"Right now. Could you please print her if you haven't already."

"We haven't so we will," said **V. Hanson**. "We started with any scrapes that might give up DNA and looking for shoe prints. No luck on the shoes, all the tree stuff on the ground messed it up."

The man said, "Whole thing is messed up. Who **does** that to someone?"

By the time Milo and I drove away from the park, the sky was darkening. Poorer visibility makes it harder to spot your suspect but the cover of night can make the quarry overconfident and careless.

He said, "I know it's probably a waste of time because even if he did drive her on Alvarado, there are all sorts of turnoffs he could've taken. But, like I said, I'll pick it up at the mouth, which is Glendale, and do some back-and-forths. Gonna make tedium sound interesting so if you need to get back, I'll take you home first."

I phoned Robin.

She said, "Sounds boring."

"No doubt."

"But you still want to. Fine, at least it's safe. Any idea when you'll get back?"

"Probably a couple of hours."

"That's not too bad, I've got a lot of billing piled up, this will force me to do it. You mind if I make sandwiches and have mine now? Haven't had a bite since ten."

"Not on my account, I hope."

"Totally on my account. Got involved with glue and lacquer and lost track."

"Go nourish yourself."

She said, "Are you on speaker?"

"Nope."

"You do the same, handsome. I've seen the trunk of his car. Grab a health-eroding snack."

I laughed. "Love you."

When I hung up, Milo said, "Nourish herself? No way she can be on a diet."

"Nope, the perils of an exceptional work ethic. Let's go."

Two round trips up and down Alvarado took nearly an hour and a half, Milo's heavy foot replaced by hesitant tap-tap crawls that evoked honks from those who managed to miss that the offender was a prowling unmarked.

The scenery alternated blocks crammed with people and stretches as inorganic as a lunar landscape. Where humans flocked, fast-food joints, gas stations, working-person ethnic restaurants, cheap motels, and graffiti-stained vacant buildings shared space with a sprinkling of residential holdovers from a long-gone L.A.: prewar apartments and ancient, sagging, wood-sided houses daring the next earthquake. Milo asked me to record any cameras I noticed, saying he'd return tomorrow to look for footage but not sounding hopeful.

We spotted several barely concealed and open dope deals, furtive figures scattering into the shadows when they saw the prowling unmarked. A couple of white Hyundais caused Milo to pull over and run the plates. No dents, legal registration, elderly owners with no records. He moved on, slowing at the sight of any light-colored compact. Nowadays, so many cars are visually interchangeable, leading to futile inspections of Hondas, Toyotas, Kias, and the like.

By nine p.m. he'd accomplished nothing and the same went for Reed, Binchy, and Alicia, who'd joined the posse an hour ago.

Milo said, "Let's call it for today, kids."

Reed said, "I don't mind sticking with it, L.T."

Binchy said, "Same here."

Alicia said, "Social pressure compels me to agree."

Milo said, "Whatever you want. I'm taking Alex home."

He drove to Wilshire, turned right, heading west and reverting to his usual gun-and-weave approach to motoring. Setting off new waves of honking protest.

I said, "Blue privilege."

"Good name for a jazz club . . . given what we just did, I figured I'd give you some entertainment."

"After you drop me off, you'll be back there looking."

He laughed. "The perils of an exceptional work ethic. And admit it: If you didn't have a girl and a dog, would you be on the couch romancing the remote?"

I said nothing.

He said, "Exactly."

When I walked through my front door, Robin was on the couch, wearing a kimono I'd bought her years ago in Little Tokyo, reading **Fretboard Journal** and listening to music. Long robe, it covered her five foot three completely and clung to her like a needy friend.

The music was James Brown. "Try Me."

I'd introduced her to the song soon after we met, joking about my old wedding-band days, the thousand times I'd played it so people could slow-dance. She hadn't laughed. The night had gotten interesting.

Now she looked up and smiled.

I said, "James at his best."

She said, "Most romantic song ever written," got up and came toward me.

I took her in my arms. We slow-danced.

31

I spent three hours the following morning in Burbank family court, subpoenaed to testify in a five-year-old custody conflict.

The kids at stake were six and seven. They'd been preschoolers when I evaluated them four and a half years ago. I'd been thanked for my input by the judge, one of the better ones, and assured the case would settle. A few weeks later, he dropped dead of a heart attack putting to the sixth hole at Wilshire Country Club. The file got transferred to another judge, known for a leisurely approach to jurisprudence, who let it sit on his desk before retiring on full pension.

Judge Number Three seemed to be industrious but abruptly transferred to white-collar crimes. The fourth Solomon, on the bench for just under a month, was baffled by the snorting, dirt-pawing tactics of a new pair of pit-bull lawyers. The kind of mouthpieces who post flashy websites and wear flashy suits, both of which suffer upon close inspection.

Today was my third subpoena on the case in a month. The day before the first two court dates I'd contacted the court to confirm as I always do, only to learn that a continuance was in place. No one had taken the time to inform me.

After the third continuance, I listed the appointment with a ?

The subpoena specified nine a.m. I arrived at five to nine but the courtroom doors didn't swing open until ten.

When you're called as an expert witness, you usually wait outside in the corridor. But occasionally you get to watch the jousting and today was one of those times. I was the sole audience at a production that was bombing, each act filled with whispered sidebars, flamboyant throat-clearing, paper-shuffling, and strutting by the Suits.

A strange alliance of opponents, both of them taking advantage of the newbie's confusion.

He squirmed a lot, finally announced a bathroom break at ten thirty that recessed us until eleven fifteen, after which the lawyerly bacchanal resumed until noon when, looking down at the bench, the newbie said, "We'll reconvene tomorrow."

No testimony had been heard.

I managed to reach the squirmer as he left the bench and introduced myself.

He blinked. "Oh yeah, sure. Good."

"Any idea when the case will come up again?"

"Um . . . hard to say."

"It's been a while since my original report and I'm not willing to rely on it."

"Oh. I see. Well, okay, then—can we just use what we have from you?"

"If I'm not subpoenaed again."

"Um . . . sure, speak to my clerk." He hurried out.

The bailiff rolled her eyes.

I said, "Where's the clerk?"

"I'll handle it, Doc."

"Thanks a ton."

"Least I can do."

When I was outside, I reactivated my phone, saw a ten-minute-old text from Milo.

ID on Katie and Alicia found the Pilot, convinced him to come in. ETA twenty-five.

That threw me for a second. Then I remembered the Wisher shots. Jack. Aspiring Top Gun.

Taking off right now. ETA thirty.

I made it to the station in twenty-seven minutes, got waved upstairs by a front-desk civilian clerk who knew me by sight, found Milo in the same room where we'd conferenced with Moe. This time, Sean was there, sitting next to Milo and facing a medium-sized man in filthy khakis.

Off to the left on a card table were a brand-new pink box and coffee machine. Nothing in the detectives' hands but their guest sipped and ate.

Milo had texted me the basics. Katie was Katherine Wanda Bouleau, forty-nine, born in Elko, Nevada, with a petty criminal history similar to that of Corinne Mae Ballinger, aka Jangles. Like Jangles and Gene Cudahy, no recent arrests, less due to behavioral change than reluctance to prosecute nonviolent street crimes. Her most recent booking photo for prostitution, eight years ago, showed the brocade of tattoos rising to her gullet. The arrest form listed the body art as "extensive," but didn't specify.

The Pilot was Jackson Leon "Jack" McReady, fifty-nine, born in Tulsa, decades of nonviolent drug possession arrest there and in Denver and Albuquerque. His record had thinned fifteen years ago, before L.A. had stopped pursuing drug busts. That might be attributed to the cool-down you sometimes saw in addicts who managed to make it to advanced middle age. The brain's craving for dope somehow self-regulating. What my colleagues who worked with addiction called the too-pooped-to-pop syndrome.

Unlike Jangles and Katie, McReady favored indoor living and was a habitué of several downtown shelters. Sean had spotted him this morning exiting the Holy Passion Sanctuary on Skid Row, coffee cup in hand, strolling through the disorder and stench of Fourth Street.

When Sean approached him, he responded with

no wariness or resistance. On the contrary, Jack McReady seemed eager to socialize, even with a detective. When Sean explained why he was there, McReady said, "The kid? Oh man, that's terrible," When Sean asked if he'd be willing to talk at West L.A. station, McReady said, "I like the Westside . . . but I am kinda hungry."

"Where your celebrity was," said Sean.

"Pardon?"

"The photography."

McReady's eyes misted. "**Nice** kid. Terrible, terrible."

"So you'll come to the station, sir?"

"Yeah but I'm hungry."

"We'll find something for you, promise."

"There you go." Big smile.

Sean said, "They didn't give you breakfast at Holy Passion?"

"They did, but not what I like," said McReady. "Too much grease. I'll eat it if I have to, but I watch my cholesterol."

Sean, a first-rate detective, said, "You've had medical tests, huh."

"Long time ago," said McReady. "Got capped and did a whole bunch of tests. Most were bullshit, some kind of rip-off, but my LDL—that's the bad stuff—kept coming up too high. My father died of heart disease when he was forty-nine so I'm careful."

"Makes sense," said Sean, keeping his voice calm.

"I **try** to make sense," said Jack McReady. "When I was on the shit it was harder to make sense but now mostly I can do it."

When I entered the room, McReady turned and smiled at me, as if we were long acquainted. Milo and Sean sat facing him. A file sat on Milo's lap.

I said, "Alex."

"Jack. I'd shake your hand but mine's full of crumbs." Brandishing a cheese Danish.

I pulled up a perpendicular chair, not wanting McReady to feel overwhelmed by a tribunal. Needless caution. His posture was relaxed, his weathered face unruffled.

Milo said, "Jack was just telling us about all the stuff Abel Rodriguez got him into."

McReady laughed. "Yup, I used to get poked like a pincushion. Hoses and stuff going up in places you don't want to know. Did X-rays and CAT scans and PET scans and whosiz all kinds of other scans. Did a lot of MRIs, my least favorite. That thing's so loud it made my ears ring and it feels like you're in a tight box. In the beginning, I used to ask what they were seeing but they ignored me or said it didn't matter so I stopped asking."

I said, "At least they paid you."

"Not as much as that kid, Donny. With those jokers sometimes it was just meal tickets at shelters and food stamps, sometimes it was like fifteen, thirty bucks. That's why when Cap saw me and said he had a real moneymaker, like real money, a hundred, even though I don't like him I said okay."

Talking about Rodriguez in present tense. Unaware he'd been murdered.

I said, "Why don't you like Cap?"

"Sir," he said. "You live like I do, you get a feel for serpents and he was a serpent." He hissed. "Crafty, you know? People said he could get mean."

"Which people?"

He laughed. "Sir, your questions, no offense but they make **no** sense. When the street tells you something, you don't ask for I.D.'s."

"Got it. So you didn't trust Cap but the money sounded good."

"I didn't trust him far as I could throw him so I didn't let him drive me over, said give me the address and I'll show up. He looked at me like sure you will, but I did. Made it right when I said I would. Saw the place and said uh-oh."

"Something about it bothered you."

"No signs, not a lot of windows, this big steel door? Looked like a place you could go in and never come out."

Gap-toothed grin. "But, there was the money and I needed to be at least a little healthy. Take the edge off, you know? So I knocked on the door and this little girl answers and she says 'Great, Donny's waiting for you.' Then she starts walking me in, turns her back on me which tells me street smarts she don't got. She walked like a rich kid, you know? Like nothing can ever happen to little old **me**."

Milo showed him Mel Gornick's DMV shot.

"That's her. Couldn't see her being dangerous to anyone but herself. But I still kept my eyes and ears wide open and then he's there smiling and telling me welcome, Jack, welcome, c'mon in. He's also got that rich-kid thing going on. Like no one ever told him he couldn't do something. I mean if I was the type, I could've, you know?"

I said, "Taken advantage."

"Taken lots of advantage. But I'm not the type, I'm live and let live, don't mess with me, I won't mess with you. So we did the thing and he paid me and that was it. The only thing was, he kept wanting to know what my dreams were. My aspirations—who I wanted to be in a perfect world. I don't dream, period, and I sure don't have **aspirations**."

McReady's face darkened. "Never experienced a perfect world. He kept saying, you must aspire for something, Jack. So I remembered the night before was movie night at Sacred Heart, they showed **Top Gun,** so I said, 'You're right, friend, always wanted to try out being a Top Gun,' and that made him happy. Real happy, he kept saying, 'Jack, that's karma. A Top Gun uniform is one of the things I have right now,' and he went into a closet and started pulling out stuff. It wasn't a hundred percent, the movie was navy and this was air force, but I wasn't going to tell him. I wanted to get done, get my hundred, get out of there."

He took a giant bite of Danish, caught white curd-like crumbs in his palm and held them there. A tremor took hold and vibrated the particles.

Milo said, "Just toss it on the floor."

"Don't feel right about that, sir."

Sean got up, fetched a napkin, held it out as McReady deposited the crumbs, then returned to the coffee table and dropped it in a wastebasket.

I said, "You finished the session and got the hundred."

"Took a while," said McReady. "'Sit this way, sit that way.' 'Relax your shoulder.' 'Look off to the side.' Finally he said, 'Got some great shots,' handed me five twenties, and gave me a hug. Which was weird, but a hundred bucks? Do your thing, pal. Then he said, 'Wait a sec,' and went into the same closet where he got the uniform and came back with a big envelope full of something and said, 'I really enjoyed hanging out with you, Jack,' and gave it to me. I figured it was a T-shirt or something. Then I looked outside and saw a whole bunch more twenties. I walked behind the building, made sure no one was around, and counted it. Another **four** hundred. So now I'm thinking I should've hugged him back."

His shoulders rose and fell. "Someone offed the poor kid, huh? Guess it makes sense but it's still terrible."

I said, "Makes sense how?"

"He was like a lamb. No wolf-smarts."

Milo said, "Clueless."

"Handing out cash to strangers?" said McReady. "A lamb invites wolves over for dinner, what's going to happen? The lamb ends up **being** dinner."

I said, "Any idea which wolf got him?"

"Wish I did, I'd tell you. You should ask Cap, he's all about that."

"About . . ."

"Doing schemes with bad people." He froze. "Hey, maybe **he** did. Cap. Figured the kid was rich and soft and went hmm."

Milo showed him seven well-thumbed before-and-after shots. Two dead women and five survivors.

"Nah, none of them is Cap."

"Know any of these people?"

Jack McReady's face creased. He smiled. "Okay, you're saying they did the same thing as me? So where's my movie-star headshot?"

Milo retrieved his "after" shot and showed it to him.

McReady grimaced. "Don't look like no movie star there, either." He returned to the other photos for a second inspection. "Y'know this one maybe . . . yeah, this one, I've seen her around."

Holding up the image of the woman we'd just witnessed dumped in the park.

"Where?" said Milo.

"Here and there."

"Could you be a bit more specific, Jack?"

"Near the Row, but she was never still, always walking. I tried the outdoor thing for a while, could never sleep, was always thinking someone would do something to me. It ain't sweet dreams at the shelters, I had my experiences. But at least it's warm." Big smile. "And you get your cholesterol."

Milo smiled. "So what's her name?"

"Couldn't tell you, sir. I just saw her around. Three, maybe four times. Moving like she was drunk. Probably why she did a crazy thing."

"What's that, Jack?"

"Lifted up her top and flashed anyone who was watching. See this?" Poking Katherine Bouleau's "before" shot. "All covered with tats." He stuck out his tongue.

I said, "Not something you wanted to see."

"Sir," he said, "you got a broke-down car, I mean a real heap-a-crap. You going to waste money painting it? Trying to take it to a car show?"

"Did everyone feel that way?" said Milo.

"What do you mean?"

"Did it gross people out?"

The question perplexed McReady. "Who knows what anybody thinks."

"We've heard she had boyfriends."

"You serious? Only one I ever saw walking away with her was this one guy and I wouldn't call him a boyfriend type. More like . . . out to get what he wanted."

"Who's that?"

"Call himself Butch. Scary dude, wears a coat even when it's hot. Couple of times we were in the same dormitory room and both times he left in the middle of the night. I'm thinking, this guy goes prowling in the middle of the night, I don't want to know."

"What does Butch look like?"

"Big. Shaves his head. Moves around like one of those wrestlers."

Standing with effort, he fought for balance, took a few lumbering steps toward us, arms dangling gorilla-like, and sat back down.

"Like that." Still dangling the arms from his chair.

"What else can you tell us about him?"

"Nothing," said McReady. "Didn't see him much more than I saw her. Two times in the shelter then maybe . . . three more on the street, the last time with her. I stayed away from him, he's got a . . . darkness around him."

"Any idea how he hooked up with her?"

"Probably her flashing and he thought easy picking. 'Cause that's what she was doing when she left with him."

He sat up straighter. "Hey. Maybe this is what happened. She gets her picture taken, sees the kid's money, tells Butch."

"He'd have no problem breaking in."

"And worse."

"He's done other bad stuff?"

"That I can't tell you," said Jack McReady, "but what I can do is know scary when I see it. Back when I was younger and real hungry, I'd see the way people looked at me when I panned them and know I looked scary. But with him it's different."

Milo said, "Anything else you can tell us about him?"

"Wish there was."

"Okay, thanks, Mr. McReady. Take this box of pastries with you. Detective Binchy will drive you back to the shelter."

"Hope they still got a bed for me."

Sean said, "I'll help you with that."

"Thank you, sir. Sirs."

Milo reached into his pocket and handed over a twenty.

Jack McReady said, "Raise that a bit and I'll pose for pictures."

When we were alone, Milo cracked his knuckles and rubbed his face.

"Good ol' Jack," he said. "Throwing out theories and coming closer than he imagined."

I said, "Only difference is he saw Rodriguez and Butch as separate suspects and they were likely linked. Rodriguez got the idea for the burglary and recruited Butch who he knew from the streets. Butch knew both the women and used them to case the studio and swipe a key. Then he cleaned house."

I paged through the Wishers photos, extracted Stella the society woman, Solomon the surgeon, Louis the explorer, Maria the ballerina. "The question now is are any of them collaborators and potential victims. Especially the women. The two men don't fit Butch's description but you never know."

He took the shots, studied. "Now all I need to do is find them. Maybe log onto homeless.com . . . things are coming together but with crappy glue. I need a stretch. Maybe a pizza."

We exited the station, prepared to walk to Santa Monica Boulevard to an Italian place he likes, and came face-to-face with a frail-looking man heading for the front door.

He walked slowly, head down. Just short of average height, with a narrow, pallid face topped by unruly wisps of white hair. A baggy, drab tweed jacket worn over a wrinkled white shirt sported wide lapels from decades past. Baggy charcoal wool slacks puddled over scuffed, bubble-toed shoes.

As we passed, he looked back at Milo. "Excuse me. Do you know where I can find Lieutenant Sturgis?"

"You've found him."

Expressionless, as if incapable of surprise.

"My name is Klement. I'm here about my youngest son."

We reentered the building with Victor Klement.

Milo said, "One flight up, sir. Stairs or elevator?"

Klement said, "I should take the stairs for exercise but my knees aren't happy today, so if you don't mind."

His voice was soft, breathy, barely audible. People

straining to hear you could be a strategic asset. But as we rode up silently, Klement worried his hands, bit his lip, clenched and opened his eyes repeatedly.

Light-years from strategic.

During the brief walk to the interview room we'd used moments ago, Milo and I had to slow our pace to accommodate Klement's stiff gait.

Once inside, Milo offered Klement the chair Jack McReady had occupied.

He sat with effort, head lowered, feet flat on the floor. **Something chronic . . .**

A man you'd never notice if you saw him on the street. Which, I supposed, was the point.

Milo said, "Sorry to meet under these circumstances, Mr. Klement. We have been trying to reach you."

"I found out, from my daughter, and made plans immediately after."

Milo said, "The main thing is you're here, sir. And, again, so sorry for your loss."

Victor Klement reorganized his facial features into the mask he'd shown when we met.

"I'm here because I know I should be but I can't be of help to you because I wasn't an attentive father to Donny nor to any of my other children. Thus, I have nothing of substance to offer. But my guess is you've done enough due diligence to know that."

Milo said, "We know the basics but we've been concentrating on finding Donny's killer."

"Killer." Head shake. "You never think your child will die before you, let alone criminally."

Flat tone.

I said, "So sorry you've had to go through it twice."

Victor Klement's face snapped upward like a sprung mousetrap and he stared at me. His eyes were the gray-blue of the ocean under a cloudy sky. Steady, appraising, piercing.

"Pardon?"

"Danielle."

"Danielle," he said, "wasn't mine. So what can you tell me about your investigation?"

"Unfortunately," said Milo, "not much, at this point."

"Do you see that changing?"

"I do."

"I'll take that as more than blind optimism."

Milo said, "Can you think of anyone who'd want to harm Donny?"

"As I just told you, I don't pretend to have any depth of knowledge of Donny. The last time I saw him was years ago, in Germany, and that consisted of a brief lunch. From what I've gathered, he was a nice boy. That came from his brother Colin, whom you've met. Colin is in the money game so I have a bit more contact with him than the others. Business discussions, nothing personal, which reiterates my point: As a father, I'm an object lesson in what not to do. I sire and abdicate. Don't ask me why I'm impelled to repeat that pattern. I've asked myself and have no answers. Now back to Donny. My daughter told me someone broke into a place he was using to photograph homeless people and shot him. Is that accurate?"

"It is, sir."

"So obviously my failings as a parent aren't relevant. Is your working hypothesis that a homeless person did it?"

"We're examining a number of possibilities."

Victor Klement's smile was lopsided, devoid of joy. "That response, Lieutenant, would have done a politician proud."

I said, "Don't want to pry but who is Danielle's father?"

Klement's head rose higher. He treated me to a second stare, longer. "Her father was my fourth wife's previous husband. Danielle was three when I met her, not yet five when I abdicated. Why are you prying into that? Surely, it's not relevant."

"Just trying to get a full picture of Donny's family."

"Digging random holes and hoping one gushes oil? That seems woefully inefficient."

We said nothing.

Victor Klement said, "My advice to you is avoid distraction. For example, your due diligence about my history. I understand why you'd go about that but as you've seen, it won't help you. You also need to realize that your sources may be corrupted."

Milo said, "In what way, sir?"

"You believed Danielle was mine because of what you read in a trashy French newspaper. It wasn't true because the source was definitely corrupted."

Broader smile, still asymmetrical, as if facial muscles had atrophied somewhere. "I'm certain of that because I did the corrupting. I'd been suspicious about someone leaking to the press and set a snare by feeding that person false information. Namely, that Danielle was one of my children. When the article appeared, my suspicions were confirmed. I have since initiated remedial procedures."

I said, "Against . . ."

"A woman who'd planned on becoming my sixth wife. You read that rag so you saw a soft-focus photograph of her with some flowers, charmingly gravid. Whether or not the child she's carrying is mine remains to be proven. If it is, I'll support it as I have my others."

"Financially."

Klement turned away from me. "Let's move on to disposition of Donny's body."

Milo's well versed in the sad process of helping families deal with the bureaucracy of death. It's a multistep slog and people usually take notes, manually or on devices.

Victor Klement listened, said, "Duly registered, thank you," and got to his feet.

Milo said, "Sir, is there anything else you can

tell us that might be helpful? Even if it seems far-fetched."

"Lieutenant, if there was anything with the slightest relevance, I'd have already mentioned it. Do your security procedures allow me to exit alone?"

We walked him to the elevator. When the doors closed, Milo said, "'Piece of work' doesn't even begin."

I said, "Unusual man."

"Aw, c'mon, be judgmental. He's a total asshole. Now I'm feeling doubly sorry for Donny. Created by **that** and an addict?"

"Easy to see why he'd reach out to strangers."

That gave him pause. He said, "Okay, triply sorry."

As we climbed the stairs and headed to his office, he said, "Didn't the original Adonis die nastily?"

"Ripped apart by a wild boar."

"Bad karma. I'm surprised Victor let her name him that."

"I doubt Victor had much input into child-rearing."

"Probably not. Because, you know, folks, he was **impelled**—like that's an excuse. If there's something colder than ice water, it's running through his veins."

"Liquid nitrogen," I said.

"Nitro Man," he said. "Nah, sounds too much like a superhero."

◆

When we'd settled in the closet-sized space, I said, "Klement made a point of coming across unemotional but one thing got to him: when I brought up Danielle. Would you do me a favor and find out how she died?"

He put the papers down. "Klement had something to do with her death because she **wasn't** his? Like animals sometimes do?"

"Nothing like that."

"Then, what?"

"Just curious. Unless you're too busy."

He looked at me. "That was cold. Don't spend more time with Bad Nitro."

Combing through death records looking for deceased Danielle's was inefficient. Instead he located Leona Gustafson's first wedding license.

Six years before marrying Victor Klement, she'd tied the knot with one Berkeley Justin Bonty.

Keywording **danielle bonty** in the coroner's file pulled up the summary.

Danielle Cherie Bonty, age sixteen, had perished seventeen years ago in Malibu, swept out to sea by a riptide. Her body had washed up on the sand two miles north. The sole eyewitness to the tragedy: her twelve-year-old brother, listed as **Donald**.

The precise location: Broad Beach.

I pictured a girl perched on the crags below Donny's house. Whipped away by a sudden gust of water running counter to the normal tides. What surfers euphemize as an offshore. What others call a death funnel.

Milo said, "Hanging out at her half brother's? The two of them had a relationship?"

I said, "One that ended in the worst possible way."

"Jesus. Still, I can't see the relevance to Donny. Someone blamed a twelve-year-old for an accident and decided to act on it seventeen years later? Everything we've learned points to a burglary gone ugly."

"I'm sure you're right."

"Oh, man, I thought we were friends."

I looked at him.

He said, "Pals don't glibly lie to each other. You are not even **close** to sure."

"Okay, there's a decent chance you're right."

"There you go, damning with faint praise. Now you've got me itchy. What's your screenplay?"

"Don't have one. Just what-ifs."

He spun around, managed to cross long legs in limited space. "Go."

I said, "I'm still assuming Abel Rodriguez was the first to come up with the burglary of Donny's studio. But the fact that his main gig had been medical fraud interests me because Danielle's mother is a physician. The person I spoke to—someone I trust—had nothing but great things to say about her. But doctors often marry doctors. What if Leona's first husband—Danielle's father—was a not-so-pure

M.D.? The kind who'd get involved in a billing scam with people like Rourke and Rodriguez."

"Fine. Now what would that have to do with Donny?"

"Maybe nothing."

"But?"

I shrugged.

He exhaled. "Failure to indulge your whims feels like a bad bet. Hold on."

The medical board offered up sparse but confirming data: Berkeley J. Bonty had indeed been a practicing orthopedic surgeon until the revocation of his medical license.

Seventeen years ago.

We checked the dates. Five months before Danielle's death. That quickened Milo's breath as he logged onto NCIC.

Berkeley Justin Bonty, M.D., had been convicted of fraud and grand theft two months prior to being de-licensed. But no record of incarceration.

I said, "Gluck said after Rourke died, the whole case collapsed and everyone pled out. Bonty's deal could've involved giving up his license. It's not jail but a doctor losing his career was traumatic. Then his daughter drowns? Someone faced with all that could crash. Maybe all the way down."

Milo said, "From surgery to the streets? He's Butch?"

"I don't see Berkeley J. making it as a street name."

"So he goes for something macho . . . okay, let's see what else we can learn about this guy."

Berkeley Justin Bonty's NCIC mugshot revealed a well-fed, heavy-jawed face topped with executive-cut gray hair. Angry eyes, angry mouth, angry everything else.

Six-two, two thirty.

Milo logged onto the department files and found three subsequent arrests, none more recent than six years ago. Battery, drug possession, another battery. Two in Rampart, one in Central. No details, no jail time.

Bonty's six-year-old arrest photo showed the same face, sagging, creased, thinner and bonier in places, more bloated in others. Topped by a skull shaved to the skin.

Bleary, puffy eyes, tugged downward by time and self-abuse, continued to glint with anger.

Four monikers.

Berk, Burk, Butch, Bonto.

I pointed out the anger.

Milo said, "Yeah, definitely not a happy camper."

I said, "For all we know, Rodriguez tried to enlist Bonty to pose before he came up with the burglary. 'Hey, Butch, you used to be a doctor, here's your chance to do it again.' Bonty learned who the photographer was and saw it as a sign. So when Rodriguez came to him about the burglary, he decided to toss in some personal revenge."

"Blaming a twelve-year-old for an accident?"

"He could've convinced himself Donny was somehow culpable," I said. "But even if he didn't, the main payback might not have been directed at Donny. It was aimed at the man who married his wife and was rich beyond belief while Bonty had nothing. Think about it: Bonty's living on the streets, addicted, childless, and Providence hands him the offspring of The Guy with Everything? Who he may have blamed for taking away his wife."

Milo got up, paced, sat back down, chewed his cheek.

"Anything else?"

"No, that's it."

He phoned Rampart Division and spoke to a patrol sergeant named Stoudemire. Asked a few questions and did a lot of listening, said, "Really?" several times before offering thanks and hanging up.

"Butch is known to them because his name has come up in three non-fatal assaults on homeless folk sleeping rough. Two were loners sacked out in downtown tunnels who got bashed on the head by a baseball-bat-type weapon, the third was a woman in a sleeping bag near the L.A. River who got hit by a car that veered off the road and shattered her legs. None of the victims remember anything but waking up in pain. The woman's lucky because another homeless was woken by her screams and he had a burner that he used to call 911. All he recalls is taillights. Without evidence, the case hasn't gone anywhere but apparently Butch has. They can't find him anywhere."

"Why's he a suspect?"

"Street talk," he said. "Same as we got. But then the sources got scared and either disappeared or denied what they'd said."

I said, "Now we've got another reason he'd kill Donny."

"What's that?"

"He enjoys it."

33

We agreed the next step was talking to Dr. Leona Gustafson. At four thirty, she'd likely be at her office, probably with a waiting room full of patients.

Milo said, "Let's show up around five, check out the situation, and wait until she's by herself."

He logged on, searched for something. Said, "Oh shit."

Twirling an index finger, he said, "But first, folks, some virtuoso dirt-eating. Just to stay in practice."

John Nguyen said, "I was just out the door."

"Sorry, John. If you could just—"

"You had it and tossed it? So get it the same way."

"My guy got it from your guys."

"So ask him to do it again."

"I've got him out doing other stuff."

"So **I'm** your gofer?"

"Sorry, John. I wouldn't ask if it wasn't important."

"It's not on your computer?"

"I deleted it."

"If you were sorry, you wouldn't be bullshitting me shamelessly. Admit it: You treated it the way you treat everything anyone sends you. One glance and toss. If that. Remember that summary I sent you last year? Crimes against people, I wanted you to comment in writing? Never heard from you. I know your game."

"A lot of flotsam and jetsam piles up, John. I didn't mean—"

"Cut the crap, I've seen you do it right in front of me," said Nguyen. "Waltz into that depressing cubbyhole of yours and sweep stuff into the circular file with drama."

"Never your stuff, John." Major-league eye-roll. Crossed fingers on one hand. The other shot aloft, the middle finger predominating.

"You actually want me to go back and find all that shit and resend it."

"Not necessary, John. Just check a name and see if it appears in the indictment."

"It's relevant to the shutterbug case?"

"Big-time. Turns out this guy—"

"Don't cloud my head with preliminary details," said Nguyen. "Get all your ducks in a row then give me bottom-line facts. What's the name?"

"Berkeley Justin Bonty."

"Fucking mouthful," said Nguyen. "Hold on."

The twenty-three seconds it took him to produce the answer said he had it at his disposal, his irritation as much an act as Milo's feigned innocence. I'd seen the show before: detective and D.A. working off stress by bickering like an old married couple.

"Yup, he's here," said Nguyen. "Guy was a fancy-ass bone-crusher, had an office in Beverly Hills."

"Have an address?"

"Why? He hasn't been a doctor in years."

"Just—"

"Fine. Here." Nguyen read off numbers.

Camden Drive. Same building as the one where Leona Gustafson practiced. Two floors up from Gustafson's suite.

Milo said, "Thanks, John."

"Thank me by solving the case and then introducing me to the supermodel. And don't ask for anything else, I'm off."

"Have a good time, John."

"Dinner with the in-laws?" Nguyen's raucous laughter was severed by the bee-buzz of a broken connection.

Milo said, "Hubby and wife were neighbors."

I said, "Joint disorders, bone disorders, plenty of opportunity for cross-referrals. That could be how they met. Or they met first and combined business with personal."

"Maybe on more than legit business."

"Gustafson scammed and got away with it? My source had only good things to say."

"Is your source God?"

I said, "Close. She's a surgeon."

He laughed.

I said, "An orthopedic surgeon."

He said, "That so?"

I phoned.

Aliza Bat Dor said, "You caught me at a good time, just finished. Did something else come up with Lee Gustafson?"

"Indirectly. Her first husband got into trouble. An orthopod who got defrocked."

"Defrocked? Like we're priests? Ha. What did he do?"

"Took part in billing scams."

She groaned.

I said, "His name's Berkeley Bonty."

"Never heard of him," she said. "How long ago was this?"

"He lost his license seventeen years ago."

"I was at Yale—hold on, one of my partners goes back thirty years and he's right next door."

Moments later, a deep male voice came on. "This is Mort Leibowitz. What do you want to know about Butch Bonty?"

Milo said, "Anything you can tell us."

"Decent surgeon for basic knees, had issues, got

involved with bad people, paid for it. Total idiot. Must've been twenty years ago. Haven't seen hide nor hair since then."

"What kind of issues did he have, Dr. Leibowitz?"

"The talk was alcohol. As far as I know it never got him in trouble in the O.R. He was also kind of a bully. Big shlub, played football for SC, thought he was God's gift."

Leibowitz stopped. "Guess I sound pretty p.o.'d. Yeah, it annoys me. Someone wasting all that training. Why's a psychologist interested in Bonty?"

Milo said, "The psychologist is sitting next to me, Doctor. My name's Sturgis, I'm a police detective."

"Detective," said Leibowitz. "Something criminal? Hope he pays for it. Loser."

Click.

Aliza came back on. "Mort's a man of few words."

I said, "You don't see any chance Lee Gustafson could've been involved in the same scam?"

"That would shock me, Alex. But I've found that life is full of surprises."

I'd come up with nothing sketchy in Leona Gustafson's background but Milo had the ability to dig deeper.

Same result. An apparently spotless reputation.

He got up, hitched his trousers, pocketed his notepad. "Maybe she's just got bad taste in men. Let's see what she does to our antennae."

34

The drive to the B.H. medical district was a smooth twenty minutes. We parked in a city lot on Camden Drive and walked a block to one of several brick-faced, brass-doored buildings.

On the ground floor a small coffee shop opened to two sidewalk tables. Above that, four additional stories, Leona Gustafson's suite on the second.

When we arrived at her door, Milo said, "You peek in. You look less threatening."

I cracked the door, then closed it. "One person in there. Blond woman in her thirties, black pantsuit. A roller bag, so likely a drug company rep."

"Two-second glimpse and you get all that." Shaking his head. "Dr. Camera." He looked up the corridor to the rear of the building. "I'll hang back there, how about you go and grab a couple of coffees, the usual."

I said, "All that covert's not necessary. Reps are into one thing: selling."

"How long does that take?"

"Depends on whether anyone's buying."

Dr. Leona Gustafson wasn't. Four minutes later, the blond woman exited, flashed us an icy smile, and rolled her bag to the next office.

Gustafson was alone in her waiting room, wearing a white coat over a navy top and gray slacks. Gold-framed eyeglasses on a golden chain were the closest she came to jewelry. They swung as she straightened lifestyle magazines arrayed on a coffee table.

Five-two, fine-boned, somewhere in her fifties. She inched backward. "Sorry, the office is closed."

Milo produced his badge. "Lieutenant Sturgis, LAPD. This is Alex Delaware."

Leona Gustafson said, "I don't understand."

"We'd like to talk to you about Butch Bonty."

"Him," she said. "My God, what did he do?"

She took us to her office, a modest, boxy space replete with diplomas, certificates, and framed photos of herself with actors and comedians of various rank, well-fed non-celebs in designer clothing. A standing frame was propped on her desktop, facing her.

Milo said, "Thanks for taking the time, Doctor."

"Sure," said Gustafson, sounding anything but.

"I haven't seen Butch in years. Please tell me. What's he done?"

"We can't say for sure but he may have killed someone."

"Oh my God! That's—a lot to take in. Who did he kill?"

"We're looking at him for the murder of Donny Klement."

She sagged. "Oh no. Donny! Donny's dead? Such a sweet boy. He's **dead**?"

Her face crumpled.

No need for Milo to use his stash of tissues. He removed one from a box on her desk and handed it to her.

She whispered, "Thank you." Sat there, frozen. "Butch? He's got problems but what reason could he **possibly** have?"

"That's what we're trying to find out, Doctor."

"Do you have him in custody?"

"Not yet."

"Not **yet**," she said. "You expect to?"

"We do."

"Well, that's good. I suppose I should be worried, Butch and I didn't part on the best of terms and every time I've seen him, he's seemed worse. Mentally. But he's never been threatening. Just sad—benign, actually."

"When's the last time you saw him, Doctor?"

"Not recently," said Leona Gustafson. "A long

time . . . maybe . . . five, six years ago? Even before
that, infrequently. Months would go by, then years."

"He'd drop by to visit?"

"He'd drop by to ask for money. It was depressing. Seeing his deterioration."

"Did you give him money?"

"Always. I felt sorry for him. For what he'd
become."

"Large sums?"

"Hundreds of dollars, not thousands. He was
always appreciative. Why would he hurt Donny? I
just don't understand what connection . . ."

She stopped, looked down, fiddled with a
Bic pen.

"Doctor?"

"The only thing I can think of—it's crazy. But . . .
perhaps it was an indirect thing. Not against Donny.
Against his father."

She put the pen down. "Do you know who
that is?"

"Victor Klement."

"Victor," she said, as if trying out a foreign word.
"Victor knows about Donny?"

"He does."

She shook her head. "Is he okay?"

"He's coping, Doctor. Why would Butch resent
Victor?"

"Because I divorced Butch and married Victor
and Butch is crazy so he scrambles everything up.

Victor and I had nothing to do with Butch, we were already over. But then Butch got into financial troubles. Because of . . . he made some mistakes. Everything went bad for him. He'd always been competitive, I can see him resenting Victor."

"Did he ever express that?"

"Only one time. One of those drop-bys for money. He said, 'You're living the high life.' I said, 'What do you mean,' and he said, 'You and your new toy.' I pretended not to understand and once I gave him a few hundred, he was out of there. The irony was by that time Victor and I had gotten divorced. So Butch had no reason."

I said, "So there was never any active conflict between them."

"None," she said. "As far as I know, they were never in the same room together."

I thought: **Doesn't matter much when you live in a fantasy world.**

Milo said, "Still, think Butch might've taken out his feelings for Victor against Donny?"

"I don't know what I think. This whole thing is . . . insane. I mean I'm not a psychologist."

Milo's lips edged upward.

I said, "Anything you can tell us about Butch will be helpful."

"I've told you what I know. As I said, it's been years."

"How did the two of you meet?"

"You're interested in that? I can't see how it would matter."

"It may not matter, but please."

She extracted another tissue, wadded it tight, flinched as if steeling herself for a painful procedure.

"It's not complicated," she said. "We were both residents at the U. and I made the mistake of going for superficiality. Butch was handsome, strong, and masculine. He'd played football at SC, had that self-assurance you get in athletes. I knew he drank a little too much but never on shift, I figured more of a frat-boy thing, the way he unwound. I knew he wasn't the most sensitive guy, but I wasn't out for sensitivity. We dated, got engaged, got married when I was chief resident in medicine. It's an administrative job so we didn't see much of each other but we were both busy so that wasn't an issue. I took a rheumatology fellowship, Butch did orthopedic surgery, we bought a house in Brentwood."

She shrugged.

No mention of the birth of a child.

I said, "At some point, his drinking got worse."

"Steadily but slowly, I didn't notice, at first," she said. "Then he began taking Ritalin and who knows what else to help him maintain alertness in surgery. Then tranquilizers, to wind down from the Ritalin so he could sleep. Eventually, I realized it had nothing to do with work."

"He was self-medicating for mood swings."

"But still," she said, "it didn't seem to affect his work, he had connections with the SC athletic department and they sent him tons of referrals for knee surgeries. What ended up taking him down wasn't drugs, it was greed."

She studied us. "Do you have any idea what I'm talking about?"

Milo said, "Jimmy Rourke."

"Rourke's the one that finally ruined him but there were others before Rourke. During the last few years of our marriage, he'd cut back on legitimate surgeries but seemed to be making as much money. My first inkling of something definitely not right was when I found a bank account he'd hidden from me. More than could be accounted for by his practice but I didn't push it. Later, when I filed for divorce I found out he'd been spending a ton on gambling and losing it faster than he made it."

Milo said, "What kind of gambling?"

"Anything he could get hold of. Vegas, Indian casinos, online, sports bets. Probably other stuff I don't know about. Why didn't I confront him? Because you didn't confront Butch."

I said, "He scared you."

"You bet."

"Did he ever abuse you?"

"Physically, no. But the way he **acted** could scare the heck out of me. He's huge. The way he talked when he got angry—hovering over me, getting in my face. Turning red. You see my size. He could've snapped me in two."

She grimaced. "His size was part of what attracted me to him in the first place. It made me feel safe."

"Then just the opposite."

"I probably sound like an idiot for putting up with it but you'd have to be in my shoes."

I said, "We don't feel that at all. We've seen it before."

"So had I," she said. "I'd heard about women in the same situation, thought it would never happen to me. But as I said, the changes were subtle. It's like that experiment where they put a frog in water and slowly increase the temperature? The poor thing's defense mechanisms are hindered so it boils to death. But finding the account was the last straw. I consulted a divorce lawyer, he looked into it and warned me to get my act together quickly or I could be liable for Butch's frauds because theoretically I'd shared in the proceeds. And even if I wasn't formally charged, everyone would suspect I was corrupt and my practice could be destroyed. So I moved out."

Her chest heaved. "With our daughter."

I said, "Danielle."

Her eyes pooled with tears.

"You know everything, don't you."

She picked up the standing frame, studied it for a while, rotated and showed us the image.

Tall, slender, sandy-haired girl in her early teens, wearing a pink two-piece bathing suit. White sand under bare feet, slate-blue ocean and white-mottled blue sky in the background. To the right, a dark corner of craggy outcropping. Rocks I'd seen a few days ago.

Milo said, "We know about the accident."

"Accident," said Leona Gustafson. "I'm anything but religious, but for a long time I couldn't stop thinking of it as divine retribution. For messing up my life by marrying Butch. For not acting sooner. He was a terrible father right from the beginning, ignored Danielle totally. But I kept hoping."

She sighed. "My idiot period. I mean, it's not like he didn't warn me. Right from the get-go, he told me he didn't want kids, but of course I figured I could change his mind. When I got pregnant, he accused me of deception, took no interest in the pregnancy. When I delivered, he wasn't there. Operating on some jock's meniscus. The next day, when he finally took the time to see Danielle, I figured, aha, the spark would be lit, seeing how cute and sweet-tempered she was."

She turned the photo back, stared, shook her head.

I said, "How old was Danielle when you left Butch?"

"Three and a half. All I took were her toys and my clothes. I didn't even put in a claim for half the house, which, it turned out, he'd mortgaged to the hilt. I rented a place in the Valley that I eventually bought. I'm still there."

"Any resistance to the divorce from Butch?"

"Nope, obviously our marriage had meant nothing to him."

I said, "No prolonged anger about marrying Victor."

"No, just that one crack. This is starting to feel like an AA meeting. How much do you know about me and Victor?"

I said, "What we've been told is he was your patient."

"He was my patient and I crossed professional boundaries. Not illegal, just wrong. And please don't ask me the exact nature of his illness, rules are still rules."

"Something chronic and painful."

"Chronic, fluctuating, rarely fatal, let's leave it at that. He was referred to me by my chairman at the U., I treated him, his symptoms improved and . . ."

She threw up her hands. "Victor was an extremely pleasant man. Everything Butch wasn't. Calm, quiet, physically understated, made no demands. And **he** said nice things about Danielle."

Leona Gustafson fingered the standing frame. "Was Victor's money a factor? You're not going to believe me but it wasn't. I knew he was well-to-do, had put **investments** on his patient form. But I had no idea how wealthy until he filed for divorce and my lawyers found out."

She smiled. "I guess divorce has been an educational process for me. The lawyers went nuts because I'd signed a prenup that I thought was pretty generous. They urged me to fight it but I refused. My relationship with Victor was so short-term I didn't feel I deserved anything more."

"Victor moved into your house?"

"Funny, huh? Billionaire in a three-bedroom Encino ranch. Victor said it was nice. Obviously, he was being polite. Which he always was. Not only was our marriage short-lived, we barely saw each other because I worked all the time and he was gone traveling. When he returned, he'd bring presents for Danielle from all over. France, China, Singapore, the Mideast."

I said, "Minimal contact."

"But I was okay with it," she said. "Relieved, frankly, because of all the stress with Butch. Then one day, barely a year and a half after we'd begun, Victor sat down and held my hand and kissed my cheek and said he was sorry but we needed to split up. He assured me it was nothing I'd done, he had what he called 'issues.' I was stunned but then I realized I'd never really had a mate, just a friend who stopped in from time to time. Another reason I didn't challenge the prenup is I didn't want my name in the gossip columns."

She patted the desk gently, as if it was a pet. "What I do here is what matters to me. And turns out, being agreeable worked in my favor with Victor.

He voluntarily added a considerable amount to the prenup."

"Amicable divorce."

"Weirdly amicable," she said. "More like a business dissolution."

I said, "We don't want to rake up unpleasant memories but could we get back to Donny? Starting with how Victor met Donny's mother?"

"No mystery, there. Vanessa was also my patient. One day, Victor came to the office, having just flown into town. We were divorced but as you said, amicable, we still had dinner occasionally, and he'd reserved a table at La Scala. I was jammed and kept him waiting, Vanessa was in the waiting room, the rest is history."

She let go with laughter, unexpectedly loud and shrill. "Turns out I'm a heck of a matchmaker. A few days before their marriage, Victor had the decency to tell me so I wouldn't find out from someone else. And Vanessa had the decency to find another physician."

"How did Danielle and Donny develop a relationship?"

She slumped, looked at the standing photo.

"**That** happened," she said, "after Victor dumped Vanessa. She came crying to me, apologized for taking him away from me. It felt like she was trying to be a gal-pal. Misery loves company. Which was the last thing I wanted. I said not to worry and went off to do some medicine. The funny thing is, we'd seen each other fairly regularly in passing because Donny and Danielle attended the same preschool. Danielle was five so I guess Donny was around two and had just started there. But we pretended not to notice each other. Then Danielle began telling me about a little boy named Donny. How shy he was, how he'd get bullied or just sit by himself. So she'd appointed herself his protector. That's how she was."

Opening her palm, she looked at the wadded-up tissue, discarded it, extracted a fresh one and dried her eyes.

"When Danielle moved on to elementary school and Donny remained in preschool, I guess they lost contact. But then, he showed up at elementary school and it reignited. I know because Danielle told me about it. She was thrilled, her little pal was back and she was going to take care of him again. At that point, when Vanessa and I ran into each other, we were able to smile and chitchat."

"Not gal-pals. Talking about the kids."

"Don't want to sound snobby," she said, "but Vanessa and I had absolutely nothing in common. Then one day, she asked if she could return as a patient and I couldn't see the harm. But shortly after, I realized she had a drug problem and I thought, what is it about me that attracts them? I'm a rheumatologist, not a shrink, so I ignored the issue and when Vanessa began inviting me to the beach and Danielle got so excited about it, I agreed. I stayed indoors, I don't like the sun, but

Danielle was a beach baby, she had so much fun. Eventually, I allowed her to visit by herself. I'd drop her off, chat minimally with Vanessa. She was a sweet woman but she sure had her issues. Do you know that she O.D.'d fatally?"

"We do."

"Fragile," she said. "No genius. But sweet and **always** nice to Danielle."

I said, "Danielle and Donny remained friends."

"Again, it was off and on," she said. "The age difference. Danielle actually ended up trying to tutor Donny because he had learning problems and she was a brilliant student. And when Danielle . . . when she passed, Donny came to the funeral and he was absolutely shattered. And now, they're both gone, two beautiful children—you really think Butch could've done it?"

Milo said, "It's something we're exploring."

"What led you to that?"

"Sorry, Doctor, can't get into details."

"Hmm," said Leona Gustafson. "I really don't want to know, anyway."

From what we'd just heard, her credo.

I said, "Is there any way Butch could've blamed Donny for what happened to Danielle?"

"How can you blame a twelve-year-old for an accident? And there was no doubt about that, it was an accident. Donny had gone inside to fetch some sunscreen, returned just in time to see Danielle swept off the rocks. He rushed over, actually got in the water and was almost swept away himself, so he clawed back onto the rocks, ran in screaming for Vanessa. She was sleeping."

Frown. "Stoned, I guess. Donny was the one who called 911. At the funeral, he looked so . . . forlorn. But I'm ashamed to say I ignored him. He wasn't my problem, my world had just disintegrated."

Two more tissues. She said, "You guys walk in here and everything gets raked up."

I said, "We're really sorry."

"It's okay, don't be, sometimes I need to be woken up. In answer to your question, yes, Butch is deranged and paranoid so I can see him getting it in his psychotic mind that Donny was to blame. Not that he cared much for Danielle when she was alive. When **he** came to the funeral, he just hung back and disappeared midway through the ceremony."

She twisted the latest tissue with white-knuckled hands. "So I can't see it being against Donny. But Victor? Maybe."

"He carries a grudge against Victor."

"Butch carries a grudge against the whole world because he's a total screwup incapable of taking responsibility for his own shitty decisions."

I said, "Other than the high-life comment, did he ever talk about Victor?"

"One time, before then, he arrived for his usual handout and said, 'How come I never see the guy, Lee?' and I made the mistake of telling him Victor traveled a lot on business and he asked what kind of business and I said something in finance. That got him going. How the rich get richer, how there's no equity in the world. No matter that he'd squandered his education and his talents, someone else had to be blamed."

Milo stood and placed his card on the desk. "You've been helpful, Dr. Gustafson. Thanks for your time."

"Sure," she said, still sounding unconvinced. She remained seated as we headed for the door.

As Milo took hold of the doorknob, she said, "Should I be worried about Butch doing something to me?"

"There's no indication of that, Doctor, but we can't tell you for sure no."

"Fine," she said. "My current boyfriend runs a multistate security company. He'll be able to handle it."

35

At five forty p.m. pedestrian traffic on Camden and Bedford was heavy enough to discourage discussion of what we'd just heard.

During the brief walk to the city parking lot, we passed a clutch of slavering paparazzi massed on the sidewalk outside a nail salon, shortly after two homeless men. Which said it all about the Westside.

One guy sat in a wheelchair, quoting Scripture as he panhandled cheerily. Sturdy-looking legs, but you never knew. The other one sat on the sidewalk near the ramps in and out of the city lot, mute, downcast, face crusted with scabs, eyes shut.

Milo said, "Down and out in Beverly Hills. Real life ain't the movies."

Once inside the unmarked, he said, "Impressions?" Before I could answer, his cell rang. He squinted at the unfamiliar number. Detectives are loath to ignore anyone. He answered and went on speaker.

"Sturgis."

A deep voice said, "Lieutenant? Hal Renton. I used to be on the job, Central and South Division Vice, now I do private security."

"How can I help you?"

"My fiancée—Dr. Gustafson—just called and told me you'd been asking about Crazy Butch. Anything I should know?"

"Just what we told her."

"He might've killed someone," said Renton, without inflection. "Okay, noted and recorded. The house we live in is excellent security-wise but my bachelor place—gated community in Calabasas— is better. It's a big drive from there to her office but if you think it's worth it."

Milo said, "Can't say for sure."

"What would you do if it was your girl?"

Milo smiled. "Gated and out of the way sounds good. Anything you want to tell me about Butch?"

"All I know," said Hal Renton, "is what Lee's told me, sounds like a loony asshole. How a great girl like her hooked up with him is beyond me. Okay, thanks. And love to hear about it when you nail his ass. Think that'll be soon?"

"If the stars align, Hal."

A beat. "Okay, then. Good luck."

Click.

Milo said, "Ol' Leona's had lousy taste in men, hope this one's better."

I said, "What I found interesting is that she saw

Victor as the anti-Butch but the two of them shared a personality flaw: total indifference to children."

"You see that as relevant?"

"It could be if he viewed Donny as evil spawn."

"Getting back at Victor through his kid."

"Getting back at what Victor represents. The good fortune that's failed him. Rodriguez contacted Butch to rip off a rich kid with no street smarts. Just a burglary. Then Butch heard who it was and decided it was a cosmic omen and started thinking about murder. Either Rodriguez or Butch enlisted two homeless women to get into the studio by posing for Donny, case the place, try to pocket a key. It backfired for Rodriguez because Butch decided to take it all. If Butch has done all the cases Rampart suspects him for, he gets off on power and violent control."

"Crazy," he said, "and a thoroughly evil asshole. Could a psychotic plan that clearly?"

"A severely deteriorated schizophrenic couldn't but what Gustafson told us about Butch's self-medication sounds more like extreme bipolar. That can also be accompanied by jumbled thoughts but there are periods of lucidity."

"Getting lucid enough to kill. Lovely. Now how the hell do we find him?"

I had no answer for that, spent the drive back to the station flooded with images.

A girl on the rocks.

A terrified twelve-year-old boy, helpless.

A man overcome by disorder, greed, and addiction, sinking to the depths. Blaming everyone but himself, as so many failed, angry people do.

Swirling all that together stuck an idea in my head. When I tried to dismiss it and it wouldn't go away, I thought: maybe.

When we reached the traffic pileup at Olympic and the 405 underpass, I said, "This is theoretical but if Bonty had a weird revenge thing going on against Victor, what better way to feel powerful and justified than to take big-time spoils?"

"Meaning?"

"First he erases Victor's kid, then he murders in Malibu. Why not more days at the beach?"

CHAPTER

36

Another sit-down in the car. Milo spent a long time digesting. Made no comment as he took Ed Brophy's card out of his wallet and punched numbers.

A female voice answered, "Char Willis."

"Lieutenant Sturgis, LAPD. I'm calling Lieutenant Brophy."

"He took early retirement. I got his extension."

"Did you also get Jangles?"

"Pardon?"

"Corinne Mae Ballinger. The homeless woman found in Rambla Pacifico."

"I'm a Traffic L.T., have no idea about that."

"Who inherited Ed's homicide cases?"

"No one here," said Willis. "If I had to guess, someone downtown."

"Any particular name you could give me?"

"Sorry, no. Like I said, I'm Traffic and we just

got a bad one up on Decker Canyon. Car versus motorcycle. I thought you were someone from the biker's family."

Several tries at the downtown Sheriff's Detective Bureau finally produced a name.

Sergeant Delmore Rush was out of the office. Milo left a message, muttered, "Never thought to call me." Sitting up higher, he drummed the steering wheel. "This hour, traffic's gonna be a bitch."

I logged onto Waze. "Not too bad except near the Country Mart."

"For theoretical, you're pretty gung-ho."

"Just tossing it out there."

"Hunh." He phoned Reed while I called Robin. She said, "A homicidal maniac? Be careful."

"Big Guy always makes sure I stay in the background."

"That's where I like you."

When I disconnected, Reed was saying, ". . . the same thing, L.T. Couple of people claim to remember Butch but no one knows his last name or where he hangs out."

"We know plenty, Moses."

Milo caught him up.

Reed said, "A doctor . . . you really think he could be shacking up in Donny's house?"

"It's a long shot but the guy's got serious mental issues and Alex thinks the motive could be tied in with some weird emotional takeover, so who knows? Also, Bonty did kill a woman in Malibu, so we know he's hung out there. We're heading out in a few. You have the energy to do backup?"

"Sure, L.T., but I'm already back home, going to take a while to get out there. I'll log on and figure the best route."

"Thanks, kiddo. Now pass the info along to Alicia and Sean."

"Alicia's out to dinner with Al Freeman," said Reed. "She's been putting in twenty-hour days, Freeman just came back, she didn't figure you'd mind. Not sure where Sean is."

"Let's give her a pass, she's entitled to some R and R. If you can find Sean, let him know but it's optional, the whole thing will probably come to nothing."

"The doc thinks it makes sense, that's definitely a factor."

I said, "You're making me blush."

Reed said, "Well . . ." and laughed.

By the time the connection broke, Milo was pulling out of the lot.

37

P er the satellite gods, the optimal route from the station to Broad Beach was Olympic Boulevard west, a brief hop on the Santa Monica Freeway, PCH the rest of the way.

Optimal is relative. Now Waze was flashing all sorts of intermittent colors.

Olympic, originally Tenth Street until it was renamed for the 1932 Olympics no city bid for except L.A., had once been a speedy conduit to the Pacific, the trip enhanced by lights timed at thirty-five miles an hour. Now it's just another L.A. cross-city thoroughfare, meaning you never knew. When exceeding thirty-five is feasible, no one pays attention to timing. When drivers find themselves slogging at fifteen mph, they curse traffic engineers.

This evening's journey featured spurts of apparent freedom squelched by jams for which no reason was obvious. Then it got worse, with the 10 freeway degrading to a crawl worthy of the drop-off zone at LAX and the coast highway turning to chrome sludge through several interminable red lights.

Finally, we were able to coast at forty-five, paralleling an ocean cloaked by a sky dotted with a few tired stars.

When we passed Rambla Pacifico neither of us said a word. From the moment we'd left the station, he'd sat stiffly, both hands gripping the wheel, staring straight ahead.

His leave-me-alone position. No problem for me, I was still sorting images, facts, what-ifs. The latest question mark: Was the culvert where Jangles had been found one of Butch Bonty's haunts? Had we just sped past him?

Milo was able to lead-foot between Las Flores and Carbon Beach, then we came up against the predicted clot south of the Malibu Pier and extending past the Country Mart on the land side.

On the ocean side, the entrance to the Malibu Colony was a hint of flicker above twin gateposts. The enclave was established decades ago by movie studios as a beachside haven for actors. Nowadays, it offered today's glitterati the chance to tweet about matters deemed profound while hunkered behind the Colony's guard gate.

Milo said, "Wouldn't it be insane if this actually accomplishes something . . . okay, finally, we're moving."

That spurt was stymied by the light near the western frontage of the Pepperdine campus. The largest lawn I'd ever seen, tonight an expanse of gray velvet.

Tired of thinking, I shut my eyes and didn't wake until the unmarked came to a sharp stop.

Red light at the Trancas / Broad Beach intersection.

Occupying this land-side stretch, another shopping center, smaller, dominated by a brightly lit Starbucks full of people and a faux-rustic, organoid supermarket.

As we waited, Milo's phone played something that could've been extracted from Chopin's nightmare.

Moe Reed said, "Hey, L.T. I'm about twelve minutes away."

"About?"

"Waze says exactly—now it's eleven. Sean left pretty soon after I did."

"Good timing, I just got here."

The light turned green. We surged forward.

Milo parked a dozen properties back from Donny Klement's house, across from a structure that resembled a giant Quonset hut and sported a **For Lease** sign. Minimal lights out at that place and most of the other houses. The few stars I'd seen at the outset had gone into hiding. The road was dark, the highway, blocked from view by a high berm, traceable only as a low drone broken by occasional shards of silence.

We got out of the unmarked. Milo walked to the back, popped the trunk, and studied his shotgun for a moment but left it in place. Retrieving his Maglite, he freed his Glock. Quick check of the handgun, then back into the black nylon holster riding his hip.

"Okay, here goes nothing," he said. "Stay behind me, anyway."

Shining the light ahead of us briefly, he switched it off, used the visual trace to direct his steps toward our destination. Bug bulbs above the door of a house two doors up helped delineate details. Enough to bring him to a full stop.

He held me back with a rigid arm. Pointed. I could hear his breathing. Rapid, shallow, rough.

Parked in front of the shabby little frame house was a car.

Boxy white compact.

Facing south.

Chrome grille.

Pulling out the Glock, he inched forward, moving slowly, pausing every few steps to check out the surroundings.

I took a few steps forward, to get a better view. The highway drone played a duet with the slosh and slap of the tide.

Milo reached the car, inspected the rear end, then

the driver's door. Pointed to Donny's house. To gritty light behind the drapes drawn on one window.

I retreated to the unmarked. When he returned, I said, "Hyundai Accent."

"Complete with dent on the door. No plates but he just leaves it here. Unbelievable. Let's back up a bit."

He led me six properties south. Phoned Reed and told him about the Hyundai.

Reed said, "Crazy. I'm right here, like three minutes."

When Reed clicked off, Milo gave Sheriff's Sergeant Delmore Rush another try. Same result.

He said, "I'm informing you that I'm about to confront a homicide subject on your turf." After reciting the address, he clicked off, looking disgusted. "I could call the Malibu substation but no matter what I tell them about discretion, they might hotshot it Code Three and alert the bastard."

His gun remained in his hand, held parallel to his body. A few moments later, headlights appeared at the mouth of the road and grew and Moe Reed drove up in his new civilian ride, a three-year-old red Camaro. He pulled in behind the unmarked, turned off the engine, and exited. Wearing all-black: sweatpants, sneakers, T-shirt criss-crossed by his own holster, the straps at their widest to accommodate his massive chest.

The two of them left me standing there as Milo took Reed for a closer look.

When they got back, Reed said, "Good guess, Doc."

Milo said, "Individuals of his persuasion don't guess. They hypothesize."

We returned to the unmarked where Reed checked his own weapon and Milo phoned Sean and caught him up.

"Wow. I'm almost there."

"What's almost?"

"I'm at the county line . . . five miles."

"We'll wait for you. Unless something happens like the asshole comes out, gets in his car and tries to leave."

"Got it, Loot. I'll speed a little. Hopefully no Chippie will radar me."

"That happens," said Milo, "invite them to the party."

As we waited for Sean, Milo holstered his gun and turned to me. "Any suggestions on how to approach this guy psychologically?"

I said, "None."

Both detectives stared at me.

Milo said, "Where'd the wizardry go?"

I said, "That's the point, there isn't any. Anything I tell you could mislead you."

Reed said, "What about all those suggestions about mental health workers riding with patrol on mental cases?"

"With a nonviolent suspect, someone who knows how to soothe could help. With a violent suspect, there'll be wounded and dead mental health workers."

Dual frowns. New set of headlights.

A tan minivan slipped in behind the Camaro. Seconds later, Sean came toward us, walking quickly.

He wore jeans, sneakers, and a black, hibiscus-patterned aloha shirt that draped his gun.

His turn for a look-see with Milo. Reed stayed back with me.

When the four of us were back together, Milo said, "It's basically a box, small, open layout except for the bedroom and bathroom. Someone in there could easily stay out of view so they're our danger zones. The front door's the only way into the house, but there are sliders on the beach side that lead to a deck. Deck's about ten, eleven feet high so it's jumpable. He gets onto the beach we've got problems so it's important we keep him away from the deck. I'd put one of you on the sand but the stairs down are crumbling and a bunch of the steps have big nails sticking out. Don't want tetanus or a broken ankle on my conscience, so we all go in through the door."

"No-knock?" said Reed.

"I don't like no-knock, period, but for sure not here, too likely to freak him out. I'll knock, we wait, nothing happens, we broach. Didn't bring a ram. You up for kicking the door in?"

Reed flexed a thick leg. "No prob."

"Okay, next step: priorities once we're in. Our main goal is keeping ourselves and him healthy. We go in fast and hope he's not carrying or near a weapon. Optimally, he'll be in the open area and the three of us can blitz him and hook him up. Given his mental status, we can expect the worst but three of us should be able to handle him. If he's not out in the open, the bathroom's on the south wall and the bedroom's right next to it in the southwest corner. The bedroom faces the beach but there's no deck, just a window too small for a guy his size to get through. The main thing to remember is if he's out of view, we get behind furniture and take it slow."

Reed said, "That puts the process under his control."

"Temporarily," said Milo. "We can live with that. In the long run, he'll have nowhere to go, so we can afford to take our time."

Sean said, "Could we have Doc do a hostage negotiating thing?"

"Nope, don't want him in there at all, the space is too limited." He patted my shoulder. "He'll be right here, enjoying the salt air."

Sean said, "He used a gun on Klement and some kind of club on Rodriguez and Katie. Big difference."

Milo said, "Good point. Gun's the worst scenario, he suicides by cop, what can we do? He comes out with the club, we'll do our best to disarm him but even with that, if he attacks us, we still may end up in the news."

Reed said, "Brutal cops injure a defenseless mental patient."

Milo said, "Bad P.R. I can deal with. DOA for anyone, I can't."

I said, "If the worst does happen, get the fact that

he's a serial killer out there as soon as possible. It'll overshadow the mental patient angle."

"If it bleeds, it leads, so use it to our benefit? Yeah, I like it. Hopefully, it won't come to that."

He flexed his fingers. Tension on all of their faces. "Okay, let's do it."

39

I remained by the unmarked as the three of them advanced up the road, weapons drawn. Waiting for something.

Getting nothing and wondering.

Feeling itchy.

They'd been gone for several minutes when a scraping noise at my back made me turn.

A figure walking toward me from the south. Shuffling. Toting something . . . a paper bag.

Probably a resident returning after some night-time shopping. I retreated closer to the berm, waited for him to pass.

Big man. Wearing a long, bulky coat—odd attire for a warm beach night.

Wide and tall even with hunched posture. Barely lifting his feet as he walked.

I tried to blend in with the car.

He got closer. The light above the Quonset hut door revealed a head shaved smooth.

He stopped.

Stood there, kept swinging the bag. If he'd seen me it was a sidelong view.

I held my breath.

He swiveled slowly. Stared straight at me. The light limned a heavily jawed face I'd seen on several mugshots.

In real life, limper, eroded, sturdy bone structure giving way to time and bad decisions.

He squinted. Came forward. Pushed his face at me, as if it were a weapon.

Jumpy eyes bounced around like pinballs. Returned to my face.

Hypervigilance warring with confusion.

The neuropsychological flux you see in some agitated psychotics.

He said, "Help you?" Low, phlegmy voice.

I smiled. "Just waiting for someone."

He came closer. "Who?"

I pointed to where he'd come from. "Friend of mine, lives up there."

"Huh." He studied me some more, said, "Fuck it," and continued shuffling. Slowing his pace, swinging the bag faster.

I pulled out my cell, sent a text to Milo.

911 he's coming toward you.

Just as I was pocketing the phone, Butch Bonty

stopped again. Put his bag down on the road. Seemed to be considering something.

Decided and came back.

Still shuffling at an easy pace.

On the third step, he reached into his coat and drew something out.

Swinging it low, as he had with the bag. Then lofting.

Shaped like a baseball bat but a bit shorter. A sawed-off hunk of something.

I took hold of the unmarked's door handle.

Locked. All that equipment and a shotgun in the trunk, basic cop procedure.

I sidled backward, hoping for an opening so I could run.

He sped up. Tripped but regained his balance and kept coming. Rotating the bat overhead like a boomerang.

I said, "Everything okay?"

"Fuck you you're out to fuck me." Rattling off words in a flatulent burst.

I said, "I don't know you."

He growled, lowered his head.

He came at me with the bat. Raising it high and bringing it down full force. I dodged to the right. The unmarked's driver's door shattered.

He coughed, exhaled like a weight lifter.

Serious job to do, working hard.

He swung again.

I shifted to the left. Got caught in the right shoulder.

Oblique blow, but enough to shoot a bolt of pain from my clavicle up to my neck and into my brain.

Then bumping down my spine, riding vertebrae like a razor-wheeled go-kart.

Right side, dominant side, not good.

He raised the bat slowly, as if wearying. A bizarrely timed sneeze interrupted him and I figured I could escape. But he'd moved too close to me on the rebound. Crowded me, big and broad, blocking any exit with his bulk.

It'd been a while since I'd fooled with karate and even back then the emphasis had been more on grace and balance than self-preservation.

But I tried, bringing my foot down hard onto his instep then jabbing upward with four stiff fingers, aiming for his Adam's apple.

Delivering my own glancing blow.

He recoiled, shook off whatever pain I'd inflicted. Roared.

He two-handed the bat and held it horizontal. Surging forward and using it to pin me against the car.

I readied myself for another defense. Go for the bridge of the nose. Then the eyes.

But as he grunted, pushed, pressed against my chest, my breath diminished and my arms were immobilized.

I kicked him in the knee. He loosened his grip

for a fraction of a second. Recovered and made wet sounds, a reptile rising from the swamp, and leaned into the bat.

Breathing became an ordeal.

Impossible.

I stopped trying to breathe, told myself I was conserving oxygen, clawed at his hands and when that didn't work, tried to push back.

Too much bulk. The bat was a vise-grip. He didn't seem to be exerting effort. Just **being** there, crushing steadily. Crazy, relentless.

My peripheral vision went first. Then the rest of my world began to dim.

Half blind, I tried to slide downward under the bat but he held me fast.

Pushing.

Then he cried out. Froze. Dropped the bat.

It rang on the pavement and bounced.

He stood there, teetered, sat down hard on the road.

Confused.

Betrayed.

I swooned, struggled to stay on my feet. Breathing was agonizing. My knees gave way, then my quads, and now both of us were sitting on asphalt.

My eyes focused minimally.

Fast-moving shape behind him.

Sean Binchy, retractable cop baton in his hand, said, "You okay, Doc, you okay?" as he took Bonty by the scruff, shoved him onto his stomach, kicked his legs wide, yanked his arms back and **snick snick** cuffed him.

"You okay, Doc? Talk to me."

Able to focus all on me while making an arrest. Impressive multitasking, Sean.

Footsteps sounded from behind him. Milo and Reed running toward me.

Firing the same question:

Okayokayokayokay?

Everyone worrying. Time to reassure them.

What I intended to say was, "Fine."

What I produced was a wet wheeze.

I tried again, was seized by a pain-burst in my shoulder, my neck, my head.

A different kind of pain in my chest. Knife-edged and dull at the same time.

Nothing like a worst-case scenario.

Then the clangor of metal rubbing against metal. Not the bat, the bat was over there, safely out of reach.

Not anything.

A noise that originated in my head and grew louderlouderlouder.

Milo was next to me, squatting. **"Oh geez, what a fuckup, so so sorry—tell me you're okay, man. C'mon. Alex? Can you hear me? Tell me something."**

I intended to smile reassuringly. Whatever facial change I produced terrified him.

He sat down next to me, used his weight to

stabilize me. Tears ran down his cheeks.I needed to reassure him. How? Clangclangclang.

"Hang in there, Alex just hang in, ambulance is on the way, no, no, forget it don't try to talk, just relax, take it easy—"

A word formed in my addled brain. I fought to extract it. Succeeded. Pronounced it.

"Peachy."

Where had that come from?

Let's hear it for the orator.

Another inspiration formed.

Another word!

"Bueno." He'd get a kick out of that.

No smile on his big face.

Tough audience. I'm dying up here!

I said, "Muy. Bueno." My world began to dim again. I swayed to the left. Kept going.

Milo caught me, held me in a seated position. Better posture for breathing when your chest is damaged. I knew that. He knew that. The world was informed!

"Stay with me, kiddo, you're gonna be **okayokayokayokayokayokay.**"

Clang clang clang.

For me, the bells tolled.

Then they stopped.

I never heard the sirens.

CHAPTER

40

I spent what seemed like forever in the E.R. at Santa Monica Hospital, most of it lying on a gurney in my allotment of curtained space. Waiting, listening to beeps and clicks and murmurs from behind the pleated fabric.

Milo was there looking ill as they wheeled me to Radiology. When they wheeled me back, he was gone and Robin was standing there, forcing herself not to cry.

I said, "Poor you."

She said, "Oh, please," and reached out to take my left hand. Then she cried.

My body continued to throb and though my breathing had eased, every respiration tweaked various nerve endings. But the X-rays and the MRI had produced good news: no breaks, just soft-tissue bruising. Even if a rib or two had cracked, treatment would've been the same: rest, ice, pain meds, and, most important, time.

I didn't bother to ask how much time because the answer's always "six weeks." I've never found hard data to back that up but it seems to make doctors feel better.

Robin held my hand and stroked my hair. I rotated my head for a kiss. Painful as hell but worth it when her lips met mine.

She drew back. "I don't know where I can touch you."

I said, "Lips will do just fine, for now. Tomorrow, we'll expand the territory."

She dredged up a smile. Her big brown eyes had dried but remained red around the rims.

I said, "Nothing broke, no big deal."

She looked away.

I said, "Maybe all the muscle I've got protected me."

"There you go," she said weakly. A moment later: "Milo was with you the whole time until I arrived. He's racked with guilt, figured he'd kept you safe."

I laughed. "Best-laid plans."

"Okay," she said. "I'll choose to see your nonchalance as a sign of emotional health rather than a crude attempt to shield me."

A beat. "Sweetie, don't force yourself. Are you really okay?"

"I **really** am."

She gave me a doubtful look. I didn't smile. The last time I'd tried it hadn't worked so well.

"Take a sip of water."

I obeyed.

Robin said, "Thank God for Sean."

"Sean thanks God regularly. Maybe God reciprocated."

"You're impossible." But managing a real smile, she bent and kissed my forehead. It barely hurt.

As I lay on the X-ray table, then in the MRI tube, I'd been thinking about Sean.

Years ago, I'd saved his life and that had complicated our relationship. Now, I supposed, we'd achieved a synchrony of sorts. Be interesting to see where that led.

Everything's interesting to a psychologist.

Robin said, "Milo said the minute he got your text they all came out running but Sean got there first."

"Long legs," I said.

"Milo said he did track in high school . . . thank **God** for his long legs. Thank God this didn't turn out . . . it could've been—sorry, I told myself not to get negative." She bit her lip.

The curtain parted and the E.R. doctor who'd sent me to X-ray came in. **E. D. Culver.**

Short, skinny, wearing a puka shell necklace. Advanced male-pattern baldness despite looking around eighteen.

His introductory statement to me had been delivered while reading my intake paper. "So how'd you get yourself in trouble?"

He'd been miffed when I pretended not to hear him.

Downright offended when I rejected the Percoset he urged and settled for Tylenol.

"Just so you know, Mr. . . ." scanning . . . "Delaware, Tylenol can damage your liver if you take too much."

"I'll be sure not to take too much."

Now he looked me over briefly and turned to Robin. "You're the sig other?"

She said, "That's me."

"You taking him home? Obviously, he can't drive."

Robin said, "Obviously. When can we go?"

"Up to me, you could go right now, he's been told what he needs to know." He glanced at me, squinty-eyed and pucker-lipped, returned to Robin.

"Just so you know, he's rejected pain meds AMA—against medical advice. Claims he feels fine but that could be delusion due to endorphins— they're these chemicals the brain makes to ease trauma. So he could start to feel worse."

Back at me: "Really worse, Mr. Delray. You might even need Demerol, if it gets excruciating. Which it could."

Thank you, kindly, Prophet of Doom.

Robin said, "I'll keep that in mind, Doctor. So when can I take him home?"

"Soon as the paperwork comes through."

E. D. Culver turned to leave.

Robin said, "What's the healing period?"

"Six weeks."

I said, "Some gurney-side manner."

Robin said, "Be honest with me. How's the pain?"

"Utterly manageable."

"Whatever you need, I'll get you."

"I'll be fine."

She balled her delicate, strong, wonderfully artful hands. Her lips twitched. "I am **not** going to get negative. I am going to kiss you again and then we're out of here."

I took one idle day. Blanche generally hangs out with Robin in the studio, but she chose to sit next to me. Careful not to press on me. I stroked her knobby bulldog head and that was helpful for a while but inertia got to me and I was ready to jump out of my skin.

The next morning, I drafted and sent reports to various judges. Two days after that, saw the patients I'd scheduled weeks ago.

E. D. Culver was no prophet, just a guy who'd taken a safe bet. For the first two days, the pain did get worse but I've got a high threshold and it was nothing I couldn't handle. When Robin was looking.

She took care of me to the extent that I let her. I kept encouraging her to go back to work and when a spasm did shoot through me, fought to hide it.

Robin noticed a couple of times. Blanche could always tell and tightened in sympathy. She was smart enough not to make a sound and I rewarded her with treats. Being with her was a great distraction. Sitting up gave my lungs optimal room to function but the first two nights, when I slept, I slid down unconsciously and woke with a burning chest.

By the time my first patient showed up, the blades of pain had dulled to butter-knife pokes.

I knew Robin and I would have to talk about what had happened. Eventually.

She kept the conversation light. When she asked how I was feeling, I always lied and said great and backed that up with a smile worthy of a psychopath.

In the shower, the right side of my body looked as if it had collided with a giant plum.

I kept the spray weak.

Ice, rest, time. The distraction of helping others. For the first time I realized that wasn't dissimilar from the way actors avoid their problems by assuming the identities of others.

All the world's a stage. I was at the stage where pain pissed me off to no end.

◆

Early on, Sean, Alicia, and Reed phoned to wish me well.

Sean said, "Probably sounds corny, but I'm praying for you."

"Not corny at all. Thanks, Sean."

"For the prayers? Sure, no problem."

Milo came by with a bottle of Chivas Blue, looking miserable. I was in the living room, reading charts and listening to a music stream I'd put together.

Paul Desmond, Stan Getz, Sonny Rollins. It's a poorly kept secret but any guitarist who plays jazz envies sax players for the fluidity of their instruments.

Breathing the right way.

Milo said, "Listen, if you don't want to talk about it—"

I said, "What's the situation with Bonty?"

That made him grimace. I felt sorry for him but not sorry enough to hear confession.

He said, "Sean gave the back of his head a nice bump, actually put a hairline fracture there. The asshole's been screaming police brutality."

"He have anything else to say?"

"Nope, lawyered up—got himself a PD. Shows how crazy he is, thinking we care. The bat's your basic sporting goods aluminum deal but with the bottom six inches broken off. Probably damaged goods he pulled out of the garbage. No handle so he made a grip by winding a lot of duct tape. Problem for him is the spaces between the strands of tape catch all sorts of crap, including dried blood. Perfect match for Abel Rodriguez and Katherine Bouleau. We also found a .22 in the house, right out on the kitchen counter, casings match Donny."

"PD's going for diminished capacity?"

"She made those noises but you know the success rate with that and I got the sense her heart wasn't in it. I did what you suggested and talked a lot about serial killings and she got that **oh-well** look."

"Veteran defender?"

"Nope, a newbie, but smart enough to know a lost cause when she sees it. John's gonna hold out for three counts of Murder One and max sentencing on each. He's pretty sure she'll settle for life with concurrent instead of consecutive and convince herself she accomplished something."

"Excellent."

"So . . . how're you feeling?"

"Great."

"Listen, about what happened—"

"No need," I said. "I'm serious."

"I thought shrinks were all for talking."

"When it's useful. I'm fine. You did nothing wrong."

He wrung his hands. "Oh sure, it was a brilliant plan. What was I thinking, leaving you out there by yourself? Asshole was known to wander."

"Who'd figure he'd go shopping?"

"My job is figuring. I shoulda put you inside the car."

I said, "Hey, Dad, am I allowed to have candy? Just one piece? Puh-**leeze**?"

He glared at me. "Glad you think it's amusing."

"Amusing is good," I said. "We should all try to maximize amusement."

"Alex—"

"Stuff happens. Find any of the other Wishers?"

"Haven't actively looked." He rubbed his face. "I mean, you goddamn **predicted** it. Mental health folk getting hurt or worse."

"Hey," I said, "don't be getting ideas."

"About what?"

"Thinking twice about having me there."

"I've already thought twice. Plus a thousand."

"Uh-uh, you think I can help on something, you damn well better call."

"You make the rules?"

"We both do. It's called friendship."

"Listen to you," he said, "all this attitude. Where'd the reserve and discretion go?"

"Time and place for everything."

"You know," he said, "I figured you were lying about feeling better but maybe you really are."

I pointed to the Chivas. "Open it."

"Booze is okay with pain meds?"

"I'm taking Tylenol. Infrequently."

"Doctor in the E.R. told me you'd need to dope up."

"He's not me."

"Oh boy, what happened to your noggin, Dr. Macho?"

"I got knocked around, nothing broke, I'm healing, now I'm thirsty."

He went to the kitchen, returned with two tumblers, cracked the bottle, poured each of us a couple of fingers, and sat back down.

"What are we drinking to?"

"Expensive scotch."

A few sips later, he said, "Can we at least talk about why he went after you?"

"He got paranoid."

"What'd he say?"

"A few F-bombs."

"What else?"

"That's about it. At first, he passed by and continued on. Then he changed his mind, came back with the bat. We'll never know exactly why. He probably has no idea, himself."

"Jesus—thank God you had the smarts to text me."

Everyone grateful to the Deity.

I said, "I didn't want him to pop in on you."

He lowered his head. Shook it back and forth slowly. Remained that way, staring down, like a buffalo grazing.

I said, "What?"

"Three of us, pros, packing, and **you're** thinking about protecting **us**."

"At the time it seemed relevant. In the end you saved my life."

"Sean did."

"He's basically an extension of you."

"Now I'm a hero? Enough. Please."

He shook his head, drank. "Moses and I were close behind but man, Sean took off like an Olympian. Turns out he ran track in high school. Go know."

A twinge—what you feel after a serious sunburn—coursed through my shoulder. I drained my glass and held it out to him.

He said, "Yessir, you bet sir, anything else for the Grand Imperial Pooh-Bah."

"There you go," I said. "Getting with the program."

CHAPTER

41

A week after the arrest of Berkeley Justin Bonty, I stood on a low knoll in Burbank. Not far from the northern rim of Griffith Park where Bonty had planted a victim.

Lovely day, sun-warmed, redolent of cut flowers. The rolling hills below were a checkerboard of velvety grass and white marble gravestones installed parallel to the earth.

Cemetery of today, pretending to be something else.

My position was at the rear of the assemblage, next to Milo, Sean, and Moe Reed. All of us, careful not to co-opt space near the front, where the casket rested in an oblong wound. Ornate casket, finished in white nacreous lacquer and trimmed with shiny brass fittings.

To the left of us, Mel Gornick, wearing a tight black dress that barely covered her butt, wept. A few feet to her left, Deandra Sparrow fooled with her phone. Black leather jacket, black jeans, black boots. To go with her new black hair.

The front tier consisted of Ali Dana in an ankle-length black dress next to a short round-faced, rouge-cheeked woman in a silver-flecked black Chanel suit who'd introduced herself as "Bianca, I'm his sister, he used to live with me," before moving away quickly.

Next to her, Hugh Klement in a black western suit, starched white shirt, turquoise string tie, held a black Stetson in both hands.

Then, a pretty redheaded woman I recognized from the photos in Colin Klement's office and Colin.

Several paces to the right, away from his surviving children, was Victor Klement, wearing the same drab clothes he'd donned for his drop-in at the station.

Hands laced, head down, expressionless.

Colin stepped forward. Turned and faced everyone else and cleared his throat.

"Recently," he said, "I'd gotten to know my little brother. I wish it had been sooner."

Tears, sniffles, everyone else's heads dropping.

With the exception of Victor Klement, who'd raised himself up, freed his hands, and was staring out at nothingness.

Lost.

About the Author

JONATHAN KELLERMAN is the #1 **New York Times** bestselling author of fifty-two crime novels, including the Alex Delaware series, **The Butcher's Theater, Billy Straight, The Conspiracy Club, Twisted, True Detectives,** and **The Murderer's Daughter.** With his wife, bestselling novelist Faye Kellerman, he co-authored **Double Homicide** and **Capital Crimes.** With his son, bestselling novelist Jesse Kellerman, he co-authored **A Measure of Darkness, Crime Scene, The Golem of Hollywood,** and **The Golem of Paris.** He is also the author of two children's books and numerous nonfiction works, including **Savage Spawn: Reflections on Violent Children** and **With Strings Attached: The Art and Beauty of Vintage Guitars.** He has won the Goldwyn, Edgar, and Anthony awards and the Lifetime Achievement Award from the American Psychological Association, and has been nominated for a Shamus Award. Jonathan and Faye Kellerman live in California.

Jonathankellerman.com
Facebook.com/JonathanKellerman

LIKE WHAT YOU'VE READ?

Try these titles by Jonathan Kellerman,
also available in large print:

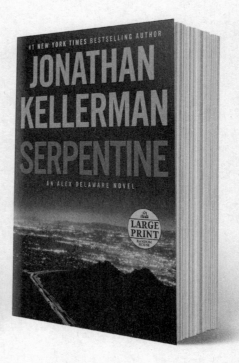

City of the Dead
ISBN 978-0-593-55876-8

Serpentine
ISBN 978-0-593-39557-8

For more information on large print titles, visit
www.penguinrandomhouse.com/large-print-format-books